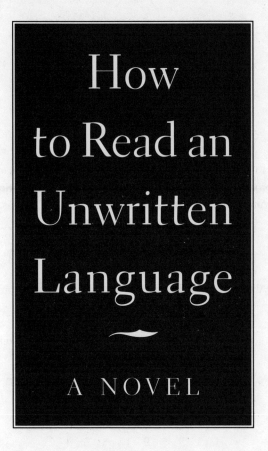

How to Read an Unwritten Language

A NOVEL

Philip Graham

SCRIBNER

NEW YORK   LONDON   TORONTO   SYDNEY   TOKYO   SINGAPORE

SCRIBNER
1230 Avenue of the Americas
New York, NY 10020

SCRIBNER and design are trademarks of Simon & Schuster Inc.

DESIGNED BY JENNIFER DOSSIN

Manufactured in the United States of America

1   3   5   7   9   10   8   6   4   2

Library of Congress Cataloging-in-Publication Data
Graham, Philip, date.
How to read an unwritten language : a novel / Philip Graham.
p.   cm.
I. Title.
PS3557.R217H69   1995
813'.54—dc20   95-11144
CIP
ISBN 0-684-80373-9

FOR ALMA, NATHANIEL AND HANNAH

CONTENTS

I would like to express my thanks for the invaluable support offered by the Corporation of Yaddo, the National Endowment for the Arts, and the University of Illinois, Urbana-Champaign, during the writing of this novel.

The things of the heart cannot be read by too many people. They burn inside like a big fire which people cannot know how to put out.

CHENJERAI HOVE

I was running to meet everything that was visible, and everything that I could not yet see.

JACQUES LUSSEYRAN

How
to Read an
Unwritten
Language

PART ONE

A Secret Performance

I've always felt that the secret life is available, whether on the chipped and lipsticked rim of a coffee cup or in a crumpled tissue's faint smell of sex, in the smudgy fingerprints of a child's frayed comic book or along the jagged flap of a crudely torn envelope. Even a single gnawed crescent of fingernail is a voice that might speak. And above all, our faces percolate with transformations, a mutating language that both invites and defies fluency.

Yet where had this belief brought me? To a bench bordering the edge of a park, weary of translation. I paged through the newspaper, from an insect blight devouring a vast arc of African forest, to a well-trimmed American backyard rife with hidden graves. Imagining such a lawn, the cropped blades of grass shivering in the wind, I folded the paper and set it on my lap.

On the path before me spread the swaying shadows of leaves from a nearby tree, and I couldn't help it, I let myself read those dark, weaving shapes: they were the leaves of a pin oak, spiky arms that seemed to grasp at each other, but faded as the light dimmed. Then a woman approached at a crisp pace down the park path, her waves of lush dark *hair at odds with the buttoned-down look of her gray skirt and business jacket. As she drew closer I saw that her steady gait was just one step ahead of something coiled inside, something ready to spring loose if she slowed only slightly.*

Then she stopped and shook that thick hair, let her hands run through it as if teasing out a pursuer. Unable to look away, I felt so still inside as she took an elastic band from her jacket pocket and, arms raised, began to gather those unruly strands into a single tame braid at the nape of her neck.

I simply couldn't let that happen—somehow that innocent grooming was also a terrible constriction, an impending, secret defeat. "Excuse me," I called out softly, glad I wore no watch, "do you have the time?"

She turned to me, her heavy-lidded eyes tinged with wariness, hesitated, and then surprised me with her own question: "Do I look like the sort of person who owns a watch?"

She regarded me expectantly, as if she thought I somehow knew her. "Well, you were walking pretty fast," I ventured, choosing my words with care. "Maybe you're . . . late for some appointment. And if you know that you're late, then wouldn't that mean you have some notion of what time it is?"

I caught a glint of amusement, curiosity in her eyes as she replied, "If I were late, I wouldn't have time to stop to talk."

"Well, maybe not—"

"Actually I don't need a watch," she said, smiling now. "Look at the sky. It's the middle of April, right? The fifteenth, to be exact. Well, read the colors." She pointed to the purple- and orange-streaked sky and took in its eerie beauty with a sigh of satisfaction. "We're cruising to mid-sunset, I'd say. That would make it about 7:10."

I watched the horizon's sinuous smears of color and marveled that she could somehow convert all this into hours, minutes. For now I saw not just purple and orange, but a fluid, smoldering red and an electric tinge of yellow as well, and I felt within me the start of my own spectacular flaring.

She misunderstood my silence. "You doubt me? We could stop someone with a watch and check. . . ."

"No, no, I believe you." I laughed. "For all I know, you might be a meteorologist."

Her eyes flickered in surprise. "So now I look like the sort of person who predicts the weather?"

The pursed and lightly mocking line of her lips was weakened by a tightening of her jaw, discouraging any thought I might have of defining her in such a simple fashion. But how should I reply, how much admit what hidden drama I'd seen in her ordinary stroll?

"By the way, my name is Sylvia Mathews," she finally said, as if this might help me recognize her.

Her name wasn't familiar, but I was glad to turn this moment into an introduction. "I'm Michael Kirby," I returned, extending my hand. We stood silently, letting this grip linger perhaps moments too long, our palms both slightly moist. I imagined messages swiftly passing back and forth between our mingled beads of sweat: two private histories now one salty residue, an improvised petri dish growing something that might tell us what to do next.

"Well," Sylvia said, slipping her hand from mine with some reluctance, "I have to be on my way—"

"So do I, actually," I said, surprising myself and certainly blushing. "Um, since you seem to be going my way . . . do you mind if—"

"Not at all," she said, her voice faintly tinged with relief.

We walked along together and Sylvia said "Beautiful park," just to say anything, and I replied, "The sugar maples are already gorgeous."

"Which are those?" she asked, and I thought, Why not return the favor of her sunset? I pointed to the lit path ahead, at a cluster of leafy shadows and their outspread, shivery wings.

She turned and offered a quiet gaze that told me she understood what I'd shown her. We continued down the path, but now, suddenly shy, we merely matched each other's footsteps. Then, too soon, we came to the end of the park and a busy intersection. We stood at the curb and waited for the light to change while cars passed back and forth, drivers and passengers speeding along together on their own mysterious destinations.

When the light turned green I realized with alarm that our paths were about to split apart. I hesitated, unwilling to leave this woman I didn't know. With a furtive glance at me, Sylvia lingered as well. Suspecting that we shared the same dilemma, I took a chance and set off across the street first, listening for the quick clip of her shoes.

I heard her walking half a step back, almost beside me, and I took another chance. At the next corner I turned left, and she followed. Encouraged, at the corner after that I turned right and still we kept apace, our intermingled steps like an echo of each other. But what in the world were we doing? Perhaps secret knowledge had indeed been absorbed into our palms and we were just beginning to understand where we were headed.

Block after block, from the small business district to the edge of my own neighborhood, our studiously casual lock-step created a bubble of anticipation. But now, with the streets nearly deserted and Sylvia still one step behind, I was afraid the spell of our pretense might burst. Quickly I led us to the block where I lived and stopped before my house.

Feigning surprise at her presence, I said, "Oh, hi. This, um, is my home." I added an awkward gesture at the ordinary brick facade, the white trim around the windows, and she offered a simple, nervous nod.

When I didn't continue, speechless from so many words inside me, Sylvia smiled sadly and said, "Well, it was good to meet you, Michael." She took one reluctant step back, about to continue on her way.

"Look, would you like to come in? Maybe have a drink?" I blurted out, immediately mortified by my bumbling invitation.

"I'd like that," she said, so quietly it might have been a thought I overheard.

Once inside the foyer, Sylvia lingered before the hutch, its shelves lined with the last of my old collection: half a scissors, its single blade dulled with age; an earring in the shape of a straight-back chair; an old, battered tape recorder; a tiny toy TV, its plastic screen painted bright blue, an airplane soaring in a corner; and a frail nest of twigs and leaves with a child's clay version of a bird nestled inside. I continued into the living room, hoping to draw her along, but she asked, "What are these?"

"Oh, just some things I've picked up here and there," I said, not yet ready to reveal any of their stories.

"And this?" she asked, pointing to the nest. Her hand hesitated above the little bird's pinched, open mouth. "Where'd you pick this up—not in a tree, I suppose?"

"Oh no—it . . . belonged to someone else, once."

Sylvia's face wrinkled in confusion. She waited for me to explain, and when I didn't, she asked, "Someone you knew?"

"No. Not really . . ." Unable to return her curious regard, I said, "So, drinks! I can offer you wine, iced tea—"

"A wine spritzer would be nice," she replied a bit airily, unhappy with my evasions.

I set off for the kitchen. Afraid of what she might pick up next, I quickly poured wine in two glasses. Then I added club soda to Sylvia's, and a fine mist of bubbles rose up, a faint, effervescent music that I imagined as thousands of tiny voices offering advice. I strained so hard to catch those whisperings that I heard the click of a tape recorder button in the living room. Then a man's desolate voice rose up in mid-sentence, speaking his strangely beautiful Asian language. Listening to those musical phrases that I'd once virtually memorized, I hurried back to the foyer with the drinks.

Sylvia's unhappy face looked up at me, and she asked, "Why is this so sad?"

I dropped both glasses. They shattered, and I could only gape at the floor.

Poised before the puddle of our drinks and the shards of glass and ice that lay between us, Sylvia said, "Hey, wake up. You dropped our drinks, remember?"

"Yes, I did," I managed, idiotically. "What should we do?"

Sylvia hopped over the mess, took my hand. "Follow me."

When we reached the kitchen I had trouble remembering where anything was, a stranger, suddenly, in my own house. "A broom, do you have a broom?" she asked. "Paper towels? We'll need a pail too."

Finally armed against the spill, we returned to the living room, and Sylvia whisked wet slivers of glass into a dustpan. I knelt down and sponged up the wine with sweeping arcs while the tape still ran, the man's voice rising and falling. Though I'd never met him I could see him sitting on a veranda while the sun set, his face unraveling from the strain of all that he felt. Squeezing the sopping sponge above a plastic pail, I stopped, astonished at tears I couldn't control.

Sylvia gaped at me, then at the tape recorder. "It is sad, isn't it?"

I nodded. "You're right."

"And why is it sad?"

"He's in love, and there's nothing he can do about it," I gulped out, my weeping now strangely pleasurable, and Sylvia knelt beside me.

"Why can't he?" she whispered.

Our lips met awkwardly, tentatively at first, as if trying on that man's alien words as he spoke. Then he paused, sighed, stopped. A few seconds passed, a woman's voice murmured in English, "Thank you very much," and the tape continued with a soft hiss.

Soon we were coiled together on my bed upstairs and fumbling with the appropriate protection. The window shades swayed and rasped against the sill, carrying in not only a warm breeze but laughter and chatter: a neighbor's party had spread to a backyard porch and they were all having a fine time.

We twisted about the sheets, our curious tongues tracing each other while a scattered, loopy giggling rose up at distant drolleries we couldn't hear. Slowly Sylvia and I improvised a sweaty, slippery rhythm, punctuated now and then by those bursts of contentment outside that might as well have been applause. Delighted with this secret performance for an audience that didn't know we were here, I wanted it to be spring forever, I wanted that party to never stop.

Breathless beneath me, Sylvia reached for my hand, held a finger and pulled, and I heard the soft pop of a knuckle joint, felt its pleasurable loosening. She pulled at another finger, and then another, each little tug a release that left me helplessly grinning.

"Oooh, you come apart so nicely," she murmured to faraway happy talk that now seemed like inner voices rising from us. Sylvia cupped my face in her hands, and her long gaze told me she wanted to be found, she wanted to find me. I nodded in unspoken agreement. Weren't we, after all, strangers who'd just begun to seek out each other's strangeness?

My Second Language

Suddenly awake—from a nightmare, perhaps, or even some budding premonition—I slipped from my small bed and stood silently in the dark hallway before the half-open door of my parents' bedroom. They sat beside each other in the soft light of their night tables, pillows propped up, Mother reading a magazine while my father balanced the checkbook, deposit slips and canceled checks lined in neat rows on the blanket. With the whisper of a sigh, Mother plucked a single long strand of hair from her head and added it to a little dark pile that looked as if it might come alive and crawl away.

My body fairly tingled with the need for whatever comfort they might be able to offer, yet I found I couldn't speak or allow myself to draw their attention. They might as well have been miles apart, though their shoulders nearly touched. While Father brushed his hand over the familiar tight knots of his curly hair and my mother pursed from habit the slender lips of her narrow face, they seemed too little like themselves—more like amateur impersonators relying on lucky physical resemblance. I padded back to bed quietly, unwilling to accept my uneasiness, but before long I understood that this had been my first hint of a secret shifting in my family, a shifting that would lead to so many dislocations.

I awoke that morning to a window lined with achingly delicate strands of frost, a cold view that begged for further snuggling under warm blankets. But I had to shepherd my younger sister and brother out of bed so Father wouldn't call up to us his well-worn list of why we were lazy.

We might have been born compliantly on schedule—I was eleven, Laurie nine, and Dan seven—but we descended the stairs to breakfast in our own particular way: Laurie's hands sleepily strummed along the rungs of the banister, releasing a resonant wooden music; Dan stopped behind her a moment to shake those rungs, pretending he was imprisoned; and I followed, nudging when necessary so we'd all arrive downstairs on time.

But Father hadn't returned from his trip to the stationery store for the Sunday paper, and we found Mother sitting at the kitchen table without her usual mug of coffee, her hands oddly cupped together.

"What's for breakfast, Mommy?" Laurie asked.

When she didn't glance at us, didn't move, Laurie repeated her question.

Mother's hands flattened on the table and she sighed. "Oh, I'm not a cook, dear. Why don't you fix something for yourselves?"

My sister stubbornly pointed a finger at her stomach. "We're *hungry*, Mommy."

"So am I, honey, but I just don't feel like a cook today."

"What *do* you feel like?"

"I don't know . . . I feel like somebody else, maybe." She attempted a weak smile, but her tired eyes so defeated her that Dan tried initiating a tease, chanting, "Mommy's somebody else, Mommy's somebody else."

Mother managed a laugh. Emboldened by Dan's success, I asked a question that forever after I've wished I never asked: "Well, who *are* you?"

"Oh, I don't know . . . a friend of your mother's."

"If you're her friend," I said, "then how come we never met you before?"

Mother smiled sadly. "It's never too late for introductions—"

"So what's your name?" Laurie asked.

"You can call me Margaret." Then, peering at us quizzically, she asked, "And what are your names?"

We introduced ourselves, pleased with this new game.

"We're hungry, Margaret," Laurie announced again. "What's for breakfast?"

"I told you dear, I'm not a cook. And since your mother isn't here, you'll have to fix your own breakfast."

Disappointed, we stared at the cupboards and drawers as if we believed they might open themselves and offer us the necessary ingredients.

"Oh, I suppose you'll need a little help," Margaret said. She stood and opened one of the drawers. "Here, Dan," she said to me, "take this spatula."

"I'm Michael," I corrected her, enjoying this pretended clumsiness at learning our names.

"Oh, that's too serious a name for a boy your age. Take the spatula, Mike."

Michael *did* sound serious. That's why I liked it. But for the moment, I could see, I'd have to be Mike. I held the spatula and then flipped it jauntily in the air, as I thought a Mike might do.

"Now, what is it you'd like to eat?"

"Pancakes," Laurie said, and I nodded. Pancakes were fine, though I couldn't imagine how we'd possibly make them. Dan loitered by the kitchen doorway and stared out at the backyard, angry at Margaret for calling me Dan. He turned and faced her. "You *are* our mommy."

"No dear, you're mistaken, though we do look alike. But I certainly wouldn't mind having a fine little boy like you. Wouldn't you like to help and get the eggs from the fridge?"

For a moment Dan hesitated, then his stubborn face softened. He walked across the kitchen to the refrigerator and Margaret turned to Laurie. "Well, honey, what kind of flour do you want to use?"

"White."

"Oh, whole wheat is better for you."

We didn't say anything. Mother had never used whole wheat flour before; we didn't even know there was any in the house. Perhaps this woman before us *was* Margaret, and not Mother.

"I like white," Laurie said.

"If you add a little whole wheat flour, it'll taste better."

Laurie didn't reply, looking to me for support. I shrugged and flipped the spatula.

"How many eggs, Margaret?" Dan called out.

"Two will be enough, dear." She turned again to Laurie. "Well?"

"I'd like white . . . with some whole wheat."

Under Margaret's directions, Dan cracked and beat the eggs, then mixed them with the milk. Laurie sifted the flour while I heated the pan and watched the butter bubble.

"Careful," Margaret said, "don't let it go brown."

I lowered the heat. Dan and Laurie, miraculously cooperative, took turns pouring the batter onto the hot greased pan, and I flipped over each irregularly shaped cake. And so, in our mother's absence, we had our first cooking lesson.

When the pancakes lay waiting on our plates, we passed around the maple syrup, one by one pouring it over our portions as if this were the most solemn act in the world. Taking small, cautious bites, we discovered that those pancakes actually tasted good. Margaret ate a bit too and praised our cooking. "If your mother were here she'd be so proud!"

We heard a car pull into the driveway. We sat still before our empty plates, listening to the car door slam and then the muffled rattling of keys. At the *whoosh* of the opening front door Margaret said, "Let's put those plates away, Daddy's home."

We stared at her. Margaret was gone, and now Mother led us to the sink as Father entered the room, the heavy Sunday paper tight under his arm. He watched us lined up and handing the plates to Mother, our faces still sloppy with syrup, and he smiled, surely pleased by our industry, by this postcard of a happy family. Yet we said nothing about our private game, which from the very first seemed to exclude him.

Father pointed to me. "Hey guy, we have some shoveling to do."

Wiping my face, I nodded and wished the futile wish that this was the last time in my life I'd ever have to dig paths through snow. Mother bent down to kiss me good-bye, and instead of trying to wriggle away I offered my cheek and held her. "Good-bye, Margaret," I whispered. Then I quickly turned away, for I didn't want to see her reaction. Something about this game unnerved me: was she Mother, pretending to be Margaret, or was she Margaret, pretending to be my mother?

Keeping to the sidewalk's thin path through the latest deep snowfall, I walked home late from school, having lingered in the library for a social studies report on Brasília, a strange, monumental city surrounded by a rain forest that even in black-and-white photographs seemed to seethe with green life. Now, gazing up at the trees' bare branches, I longed for leaves, for spring's distant warmth.

A car horn rang out harshly, and I turned to see Mother at the wheel, easing over to the curb behind me. I could only stare as she rolled down the window: Laurie and Dan sat scrunched together on the front seat beside her—a treat seldom offered—and, though she never wore such things, a blue scarf covered Mother's unruly hair.

She was someone else again. "Hey, kid, want a lift?"

"No thanks," I replied, coolly regarding my brother and sister. "My mother told me never to ride with strangers."

She laughed. "You're a good kid. Toodle-loo!" Waving the tail of her scarf like a handkerchief, she drove off, and Dan and Laurie turned around in their seats and made foolish faces at me.

What's your name? I almost called out, but the car had already slipped around the corner, disappearing behind a snowbank. Angry that I'd been left alone for being so safety-minded, I turned in the opposite direction and thromped through the deepest drifts I could find until icy chunks encrusted my pants. My shoes damp and socks thickened, I eventually found myself at the edge of a mall's slush-stained parking lot, thoroughly chilled and farther from home than I'd planned on.

When I finally returned and peeled off my stiff clothes, I could hear the faint sounds of Mother in the kitchen, now herself again and preparing dinner. I sneezed, and Laurie and Dan ran up and gleefully let me know what I'd missed: a woman named Dot had driven them to a stationery store in a distant neighborhood, buying them comic books and all the candy they wanted. I nodded, noting without comment that they hadn't saved me a single goodie. Worse, Mother hadn't saved a thing for me either, but then she'd been Dot, hadn't she, and I'd been merely a cautious stranger.

By evening a soupy congestion forced me to suck in raspy breaths, and Mother wrapped me under extra blankets in bed and hovered over me with a reassuringly familar fluster. The next morning she kept me home from school, offering me hot raspberry tea laced with honey, and I luxuriated in my fever and aching limbs as I listened to Laurie and Dan being hustled off to the bus stop.

When I woke from a sweaty nap she even served me my favorite meal—chicken broth and crackers, cheese wedges, and ginger ale— but after lunch she was almost unnervingly businesslike when she held out a spoonful of thick and bitter medicine. She shook her head quizzically at whatever I said, until I realized she knew no English. I tried communicating in elaborate sign language, which delighted her, and just when I managed to wheedle out her new name, Rosario, the phone rang.

"Adios," she said with a grin and what seemed to me to be the right accent, her drawn-out o so richly foreign.

She returned with the thermometer, speaking English and herself again, and the shocking thought occurred to me that my mother lived a secret life at home while we were away at school, improvising these characters to fit her changing moods.

As if the bare trees' new green buds sprouting into bright waving leaves were a surrounding inspiration, Mother flourished too, displaying surprise after surprise for the three of us: Marcie the policewoman, who always wore a long-sleeved blouse to hide her scar from a bullet wound; Tina, a dancer famous for her flying leaps, who huffed through stretching exercises all afternoon, trying to coax us from the canned laughter of the reruns we watched on TV; Valerie the photographer, who specialized in groupings of potatoes, onions, single-pint milk cartons, or reconstructed egg shells that she called Family Portraits. But Mother was never Gladys, the name Father called her.

Whenever he came home from work Mother returned to herself—our feigned innocence on that morning of the pancakes had set a pattern of secrecy—yet even though she sat on a chair at the dinner table or in front of the television, she managed to announce the reappearance of a character with the slightest change: whole histories were implied by any of a dozen slightly different nods or shrugs or shaded glances. A stifled yawn, its faint strain turning into a tiny, hard smile, and I knew Mother was now Susan, the woman who wouldn't laugh, no matter what jokey histrionics Laurie, Dan, and I might perform; a bitter sigh and tight shake of her hair while washing the dishes and she became Melanie, the big-city reporter who'd seen it all; a single, knowing peek at the ceiling fan announced Tamara the Magnificent, a retired juggler who demonstrated her talents with invisible plates and balls, candlesticks and swords.

Often during breakfast I watched Mother's hands cupped against the formica surface. Her fingers curling inward suggested the imminent release of another new character, and I honed my skill at identifying her thicket of selves. In this way I grew up bilingually—learning both the sometimes exasperating rules of English grammar at school and Mother's secret, impersonating gestures at home. My first language helped me make my way through the world; my second language helped me see through it.

With the return of spring Father kept every inch of our lawn finely mowed and trimmed. The owner of a nursery and landscaping business, he made sure the tidy green world around our house was an example for the neighbors, an advertisement for any present and future customers, and it was my burden, as the oldest child, to help him. Toiling under the sun, I admired the persistence of weeds and creepers for their ability to turn up in the most unlikely corners, and even as I tore them out I wished them well. But all that hard work was a kind of dream for Father, a dream no one else could really enter, and sometimes, as he laid mulch about a flower bed or raked up lawn clippings, he occasionally glanced my way without recognition.

One afternoon Mother came out to announce BLTs and lemonade and Father didn't turn to acknowledge her; instead, bent over a hedge, he continued snipping away with his usual fervor. She surveyed the smooth green expanse, her eyes darting back and forth, her body eerily still, and I recalled that night when I first noticed how far apart my parents seemed from each other.

After lunch, Father packed us off to the local bowling alley, as he did every Saturday, giving Mother her weekly "rest," as I once over-heard them call it. On the way there, the radio news detailed a hur-ricane's path through a chain of Caribbean islands, and despite myself I imagined uprooted palm trees swirling in the howling wind. When Father finally parked the car in the lot I looked out the win-dow, surprised to see such a startlingly clear sky.

We all emptied out of the car and followed him into the bowling alley, where Top 40 music jangling from the lobby loudspeaker was punctuated by the silky growl of speeding balls and the clatter of falling pins. At the counter we faced the open shelves of shoes—with their forlorn laces and frayed tongues, they looked embarrassed by their disreputable familiarity with hundreds of different feet. Father checked the soles, the wear of each heel before ordering our shoes, and then, with the huge scoring sheet nestled lightly in the crook of his arm, he led us to our lane.

Head bent, he listed our names on the score sheet and we hud-dled beside him, taking in the competing aromas of his hair tonic, his Clorets. Then we searched through those long racks of bowling balls lined up like a complement of bombs, the same kind that in cartoons would roll with a lit fuse into the lair of a hidden villain. Somewhere among them a bowling ball waited for the grip of my hand, and after much consideration I slipped my fingers into one with a blue streak circling it and approved of its round, easy weight.

As the youngest, Dan had the privilege of starting. Ignoring the fingerholes, he hugged the huge ball against his chest and knelt down at the double line, carefully setting the ball on the polished surface. He aligned it with the distant pins, pushed, and the ball rolled slowly away, arriving at the center of the pins with almost no force and barely breaking through them. His next ball uncannily crept down the same path and missed the remaining pins.

"Good try," Father said, his voice holding back something less pa-tient, but it wasn't enough to ease Dan's sulk.

Laurie was up next, and she swung her ball at such a sharp angle it careened dangerously close to the gutter, then curved away to the other edge of the lane. The ball just managed to clip a corner pin, sending it flying. On her second try the ball wobbled into the gut-ter's polished groove.

She moped back to Father, and his hand encompassed her wrist, twisting it back and forth experimentally. "You have to keep this straight," he said. Laurie regarded her hand with curiosity, as if it might speak and explain why it wouldn't obey her.

I studied the distant pins carefully, willing my own wrist straight. I swung and released and watched the quivering pattern of the ball's blue stripe repeating again and again until it toppled nine pins.

For me, a disappointment, but Father said nothing and looked away at a ball coursing down another lane: I was too old for advice. When I smacked the last pin for a spare, Father's reward was letting me draw the slash through the corner box of my frame. I bore down on the pencil, imagining a long succession of thin X's for the rest of my score.

After rubbing rosin on his hands, Father picked up his ball, took a few swift steps, and with a graceful backward arc of his arm shot it down the lane. Its dark surface flashed in the light, and Father stood so still, watching the distant wooden stutter of flailing pins. A strike. He stood there until the pins were reset and then he turned back to us, his lips tightly curved. But there was no real pleasure in Father's smile. Instead I saw something fierce and not quite knowable.

As the game progressed I began to dread that hint of grimace in his grin, a strange mixture of suppressed anger and exasperation that appeared whether or not he bowled a strike. If Father didn't really enjoy the game, then what attraction *did* it hold for him? Waiting my turn, I listened to a ball purling swiftly down the next lane, purring like the sound of a well-oiled mower, and I thought all those falling pins, in lane after lane, were a particularly exotic lawn, and their explosive clatter was the harsh music of some intimate battle. And if this was a battle, then Father reenlisted us with every frame, for when the pins automatically set up again, another noxious overgrowth needed to be mown down.

Now my mother wasn't the only person I saw with new eyes. In the days that followed, my father's usual remoteness—which I'd so long taken for granted—grew increasingly uncomfortable. His silence seemed everywhere in the house, surrounding even the screech of a teapot, an alarm clock's grating buzz, and I began to suspect why Mother's varied identities squeezed themselves back inside her whenever he was around. My parents were locked in some mysterious adult dispute, an argument perhaps far more serious than I was willing to believe. My ability to imagine this horrified me, but the vision I'd acquired wasn't something I could turn off, like a flashlight. It was now a part of me, shining into places I'd never noticed before.

Mother's characters continued chatting up entire breakfasts and whole afternoons—a string of women who were their own story-books: Stella the usher who could recount the smallest details of movie after movie; Christie the bag lady, whose past privileged childhood overwhelmed the present in sudden bursts of memory.

One morning Mother was unusually quiet, and after cleaning up all the soggy little O's of cereal Dan had spilled on the floor she sat back at the table, her thumb stroking a spoon's concave smoothness. "I ever tell you the time I got lost in a department store?" she asked, in a husky voice that proclaimed the arrival of Danielle, the op-tometrist who gave us free eye exams.

"Nuh-uh," Laurie managed, mouth full.

Dan pushed away from the table, leaving his second bowl of ce-real untouched, and muttered, "I have to go to the bathroom."

Danielle barely noticed, and with a faraway look, as if savoring the story to come, she swept her hair back and curled it behind her ears. "I remember walking down an aisle of toys, staring at the rows of dolls while my mother browsed in the kitchen section next door. I knew she'd drag me along to the linen department pretty soon, so I pretended all the beautiful dolls with their lovely little smiles were asking me to stay.

"I could see my mother reaching out to touch a toaster that was so shiny it reflected her hand. I thought how cold it must feel and I shivered, and I turned to a shelf lined with clear bags of marbles. One of them was filled with cat's eyes, and they reminded me of those dolls' eyes, you know? A bag of eyes that seemed to see some-thing in me that I didn't know was there . . . have you ever felt like that?"

Laurie looked down at her toast, but I shook my head *yes*. I felt that way almost all the time now.

"So you probably know how strange I felt at that moment," Danielle said wistfully. "Anyway, whatever that something was, it made me want to touch one of the marbles, see what it felt like in my hand. The bag was tied shut with a red string, and when I finally undid the knot I realized that I'd forgotten about my mother—I glanced around but she wasn't anywhere. Then I called to her in such a tiny voice that I realized I really didn't want her to hear me.

"Now that was a very interesting thought, one I imagined the marbles had somehow given me, and it made me want to touch them even more. But when I reached into the bag my hand slipped and all the marbles rolled on the floor—so many little eyes trying to see me!

"I ran away before a saleslady could discover what I'd done, and I ran away from my mother, too—wherever she was—because I was sure she'd be angry." When Danielle paused, I imagined those marbles spinning on our kitchen floor, the cat's eyes catching a dizzy swirl of shelves and ceiling and counter and us.

"Well," she continued, "I ran through the furniture department and then up the escalator two steps at a time. I kept rushing down aisles on the second floor—the department store was so big! The thought suddenly hit me that my mother might never find me, and I stopped. I was in the middle of the perfume department, and there were posters of women with shaded eyelids and streaks of blush and long lashes everywhere. They looked so serious I was sure they knew why I was there.

"Then a saleslady behind one of the counters said, 'Why so glum?' She looked a little like the women in the posters, and at first I almost believed she'd walked out of one of them. I started to back away, but she gave me such a friendly smile I had to stop.

" 'Not talking today?' she asked. I shook my head. If I didn't speak, then I wouldn't have to confess what I'd done.

" 'So, how about a little makeover?' she said. 'It's a slow day, y'know.'

"I didn't know what she was talking about. 'C'mere,' she said with a little wave, 'I can make you look like a big girl in no time.' She pointed to a stool in front of the counter and I climbed up, and when she bent down we were almost the same height. Already I felt big! She brushed my cheeks and forehead with a sweet-smelling powder, and I crinkled my nose in pleasure and tried to hold in a sneeze.

"She let me pick the color of eyeliner—the deepest, darkest blue.

'Close your eyes,' she said. I felt a soft pencil against my eyelid, tugging a bit at my eye underneath. I thought of those marbles again and shifted in my seat, trying to imagine what my new face looked like. 'Hold still,' the woman whispered, and worked on my other lid. Then I felt the tickle of a brush sweeping along my lashes, the pull of something over my eyebrows."

Danielle paused to flip her hair behind her ears again, and she offered us a wan little smile. Laurie stared back intently, her hands clutching a napkin beside her forgotten breakfast.

"Well, then that saleslady said, 'Now it's time to pick your lipstick.' She spoke so softly I almost didn't hear her, and just as quietly I said, 'You pick.' My eyes were still closed, and I felt a cool stickiness rub against my lips—first the top, then the bottom, and I wished my lips were a mile long so she'd take forever. When the saleslady told me to press them together I did, two or three times. 'Open your eyes,' she said, and there I was, just inches away in a mirror and with something like cat's eyes, so grown up I could walk right by my mother in the store and she wouldn't recognize me at all. Who am I now? I thought—"

"But your mother *did* find you, didn't she?" Laurie broke in.

"That's the funny thing," Danielle said, escaping again into a dreamy look, "I can't remember . . ."

She had nothing more to say. I pushed away from the table, motioning to Laurie that we might be late for the bus, but she hesitated, not at all satisfied with Danielle's answer. Then I noticed Dan standing just outside the kitchen doorway, waiting for his absence to be noticed.

"C'mon, it's time to go," I insisted. While I hurried my disappointed brother and sister out the door and down the steps, I couldn't stop imagining those marbles spinning and spinning. Were they somehow us, trying to catch a glimpse of who our mother really was, or were they all the parts of Mother we'd recently discovered, casting strange and different gazes on us? I tore down the sidewalk, afraid of missing the bus, again afraid of seeing what I never dreamt I'd ever see.

The Collector

Mother's characters now lodged inside me, inner voices that chattered away even during school hours, sometimes branching off into conflicting paths that confounded me. *There's no instrument panel that can't be mastered,* whispered Joanna, a test pilot, spurring me on as I struggled with algebraic equations in math class. Yet the numbers and letters blurred into smears on the lined paper when Maureen the gossip columnist spoke up, insisting, *Secrets? What are secrets? If I can't find out, I make it up.*

These voices so preoccupied me that everyone else at school became irrelevant background: the thick-glassed, stuttering teacher who rapped out chalky math problems on the board, the bully who patrolled the school entrance, even the new girl—all blond waves and piercing green eyes—who sat at the desk beside me. And what *were* those lyrics I sang during chorus practice? Only one moment, echoed over and over during those last weeks before summer vacation, stands out: passing Dan or Laurie in the halls as we were herded along in our separate classes, catching their faces, holding their eyes for a moment and knowing that they, too, were peopled with Mother's cast of characters.

One afternoon as school let out, Laurie made her way toward me through the crowd of kids waiting for the bus. "Mom's here," she said, Dan in tow. Nearly breathless, she pointed out our dark blue station wagon idling at the edge of the parking lot.

Mother caught our gaze and nodded in an odd, crisp fashion: a new character awaited us. Dan frowned—he'd grown less and less patient with Mother's stories, and Laurie had to drag him by the hand, tempting him with visions of comic books and candy. Finally they raced for the prized front seat and this time I followed, determined not to lose out on any treats again.

Laurie pulled ahead of Dan with a triumphant whoop, but all she won was a locked door.

"In the back, in the back," Mother said, waving us away from the front door. "What do you think this is, a private car or something?"

She tapped her fingernails on the steering wheel as we quietly settled in the backseat. "Where to?" she asked.

My brother and sister looked to me for an answer and I hesitated—where *did* I want to go?

Mother turned and offered us an impatient frown. "Well, don't most kids go home after school? Or don't you have a home?"

"Of course we do," I said.

"And where *is* home? Take all day if you like . . . the meter's running, y'know."

His hand on the door, Dan shifted impatiently, perhaps contemplating escape, and I spoke up so he wouldn't be left behind. "432 Porter Lane. Do you want directions?"

She laughed. "I know this city like the back of my hand."

"City?" I asked, but she ignored my question and started out of the school parking lot. "What do you kids study in there, anyway? Reading, arithmetic, all that stuff?"

"Uh-huh," I replied. "And—"

"Well, I'm sure you don't get taught what you really need to know."

Dan leaned forward, suddenly interested. He hadn't cared much for kindergarten or the first grade, and now thought even less of the second. "We don't!"

"Just like I thought. It seems to me that what you need to learn is the first and last lesson of life: Don't never take nothing from nobody."

Dan nodded at this wisdom. Laurie and I said nothing.

"*Hey*, you all deaf back there?"

"No, we heard," I said. "Don't ever take anything from anybody."

"Good grammar, kid," she said, eyeing me from the rearview mirror. "But it doesn't matter how you say it, just remember it. You want to know my opinion? Kids shouldn't go to school. They should all drive cabs."

"We're too young to drive," I said.

She snorted. "Details, details. Bring down the age for a license, prop up the driver's seat with a few pillows, and everything's set, right?"

"*Right*," Dan replied.

"Yeah, well *you're* a smart kid, that's for sure. So listen to this: drive a couple of days in a cab, and you'll see the world. All kinds of people, all types. Some of them rough, too. But everyone can be handled, see? I remember when I picked up two guys, big beefy types, and when they got in the back I could smell that they were pickled . . ."

Laurie giggled. "Pickled?"

"Yeah, you know: snookered, *drunk*. I didn't mind. Money's money. But it turned out they were creeps—one of them said, 'Hey, look at this knife we just bought.' I looked in the rearview mirror and they were passing it back and forth, admiring the nasty-looking thing, and it *was* nasty looking, I'll tell you that. I knew they were trying to scare me, so I just said, 'Nice, where'd you buy it?'

" 'We didn't buy it, we stole it,' the other creep said, with a laugh I didn't like. Then he leaned forward and waved it near the side of my face and said, 'And we'd really like to try it out.' "

Laurie's lips pressed tightly together, so I said, "But here you are now, so this story has a happy ending, right?"

"You bet, that's the whole *point*. I looked at that blade wiggling at me and I said, 'Hey, that beauty looks a lot like a knife I got in *my* collection. Lemme take a look.' So I held out my hand and—you won't believe this—the dope *gave* it to me. Too much to drink, right? I slammed on the brakes and waved the knife at *them*. 'Okay, assholes,' I said. 'This ride's over. You pay full fare, and I expect a big tip.' "

"They threw their money at me real fast, just like *that*." She snapped her fingers. "But then one of the dopes said, 'What about our knife?'

" 'You like me so much you gave it to me as a gift, remember?' I waved it a little closer and they popped out my cab toot sweet. 'Course, once they were safe they started calling me every name in the book. Tough guys! And I drove off a little richer, with a nice souvenir."

Mother turned the corner, driving by the same stone church we'd passed just a few minutes ago, and I remembered Father once complaining about a cabdriver doing this to him in New York City—now our own mother was trying to cheat us, driving in circles around a block that wasn't even ours. "Excuse me," I said, "but this isn't the way to our home."

Her eyes in the rearview mirror caught me again. "Don't you live on Carter Street?"

"Porter Lane."

"Well, well. My mistake."

We drove on in silence the last few blocks, and when she stopped in front of our house, Mother said, "So there you go, kids—I get you home safely *and* teach you a valuable lesson you should never forget, right?"

"We're not paying full fare," I said.

"Don't worry, it's on the house—I don't usually drive such well-behaved kids around."

"Thanks," I said. I opened the car door and we all scooted out.

Mother kept the car idling. "Aren't you coming too?" Laurie asked her.

She didn't even turn to look back at us. "I'm not a baby-sitter, little girl. I've got a job to do."

We stood on the sidewalk, stunned as the car drove away from us. "*Asshole!*" Dan shouted. He kicked at a rock and it bounced ineffectually a few feet. Only after the car disappeared in the distance, only after we couldn't hear the faint purr of its engine did we listlessly approach the front door.

It was locked. Laurie's lips quivered but I shushed her and steered everyone to the backyard. The arc of hedges and shade trees, the well-trimmed lawn and slightly rusted swing set in the corner looked as if it could belong to any family, even a happy one. Laurie grabbed the swing chains and I pushed her to giddy heights, while Dan sat cross-legged, pulling up tufts of grass, and we all waited for one of our parents to come home.

Now whenever Mother changed, Dan fled the house, and when he returned he refused to speak, even to eat, until she apologized by being herself again, by simply offering us her uneventful attention. As for me, I couldn't help feeling that every one of Mother's characters hid a story about her, and in the evenings Laurie and I tried to guess the motivations of the latest addition to our family.

"Why did Daisy do that?" Laurie asked me while we sat together on the edge of my bed—earlier in the day Mother had been the brooding Daisy, who borrowed Dan's crayons and drew over a few days' worth of newspapers that hadn't been thrown out yet by Father. Laurie thought they were just messy squiggles, but to me they were different kinds of furious weather: multicolored tornadoes; dark red, brooding clouds; complicated storm patterns that ranged across the comics page and the TV listings.

"*Stupe*, she's an artist," I said, surprised to hear myself echoing Mother's cabdriver voice.

"Oh," Laurie said, grabbing an edge of the pillow and working it with her fingers. "So why didn't she draw pictures?"

"Because that's not what artists do any more," I said, recalling a field trip last year to the local university's museum, when I'd found myself in a room filled with huge canvases that looked as if the artists had danced and twitched while they spread their brilliant colors.

"Why *not?*"

I regarded Laurie's pained face in the dim light. This wasn't the route I wanted our discussion to take, so I ignored her question and offered another: "I wonder why Daisy became an artist?"

"Because she can't draw pictures?"

"No," I snorted, though I wasn't certain of this either. "Maybe," I said, remembering a bit of the museum guide's lecture, "maybe she became an artist because she just *had* to."

"You mean, like going to the bathroom?" Laurie kicked her feet against the side of the bunk bed, an odd little laugh gurgling in her throat.

"Very funny, I'm sure. No, I mean maybe when Daisy was a little girl she grew up in a place where there was a lot of . . . bad weather."

"When she was a little girl," Laurie repeated, as if this were extraordinary information. "So why would bad weather make her an artist?"

"Well," I said slowly, uncertain of my logic, "if she saw things like hurricanes and ice storms, then maybe when she grew up that's what she wanted to draw."

"How come?"

"I don't know. You'd think she'd want to draw nice weather, right?"

"Yeah," Laurie replied, nodding with satisfaction that we finally agreed. Yet I tapped my heels against the sideboards of the bed, unsettled by the implications of my version of Daisy. If something in her childhood had led her to dash off so many shades of bad weather, then what would *we* do when we grew up?

Dan appeared in the doorway, frowning his disapproval, and I glanced at the clock. Once again Mother had forgotten our bedtime, and once again Father hadn't noticed. So we formed a quiet, furtive line at the bathroom sink, as if we were guilty of something, and after our various toothbrushings and handwashings we put ourselves to bed.

I lay miles away from sleep that night, lost in a crowd of Mother's someone elses. Where was she among them? Would she ever let us find her again? With this thought, I felt some hidden part of me struggling to open, and I pushed away the covers and paced in the dark, fueled by an anxiety I couldn't name.

The window offered an antidote: the comforting view of a quiet street. I reached out to hold this sight but instead touched glass, felt its faint chill. I pressed harder at the window. If something so solid could be so easy to see through, I thought, then why weren't people the same way, open to any search, available to anyone's curiosity? If this were possible, we could finally catch our mother! But then wouldn't Mother also be able to discover, even with a single glance, my growing fear of her?

I pulled my hands away from the window's smooth touch. Suddenly cold, I clutched the open neck of my pajamas. A button dangling from the collar somehow oppressed me and I tugged at the thread, tugged at it again. Yet when the button snapped off I was filled with regret over this small loss. Still grasping the button, I returned to bed and rubbed at its distinct circle—so alone in my warm, sweaty palm—until I fell asleep.

Mother slept late that morning, the bedroom door shut to us. While Laurie prepared breakfast, I hurried my way down the basement steps to the sewing machine, where Mother kept an ashtray filled with old buttons of varied colors and sizes. Fingering through these other victims of loose threads, I listened to their crisp clicks and decided they deserved a better home than this musty basement. I padded upstairs with the ashtray and set it on a shelf beside my model airplanes.

The thought of those buttons—a little pool of circular waves—distracted me all through my day at school until finally, during social studies, I abandoned my textbook in exasperation and chewed a little arc of nail from my thumb. It peeled off smoothly and I stopped to examine it: one edge curved and stiff, the other ragged and surprisingly soft. I worried the rest of my nails until I had a tiny pile of crescents on my desk that could have been miniature white eyebrows, boomerangs, disembodied smiles or frowns. Why not collect these too? I thought, and slipped them in my pocket.

Back home I took a shot glass from the pantry cabinet and this soon sat brimming with nail clippings, right beside the ashtray of buttons on my shelf. Over the next few days I collected chicken and fish bones from dinner plates and crammed them into a Flintstones jelly jar: a potential dinosaur skeleton, they were the perfect background for Fred's stenciled face smiling from the curved glass. I liked to imagine that if I fit them together the most extraordinary creature would be revealed.

My collection grew in the following weeks: a sandwich bag of stray feathers, gathered from the park; a long-stemmed glass half filled with paper clips; and an old bowling bag so stuffed with white styrofoam peanuts that it seemed a real bowling ball nestled inside the cracked imitation leather.

When summer recess began I had to forgo gathering leftover

chalk scraps from the classroom blackboard, but this was a minor setback. Already I had plans to scour back lots for stray bottle caps. I would have asked my increasingly restless brother for help—he knew the secret byways of our neighborhood far better than I—but he couldn't stand the sight of my collection and its fussy arrangement. It was true that I had to place each container just right on the shelves, its own little pocket of order. Alone in my room, I could settle so easily into the solace of things and stare at them for hours.

Arguing over whether to eat the cantaloupe or the grapefruit—all that was left in the kitchen that might make a breakfast—Dan and Laurie rolled them back and forth at each other across the table. A ripe scent, hinting at decay, filled the room. Mother stood by the sink, feigning indifference, though when she scratched at her elbow I realized she was really Patricia, the woman who suffered violent fits of itching. Before I could hush Dan and Laurie, Patricia grabbed an unwashed glass. With one deft swing she broke it in half against the faucet and glass shards scattered across the counter.

We stared, unable to move, to protest, as she approached our table with the jagged bottom. She stuck it into the cantaloupe, where it sat firmly like a horrid hat.

We decided on grapefruit and ate dutifully, listening to one mower after another start up down the block. Patricia scratched at her arms, the back of her neck and then, a cigarette dangling from her mouth, she smoked—a habit Mother had quit over two years ago.

"It's hot in here," she murmured, as if to herself. "Where's the fan?"

She left the kitchen and rummaged in the hall closet, where Father had stored our old fan after installing the air conditioner. When she returned, none of us dared ask Patricia how she knew our house so well. Our mouths were full, or if they weren't we pretended they were. Even Dan chewed silently.

She placed the fan on the counter, close to the screen door, and punched the switch. The metal blades spun to life, the circular cage rotating back and forth. Patricia blew smoke out through her nose, the light-blue wisps curling in the direction of the fan's luxurious whir. Those delicate smoky trails sped through the grillwork and past the blade, rushing out as an indistinct cloud that vanished through the screen door.

"Do that again," Dan said in awe, actually daring to speak up, but Patricia had already exhaled, as though anticipating the request. Again the smoke spread out in intricate, sinuous lines, then curved quickly through the blades and came out a gray stain.

Patricia turned to us. "Here," she said, holding out her cigarette, "any of you want to try?"

None of us did, but none of us wanted to say so. We waited for each other to speak.

"Don't worry," she said, her outstretched hand still offering the cigarette. "It's filter tipped. It's *low tar*."

"Sure," I piped up, the grapefruit still bitter and raw in my mouth. "Pass the damn thing over."

Patricia stepped back against the counter, a knowing look in her narrowed eyes. Did she suspect that I too had a secret life? She laughed, flipped the cigarette into the sink, and then turned on the faucet and the disposal. After unplugging the fan she hurried out of the kitchen, the thin cord trailing behind her, away from the mashing whine that seemed to surround us.

We Want You Back

My search through the park had been a success: two ancient bottle caps, their fluted edges rusted; a few sharp brown shards of a broken beer bottle; and a dark iridescent crow feather. After stowing them in a backpack, I simply had to return to a special corner of the park that I'd discovered: a little circle of trees that offered a green tunnel to the sky, its borders subtly altered by swaying branches. I stretched out on the grass and watched bits of cloud pass by, wispy expressions that dissolved into a sheer blue so calming that I felt ready for whatever new characters Mother might be concocting back home, even if I didn't know *why* she might be concocting them.

At the time I hadn't heard of anything called a multiple personality disorder and so couldn't consider this possibility, yet even now I doubt that term could ever explain my mother. She'd simply started a game, a silly game out of boredom or sadness, and too soon that game's logic led her away from where she'd started, led her away from us.

If only I'd known how far, that day when I returned home and stood before the open side door, listening to Laurie and Dan in the backyard arguing some variation of It's My Turn. Their dispute wasn't very serious—the squeaks of two swings punctuated a lazy sparring that seemed mostly designed to trigger Mother's intervention, though she didn't seem to be taking the bait. Where was she?

I ventured into the quiet house. "Hello?"

"Is that you?" I heard her call from upstairs. "*Finally.* I've been waiting for *hours.*" She barged out onto the landing, an exasperated smile on her face. "*There* you are. What kind of a repair service do you run, anyway?"

She waited for me to explain myself and enter whatever drama she was plotting, and her toe tapped away at the banister like an improvised, impatient timepiece.

So I once again entered into another game with the simple phrase, "Excuse me, ma'am?" though I also couldn't help wishing that I could take back my words.

"I *said*, you should've been here hours ago."

I sighed. "I had a big job over at the Carleton place. If I were you, I wouldn't complain. You're lucky I showed up," I groused, secretly exhilarated that I could reprimand her. Was *this* the sort of freedom adults enjoyed every day?

She chuckled bitterly. "Oh, do I feel lucky." Setting off down the second floor hall, she called back, "At least don't take your time now that you're here."

I hurried after her and she led me to the one room in the house I never felt comfortable entering, even on Christmas mornings when Laurie, Dan and I dragged our parents from bed as early as we dared. Hesitating at the doorway, I surveyed the night tables and their mysterious drawers that none of us could ever bring ourselves to open, the large bed and its plush covers, and a seascape painting on the wall with waves always about to crash down on the headboard.

"Excuse me," Mother said, "but you *can* come into the room; we don't have problems with the door hinges. Actually, the problem's right over here," she said, struggling to open a screen window. She peered outside and then she was halfway through, her legs dangling in the air for a brief awkward moment as she scrambled out onto the roof.

"Wait!" I shouted in my own voice.

She peered back inside, her face framed by the window, both hands clutching the sill. "You *are* wearing your workboots, aren't you?"

I glanced down at my sneakers—they'd certainly keep a good grip. "Sure," I repeated, trying to recover my confident repairman's tone. "But ma'am, why don't you let *me* see what the trouble is?"

"How are you going to find it unless I show you?" she said, and scrabbled away on the roof.

I stood before this window that was now much more than a window: if I crawled through I'd *really* have to become the workman in my mother's story. Except she wasn't my mother, I reminded myself, she was just a very odd woman who was going to give me a rough time on this job.

"I know you get paid by the hour," I heard her say, "but as far as I'm concerned the clock doesn't start until you're out on the roof."

I clenched my teeth. The customer's always right, I thought, easing myself out feet first, testing the shingles' gritty surface on this roof that was tilted like the deck of a dangerously listing ship. Only when I was sure of a steady grip did I turn around.

The front yard seemed miles away, unaware of me and yet at the same time waiting for my feet to slip. Queasy at the first hint of the shingles' faintly tar-ish aroma, I was ready to scramble back inside. But Mother had already clambered to the peak of one of the dormers, and I fought my fear and followed. Using a bird's nest in a nearby shade tree as a guide, I kept my eyes from the shifting clouds and the patient ground below. Finally I reached her, unable to hide my nervous little gasps.

"How long have you been in this business?" she asked quietly.

"Longer than you think, ma'am. Now what's the problem?"

Tapping the angled shingles with her feet, she said, "Just look at this roof. It *leaks*. It started in the bedroom—there's a terrible stain on the ceiling. That's not all, of course—you can't imagine what else's been ruined inside. And it's spreading everywhere!"

With a slow sweep of my head I regarded every shingle: each was as ordinary as the other. "The roof appears all right to me. Are you—"

"Oh you! Where are your *eyes*? Look at *this*." She stamped her feet. "And this *here*."

"Well, maybe I was a bit hasty—"

"And this, and *this* . . ." Mother pounded at the shingles with her fists, working her way up to the crest of the roof.

"Wait!" I shouted, climbing after her, "I see what you mean—"

"Mommy!" I heard Laurie cry out. "Mommy come down!"

I reached the top and there were my brother and sister below, rushing to the edge of the house. Laurie began weeping. "Please, please," was all she could manage, staring up at us.

"It's just the brats," Mother said. "Ignore them, they're always crying about something."

I sucked in my breath at her words. Was Mother playing a mother who didn't love her children, or had she confessed something? Her steady gaze waited for a reaction. Was I still a workman in her eyes, or merely a child who impersonated one? Once again the awkward angle of the roof pulled at me. I knelt down, my eyes squeezed shut, and decided I'd lost my patience with this woman—it was time to wrap up the job.

"Ma'am?" I ventured, "I've seen this sort of thing before. So I've just applied . . . Protecto-Guard. On all the problem areas."

She didn't move, she just kept watching those poor wailing kids, not a touch of concern on her face, and I tried again. "Excuse me—"

"Protecto what?" she replied, her voice husky, barely audible.

"Guard. So if you'll just follow me," I said, assuming a tone of professional impatience. "I can get to my next job down on Sycamore Street."

I tugged at her resisting elbow until she nodded silently and let me lead her carefully down the roof. Emboldened, I kept up a distracting patter: "As you can see, Protecto-Guard dries quickly, and gives off no unpleasant odor. And it's inexpensive too."

The woman didn't say a word, though I could tell from the amused line of her mouth that she was listening. I decided to charge her extra just for being such a pain in the ass. But first I had to get her off the damn roof, so when we reached the window I shuffled to the side and motioned for her to climb back in.

She grabbed the sill with both hands, then closed her eyes and leaned back.

"I'm in a *hurry*," I grumbled, alarmed that she might let go and fall. "*Please*, after you."

With a sharp grunt she pulled through the window, as if returning inside were painful. Following too quickly, I scraped my shin but kept quiet—I was a grown-up, after all, with no mother nearby to offer any sympathy.

I could hear the woman's two kids running up the stairs, bawling. She turned to me and looked as if she might start complaining again, so I pointed to the ceiling. "See? No unsightly stain. I've fixed everything. Protecto-Guard really works wonders, and you'll find that the ceilings everywhere in the house are just as stain free."

"It'll come back," she murmured, and then she took my brother and sister into her waiting arms.

Pretending that what had just occurred could somehow be forgotten, we settled once again into our unspoken pact of normalcy: Mother set to work in the kitchen, while we took our places on the living room rug before the television. But I found no delight in the transformations of Felix the Cat's magic bag, even when it unfurled into a tank and routed his enemies.

Dinner that evening at first maintained its usual dreariness, with Mother matching Father's silence, but after a few minutes Laurie set her head on the table and wept, her shoulders shaking. When Mother leaned over, cooing comfort, Laurie shivered away from any touch and slunk down in her seat.

"Gladys?" Father asked. "What's the matter with Laurie?"

Before Mother could reply Laurie wailed, "Mommy climbed up on the roof today!"

"The roof?" Father repeated, and with those words he unknowingly entered into our secret life.

Mother said nothing, her face strained with surprise. She turned to Dan and me, the two other witnesses to today's extravaganza. What she saw in our hard faces couldn't have reassured her.

"I want an answer," Father said, glancing around the table.

"It was nothing at all . . ." Mother began uncertainly. "I thought there was a . . . a squirrel in the attic, and I wanted to check to see how it maybe . . . might have gotten in—"

"Michael was up there too," Laurie said to her plate in a small, sniffly voice.

"Yes, I forgot," Mother replied, eyes wary. "Michael helped me look, didn't you honey?"

I simply couldn't take part in another of Mother's stories. "We were up there because you said the roof was leaking."

"*I* said?" was all she could manage, openmouthed at my desertion.

"Well?" Father asked, an edge in his voice. "Squirrel or leak?"

"Squirrel," Mother said.

"Leak," I repeated less confidently.

Mother attempted a breezy laugh. "Really, it's plain to see that the roof doesn't leak."

"We don't have a squirrel in the attic, either," I forced myself to say, "but you *said* there was a leak."

"I don't know what's come over your son," Mother announced, turning to Father.

Your son. Was she once again looking out at us from behind another character? "You're lying," I squeaked out, amazed at my daring.

"*What* did you say?" Father hissed. Mother's thin smile made me realize my misstep—with no one else on the roof, it was my word against hers.

"I asked you a *question*," Father barked.

Laurie hiccupped with teary misery, but I wouldn't allow myself to cry. "I, I said—"

"Michael's telling the truth," Dan said, breaking his silence.

"I suppose *you* were on the roof too, young man?" Mother replied airily, her triumph nearly at hand.

"No. But you lie all the time. You pretend you're not our mom."

"What is the *matter* with you kids?" Mother said, backing away to the refrigerator.

Now Father stood and pinned us with a stern gaze. "It's time to apologize to your mother."

Refusing to back down, Dan shook his head. "We *won't*. She tells lies all the time. Every day."

"This little *game* you're playing isn't funny!" Mother said, striding toward him, her finger poking in the air. "Not one little bit!"

Dan didn't blink. "We don't want those other people, Mom."

"We want you," I added. "We want you back."

"We do, we do," Laurie croaked out, her voice raw from stifling sobs.

"I won't allow this!" Mother cried out, fists raised and shaking. "I won't allow this!"

Father reached out and held her wrists. "Gladys," he said in a surprisingly tiny voice, "what's going on?"

Dinner abandoned, our parents locked themselves in their bedroom, where they spoke in angry whispers, indecipherable even with my ear to the door. Dan and Laurie sat hunched before the television like defendants waiting for a jury to announce its deliberations, and I joined them. We stared with little pleasure at one show after another: comedy then car chases then comedy. When the news anchors casually offered us the world's latest disasters, Dan and Laurie lay on the rug, their eyes barely open. I turned off the TV. Harsh whispers still drifted from our parents' door—who could tell when they'd be done? I gently shook my sister and brother and led them up the stairs.

The next morning we found Father alone in the kitchen, preparing a breakfast of slightly runny scrambled eggs and toast with only the crusts burnt. We ate without complaint, feeling so guilty over our well-kept secrets, and we waited for him to ask us just what had been happening these past few months. Instead he stood by the sink, hot water pouring over last night's dirty dishes, and he stared at us as if our school portraits on the wall had suddenly come to life, as if there was far more to us than our minor daily disputes, our culinary prejudices, our unpredictable nighttime fears.

Father left the kitchen and returned to more long hours with Mother in their room, so long that Laurie had time to break into Mother's makeup kit in the bathroom and smear her lips an awkward, off-centered red that I made her wash off. Then Dan began to fret. "It's our *bowling* day, when are we going—"

"Oh, be *quiet*," I said.

Perhaps Father heard us, for he appeared minutes later, strangely cheery. "Anybody ready for bowling?" he asked, adding, "And guess what? Your mother's coming too."

At first we were silent. I couldn't imagine Mother would enjoy the bowling alley with its toppling pins and unruly din, but how could I explain this to my father? "Does she *really* want to come?" I ventured.

He hesitated. "Of course she does!" he replied too loudly, trying to convince himself as well as us.

"Dad, I don't think—"

"Look, we could *all* do with a little healthy athletic activity," he said, his voice defying contradiction. "Off you go to the car—we'll be right with you."

We sat in the backseat for several long minutes, anxiously waiting, yet when our parents finally appeared they walked down the front steps together with an offhand ease, Mother nodding agreeably to something Father whispered in her ear. She settled in the front seat and turned to gaze at us with affectionate indulgence, much like our old, familiar Mother. But as I stared out the window, at the storefronts melting together as we sped by, I wondered if the woman sitting in the front seat might just be artfully impersonating my mother.

When we pushed open the bowling alley's glass doors, the explosive clatter of pins echoed about us. Mother winced, but entered bravely into the air-conditioned air, following after us to the main desk, where Father went through his ritual inspection of the bowling shoes. Mother held her pair up with two fingers, swinging them in unison. "What strange creatures," she said, feigning astonishment. Then more pins smashed behind us and she closed her eyes.

We claimed our lane, laced up our shoes, and Mother accompanied us to the racks of bowling balls. Tentatively running her hand along the rows, now and then she'd turn a ball so that its three fingerholes faced out, and she'd peer at the dark round eyes, the open mouth.

Mother returned to our lane empty-handed. "Nothing to your liking?" Father asked. "Want to borrow mine?"

"No thanks. I think I'll pass on the first game and contemplate my fashionable feet," she murmured.

"What?"

"Oh, I'm just a little tired," she replied, her teeth set in cheeriness. "I'd better rest up for the second game."

Mother didn't rest at all. She paced behind us, back and forth and back again as we took our turns, and with each new clash of pins her face stiffened. Father never looked back at her, determined not to condone her unsportsmanlike behavior, but Laurie's lips trembled at the sight of Mother's brittle mask, and I couldn't stop gnawing my fingernails.

Mother paused only once, after I'd clinched a spare. She stared at a last, lone pin that spun swiftly on its side; then she turned away with a stricken look as it was scooped up by the reset mechanism. Surely by now she understood that this entire game was target practice against what refused to stay down.

I decided I simply couldn't add to her misery: on my next turn I sped the ball at a sharp angle, directly into the gutter. Father restrained himself from offering advice, even when I repeated my mistake. But I offered Laurie a knowing glance and she caught on to my scheme and followed along. Then Dan joined in, simply for the love of mischief. Gutter ball after gutter ball confounded Father while Mother's face seemed to soften, and once again we were in her thrall.

"What's going on here?" he declared. "Wipe your hands before you bowl—what's on those fingers? Don't I always say absolutely no to potato chips during the game? Where are you hiding them?"

"Sorry, Dad," I sighed, feigning despair. "It's just—bad luck, I guess."

We continued to ignore his complaints. Father threw three stunning strikes in a row as a rebuke to our miserable performance, yet still he seethed.

When Dan stopped at the line as he always did, preparing to push the ball, he so overtly aimed it toward the gutter that Father sputtered angrily. The bowling ball slipped from Dan's hands and it crept down the lane, aiming straight for the pins.

"No!" Mother shouted. She rushed past us, down the lane after the ball.

"Gladys! Back here—get back here!" Father called after her.

She never looked back and caught up to the ball, her hands framing its curve. Kneeling, she cradled the ball in her lap and I knew what she saw: the deep-pitted eyes of its face, its silent, howling mouth.

The pins in the next lane erupted and Mother clutched at her head, the same way she'd held the bowling ball. "Stop!" she cried out. "Stop!"

A few balls continued speeding down the lanes, their distant clatter echoing. Then the entire bowling alley was quiet, except for the churning hum of fallen pins being reset.

"Stop," she repeated, her arms stiff and palms up as if she were directing traffic. "It's . . . very important . . . that everyone . . . *stop*."

Laurie began to whimper, and Father called out wearily, "Gladys, that's enough." She stared back at us without recognition—whatever she was about to do, we'd only be minor obstructions.

Three lanes down, a fat man laughed and shook his head in bemusement before reaching for his bowling ball. He lifted it before him and eyed the distant pins.

"No, you mustn't. You mustn't!" Mother screamed, her mouth an open wound.

The man shook his head again, took a few lumbering steps and released the ball. At the crash of flying pins Mother shook so violently I imagined all her hidden selves shuddered within. Father ran down the lane, nearly slipping on its polished surface before he reached Mother. Her face now immobile as a statue's, she offered no resistance as he led her away.

Somehow we managed to make our way through the confusion of a gathering crowd to the main desk. We returned our bowling shoes, filled with shame and misery, and the register rang and Father fumbled with his wallet as he kept a grip on Mother's arm. Laurie, Dan and I huddled in a tight circle of misery about them as we left the bowling alley, a misery that, as piercing as any siren, enveloped our car when Father drove from the parking lot.

Back home, our parents once again disappeared into their room for another mysterious conference that would last all day. At the click of the locked door, Dan fled from our house for the call of the neighborhood, and Laurie ran downstairs and threw herself on the couch, face pressed tightly into the pillows. Her body heaved with sobs.

I gently shook her shoulder. "Hey, Laurie, hey, it'll be all right," I murmured, my voice utterly without conviction as I gazed out the living room window. The ominously darkening clouds tempted me to chase after Dan, but I was afraid to leave Laurie alone. When my sister was finally done with all that weeping that no parent came to comfort, she rose from the couch, and her pale face seemed emptied of all tears forever.

Unable to bear the sight of that stricken look, I had to turn away. Remembering that I had a few fingernail slivers to add to my collection, I escaped to my room. As I approached those containers, so neatly spaced apart from each other on the shelves, a terrible thought ran through me: they were just a bunch of shreds and scraps and castoffs that added up to nothing, pieces of a puzzle that could never be put together. My throat constricted, for a moment I had trouble breathing, and then that thought disappeared, banished, surely, by my collection's soothing qualities. Yet when I slipped the slivers into the shot glass, it was without my usual twinge of pleasure.

I woke that night to reverberating thunder that uncannily echoed the afternoon's din of flailing bowling pins. Please don't let it wake up Mom, I thought, *please*. Between those claps of thunder, a rhythmic banging kept up outside, an unnerving *slam . . . slam . . . slam* that seemed as if it might never end.

What could that be? I crossed the dark room and peered out through the windswept torrents of rain lashing against my window, just able to make out our neighbors' porch, illuminated by a dim outside light. The screen door swung open from the wind and then its spring pulled it shut, again and again, opening and closing like a perpetual coming and going of invisible guests.

A brilliant shaft of lightning cast our own rain-streaked house into momentary relief, and I caught my breath at the sight of Mother standing at the hall window, staring down at that swinging door. Then it was night again. Had I imagined her? I stood and waited for another bolt of lightning, all the while listening to that awful, insistent banging, but when a shivering light again surged through the darkness, the hall window was empty.

Morning brought the distant, disembodied chatter of birds, and the sun streaking through the curtains. Our parents' door lay open, though the bedroom was empty, and we found no one downstairs. I looked out the window at the driveway—the car was gone, so perhaps Father had left for the Sunday paper. But where was Mother? We hurried out to the backyard and called her name, and received no answer.

Small branches littered the lawn, and a single wooden shingle dangled at an odd angle on the side of the house. The soaked grass was spongy beneath my feet, and above drifted one lone cloud, a straggler from last night's storm.

It was a round tiny cloud, and I turned in a slow, tight circle as I took it in, my head stretched back, and then I turned a little faster, enjoying the spinning. I spun more and more, creating a circle of sky as if I were that funnel of trees in the park, and I closed my eyes and imagined I could separate from my body and float away. Yet when I felt in danger of sweeping out of myself I stopped suddenly, opening my eyes to the world dashing dizzily around me: the neighbors' houses elongated into a circling, speeding train, my brother and sister squeezed into one blurry child, and that single cloud spinning above like the point of a top.

Without speaking, Laurie began to twirl herself too, her arms extended. Even Dan joined in, and we twisted about the backyard, whirling until we were giddy from our dizzy steps. We stopped and let the world slow down and suddenly there was Mother, watching us from the edge of the lawn, her arms folded across her nightgown.

She took a few groggy steps forward and her lips moved oddly, silently. Then she managed to gurgle something, her words so slurred we couldn't understand her. Was this morning's character supposed to be some sort of derelict? We turned our backs on her, unwilling to enter into any new game, and we kept up our own, turning in circles before our swaying mother.

She shouted, shouted out words so undone by a thick tongue that we stopped our twirling. But she wasn't looking at us, her eyes were on that loose shingle on the wall.

She lurched past us and her hands scrabbled at the rough wooden square until she tugged it off. She flung it behind her, just over our heads, and it sliced into the hedge. Then Mother pulled off another shingle, and another, revealing an underlying layer of coarse black paper that her fingernails scratched at, and I couldn't tell if she was trying to tear our house apart or somehow work her way back into it.

Pieces of the house, like scattered tiles, littered the lawn, and we ducked as more shingles whirled in the air above us. Finally Dan grasped at Mother's arm and he tried to pull her away, but she shook him loose with an awkward shove, almost falling herself, her hair swinging wildly.

Swaying on woozy legs, she clutched at her stomach as if it, too, held something that must be torn away, and her face split wide open into a long, terrible moan. Mother turned to us, her eyes filled with what I have always since believed was sorrow and regret, and then she toppled over.

She lay so still, staring straight at the sky, and we encircled her, unsure of what to expect. "Mom?" Laurie whispered. We knelt around her, waiting for any slurred answer, and we bent so low we saw ourselves contained in her unblinking eyes like a tiny, concave photograph. We were Mother's secret audience, caught together for one last long moment before we allowed ourselves to understand, before we split apart in terrible grief.

PART TWO

I Have a Hunch about You

I lay on the bed, my knuckles still loose from Sylvia's sweet tugging. This woman I'd met merely two hours earlier now stood naked before my bureau mirror, combing her thick brown hair, and though her back was to me I could imagine the already familiar shadows of her collarbone, the tiny oval birthmark beside her left nipple, the ghostly line of an appendectomy scar.

Sylvia kept at her hair, setting off crackles of static, and her face in the mirror watched me watch her until a sudden recognition flared in her eyes, something I couldn't quite read. She shifted her gaze to the flowery design on the brush's handle.

"Pretty," she said, adding carefully, "left behind by an old lover?"

Her eyes met mine in the mirror and I shook my head no.

She stopped brushing. "Current lover?"

"No. It's just something else I've collected." I sat up, deciding it was past time to tell her all about what remained of my objects. Why not begin with the bewigged and terribly thin woman at a yard sale who'd confessed that, after chemo, she'd hoped the lush tendrils and petals etched on that comb's handle might somehow induce her hair to return?

Sylvia turned and regarded me coolly. "Secrets, secrets."

"Not at all," I returned. "I can tell you all about that brush." I hesitated. "Or the tape, or—"

"Wait," she said, a wry pleasure returning to her lips. "Actually, I think I'd like to keep you mysterious for just a little while longer. Let me start."

"Oh?"

"I could tell you a story."

"A story?"

"Uh-huh. About how my parents met. It begins with my grandfather, though. He was a magician."

"A story," I repeated. I'd heard so many tales in my life, tales that took me to such unexpected places, and now Sylvia was about to tell me another.

She turned back to the mirror and her hair. "My grandfather mostly worked small towns in the Southwest and Texas," she began. "He wasn't much of a magician, apparently—just the usual dopey tricks. But he did have one big drawing card. He'd bury an assistant alive in a box not much bigger than a coffin, always on the outskirts of some sleepy town. He charged good money for a peek down the periscope. One summer, he took my mom along on the tour. She was barely seventeen, and she certainly didn't know what her father was planning for her."

"C'mon," I said. "You're kid—"

"Nope. My parents could really embellish a story, I'll admit, they liked to do that, for sure. But they wouldn't mess with the basic facts. Anyway, it's crazy, huh? What could he have been thinking about, burying his own daughter?" Sylvia shuddered. "I don't like to imagine.

"Anyway, the first time he buried her, Mom just went, well, batty, crying and moaning until my grandfather dug her up. But he had no real show without this big draw. And no show, no money. So he gave her a lot of crap about how all his other assistants had managed just fine, and somehow he convinced her to go down again, this time with a bottle of raspberry brandy.

"Even so, Grampire—that's how I think of him—Grampire realized that with Mom being so much trouble he needed extra help, and this is where my dad comes in: he got the job to bury her. Before every show he dug the hole, set the booze in the box, checked the periscope and airhole pipe, even a string of light bulbs that would light up Mom's face.

'Christmas decorations,' she always called them. That's why we never had a Christmas tree when I was a little girl."

Sylvia's hair now fairly bristled as she stroked it, and she looked at me again. "You know, almost no one else knows this story, so why am I telling you?" She paused, then answered her own question. "You make me feel like a faucet."

I shrugged, trying to hide any hint of how often I'd heard similar comments. "I'm just listening."

"Well, listen away. Whenever Dad helped Mom into the box he didn't dare look at her, not even when she whispered she was ready. He just closed the lid and started shoveling dirt, and then he helped Grampire sell tickets to the customers—creeps who came to peep through a hole at 'The Lady Who Dares Death in the Face.' My dad always refused to look in. But as he once told me, he realized pretty quickly that this was a rather mild form of protest.

"So one afternoon, after everyone left, my dad gave in and peeked. I could never get him to tell me what Mom looked like. All he'd say was, that's when he decided to save her."

My own mother's bloated death mask suddenly appeared before me. If any of us had managed to really see her, to see through her disguises during those last terrible months, would that have changed what happened?

Sensing my distraction, Sylvia waited, the brush idle in her hand.

"It's okay," I said, offering her a reassuring smile.

"So. That night, while the 'great magician' slept, my mom and dad whispered for hours. The next night, too. They have different memories of what they talked about, but at least they both claim that's when they fell in love. When they traveled to the next town and Dad had to bury Mom again she was probably pregnant—I was born nine months later. Just think—I spent the first days of my existence in the womb of a woman buried alive!"

"C'mon, you're making this up," I said, trying to shake off any thought of all the people buried within me.

Sylvia laughed. "It's as true as any story your parents tell you can be true. Anyway, I've believed it since I was a kid, so it's a part of me now, you know?"

I nodded. "I certainly have some experience in that area."

"Oh? Well, pretty soon my parents started to plot escape. What they

came up with was very dramatic, very B-movie-ish, actually—just like
their situation. Instead of burying Mom, Dad knocked out Grampire
with the flat side of the shovel and they stole his car. My mom never
had to be pored over through a peephole again. And she never saw her
father again, either."

Sylvia turned from the mirror. She tossed the brush on the bed and
then sat beside me. "Y'know, I've always tried to imagine how those
men stared at her, with just what kind of intensity. The way you look at
me reminds me of that."

"Me?" I said. "Hey, what are you trying to say?"

"No, wait, hear me out," Sylvia replied. "Remember, one of those
men was my dad, and he saved her." Suddenly embarrassed, she
grabbed a pillow and covered her face.

"I have a hunch about you," her muffled voice said.

Our Phantom Limb

My brother and sister wouldn't even approach the coffin. I forced myself to look inside, and I flinched at the sight. Nestled in a brittle cushion of brown hair, Mother's puffy face had become another stranger. She seemed almost serene, as if she'd silenced those voices and finally escaped them. But she'd also escaped us, and with that bitter thought I returned to the milling crowd of Father's respectful employees, the few curious neighbors, and our mere handful of extended family.

Dan and Laurie and I accepted what seemed like standard expressions of condolence with a simple nod or a mumbled thank you. We mingled among the guests, trying to avoid Father and his haggard face, his sleepwalking steps. Guilt and regret held us back. We'd kept Mother's gallery of characters a secret from him for so long, how could he not resent us?

For weeks after the funeral, there were entire evenings when Father locked himself away in a dark room with terrible migraines, groaning from behind the door for aspirin. Once, as I struggled to find the bottle among hand towels, toilet paper and the sad remains of Mother's makeup collection in the cluttered bathroom closet, he lurched into the hallway.

His eyes were covered by a damp cloth, and his voice was a tight knot. "It hurts so bad I can't see straight."

My fingers fumbled past a box of band-aids, a bottle of cough syrup.

"*Hurry.* Everything . . . is *stuttering*," he rasped, his large hands grasping his head. "Like a broken TV."

Then I understood: some sort of Hold dial had gone loose inside him. I called to Dan and Laurie for help and they squeezed past Father's faltering steps to join my search for aspirin. His mouth opened in horror at the sight of his three anxious children, and his shocked face has never left me. I can still imagine how we must have appeared, our image skittering before him like a family film gone wild.

Even on the best of days we confounded him—we wouldn't stay in place, just as, day by day, our various toy collections slowly unfurled themselves across the floors of our rooms. Without warning, we shed our sadness and threw ourselves into desperate games of tag, for the thrill of outrunning grasping hands and chasing after fleeing figures just beyond our reach, and Father could only watch in numbed silence, unable to shout a warning before a lamp overturned.

Yet our racing leaps concealed this secret: Mother had become our phantom limb, and we each had separate, invisible limps. Laurie dipped anything at all into the sugar bowl, even cubes of cheese, trying to satisfy an insatiable urge as a sticky cosmetic sheen of sweetness covered her lips. Dan quite methodically made a mess of his toys, slowly pummeling them to bits; or he took yet another reckless tour of the neighborhood, ringing doorbells and then running away, or "borrowing" a bicycle left on a front lawn. As for me, I took on family chores that Father could barely manage, so that in work I might lose myself. Slowly supplanting an array of indifferent babysitters and domestic help, I washed and dried the dishes and set them in the pantry; I organized shopping lists; I picked up after my brother and sister, and in the evenings I made sure they took their baths and brushed their teeth; I read bedtime stories.

Father tried to do his best, however inadequate his best might have been. Now that school had begun again, he specialized in breakfasts, serving up long strips of crunchy bacon, cold glasses of orange juice, and syrupy waffles. But he still hadn't learned what the various drawers in our bedrooms held, how to set the timers on the washing machine, or how to coax calories into picky eaters. And when it came to offering us patient attention, it was clear there were nuances he could not grasp. Merely having the name Father, I realized, didn't always make a person a parent. Acting more like a parent would be just that for Father—acting, and then he might march down Mother's dangerous path.

Yet there was no question that we were his responsibility: what family did we have left? Only one of our grandparents was still alive—Father's mother, Nani. She lived in a rest home, always hunched in a wheelchair, long past the ability to speak, lost in a smock-like garment. On our visits Father would sit silently beside her, stroking her withered arm as a substitute for words, while her eyes followed the movements of her grandchildren. I always tried to avoid that gaze. Ashamed of my unfairness, I still couldn't help imagining Nani as the oldest thing in the universe, her eyes like those Black Holes I'd learned about in school, whose gravitational pull might draw us all in if we weren't careful.

And then there was Aunt Myrna, Mother's unmarried older sister. She'd rarely come to see us when our mother was alive, and now, perhaps shamed by her earlier neglect, she spent many long hours driving to and from her distant town to visit us on a Saturday or Sunday. Gone were our weekend trips to the bowling alley—none of us could even bear the thought of that awful game, and if Father still played, he did so alone, whenever Aunt Myrna hauled us off to a park or a mall.

These jaunts always included a visit to a cafeteria rife with overcooked vegetables and soggy fruit suspended in Jell-O molds. I'd poke away at dark, pungent spinach on my plate and try to see where my mother's features fit in Myrna's round face and jutting chin, her reddish hair that just seemed to lie on her head. I could never do it, just as I was always on the verge of asking her any and all of the questions brimming inside me: *Does Laurie's voice remind you of Mom's when she was a little girl? Which one of us most reminds you of our mother? What was she like when you were young?*

Instead I listened, along with Dan and Laurie, to Aunt Myrna's incongruous quoting of dialogue from her favorite television shows. Wiping at a puddle of Dan's spilled milk on the cafeteria table, she announced, " 'I could never do that—she's my best friend!' " If Laurie lingered too long at a drugstore's cosmetics counter, Myrna said, " 'Now Barney, calm down.' " And whenever she parked the car and we trooped out into another parking lot of another mall, our aunt loved to declare, " 'Why, there's a fortune in unmarked bills in this pillowcase!' "

Soon we followed her lead, spouting lines out of context whenever we could. " 'Not in my bathtub, you won't,' " Dan muttered as he struggled with his shoelaces, and once, when Aunt Myrna took us on a long drive in the country, Laurie woke from a nap, glanced out the window and announced sleepily, " 'Look, all the food's in French!' "

The repetition of these and other special phrases became an invisible glue that seemed to hold us together. So during one cafeteria jaunt, right after Aunt Myrna graciously exempted us from candied yams, I finally found the courage to ask, "Did you and Mom ever play pretend games when you were little?"

Dan and Laurie stopped their clowning over the sugar packets, their sudden quiet an unspoken echoing of my question. Aunt Myrna held her teacup in midair and stared at the wisps of steam rising before her eyes, and I thought with relief and disappointment that somehow she hadn't heard me.

Then she replied in a surprisingly flat voice, "No, I don't recall anything like that." She sipped her tea, she dabbed her lips. She regarded us as if we were contagious.

In the park Aunt Myrna settled quietly on a weathered bench while Dan and Laurie careened from seesaw to jungle gym. I sat beside her moody silence and I realized the terrible mistake of my question: I'd stirred up a fear that Mother's impulses lurked inside her too, waiting for escape. When my brother and sister chased each other around the sandbox, flinging arcs of sand in the air, Aunt Myrna simply looked away, and I somehow knew that she would leave us slowly, over many months of shortened visits and deferred or broken dates.

Before beginning the bedtime story for my brother and sister that night, I wondered how I could possibly soften Aunt Myrna's inevitable leave-taking, and I anxiously snapped the book open and shut until Laurie yawned and muttered, "The better to eat you with, my dear." She extended her hand toward me, a restless hungry mouth.

I slipped the book behind me and answered with my own quotation: "You can't catch me, I'm the gingerbread man!"

Catching on, Dan sang out with witchly glee, "I'll get you, my little pretty!" and he wrestled the book away.

We tossed phrases back and forth from a wealth of bedtime stories, transforming our evening ritual into a fractured tale that ranged from Mother Goose to Disney, Dr. Seuss to Robert Louis Stevenson, Babar the Elephant and Marvel comics. Our stepwise narrative continued flirting with disaster until we wearily left off and went to bed, still short of a happy ending.

We continued that convoluted story the next night, and the night after that, exploring the odd corners of books we thought we'd forgotten, and eventually, during a lull in the narrative, we came up with a game we called Name That Dwarf. If a teacher or friend or schoolyard bully were really one of the Seven Dwarfs, which one would he or she be? Our mournful principal Mr. Donners, famous for school assemblies alerting us to the dangers of current infectious diseases, we dubbed Happy. Miss Milbane's habit of crinkling her nose as she corrected homework assignments at her desk earned her the title Sneezy.

"What about the popcorn lady at the movies?" Laurie asked to our anticipatory laughter. "What about Tommy Vickers?"

"What about Dad?" Dan asked.

We fell silent at this deliciously forbidden thought.

"Bashful?" Laurie suggested.

"No—Grumpy!" Dan countered.

They both looked to me, the possible tie breaker. "Sleepy," I said without thinking, and Dan snorted with disgust. "*Sleepy?*" he said. "It's no fun playing if you don't even *try*."

"I *am* trying," I protested, but Dan turned away, suddenly concerned with the bits of lint that clung to the blankets.

"You're *Dopey*," he murmured offhandedly.

I refused to be provoked, refused to allow Dan's tightly coiled emotions to release yet again. At school he pushed classmates off swings, threw his milk carton against the hamster cage, and he spent so much time on the principal's bench that already, in October, there was talk of his repeating third grade. At home he probed the edge of Father's patience, risking an enforced early bedtime or withheld dessert.

Laurie sighed, disappointed that our new game had ended so abruptly. I said nothing, content to mull over the aptness of my choice: Dad *was* Sleepy, and I wanted him to wake up.

Interrupting my thoughts, Laurie asked, "What about Mom?"

"What about her?" I replied cautiously.

"Which dwarf was she?"

I shook my head. "Game's over, Laurie."

"C'mon, guess."

Dan, his interest rekindled, abandoned the little ball of lint he'd begun and waited for my reply.

"I don't want to guess," I said.

"Because you just don't know," she snorted. "But *I* know."

"Well?" Dan asked.

"She was all *seven* of them—"

"Nope," he interrupted, his eyes bright with challenge, "she was the Seven Hundred Dwarfs!"

When Laurie giggled I decided to up the ante: "Seven thousand."

"Seven hundred thousand," she added, and we continued this bittersweet, liberating disrespect to the edge of our mathematical abilities. And yet when we were done, all our addition and multiplication still added up to less than one mother.

Schoolwork now afforded me an escape much like my household chores, and I plunged into the class assignments as if every correct answer bestowed a mysterious, healing grace. But I was hindered in this quest by my teacher, Mrs. Lawler. She always rushed through Today's Lesson, leaving little time to consider the hurried facts we'd just been offered, facts which then threatened to simply vanish in the air.

One morning I tried to keep up with a lesson about whales that, typically, brimmed with sociology, history, ecology, music, art and more. After a breathless few minutes devoted to What is language?, Mrs. Lawler set the needle down on a record album she'd brought from home, a recording of a symphony featuring whale songs. After a woozy rasp for a moment or two, violins and horns announced their alternating melodies above scratches and crackles. This was a record that had been played too often, suggesting a secret about my teacher I didn't have time to consider, because a distant whale moan seemed to grow out of the speakers, joined by another moan, higher pitched, and then another, barely audible. More eerie voices entered at a stately pace, rising above the distortion of the record and so entrancing us that no one laughed when Joey, the class clown, slumped back in his seat and silently pursed his lips to the whale songs as if he were a dog howling at the moon.

Those large creatures gliding deep under the water spoke to each other in strange, slow tones. I imagined they also spoke to me, and that in the pauses between their plaintive moans they waited for my reply. I listened closely, just on the point of understanding, when an ugly amplified scrape cut through the room—Mrs. Lawler had wrenched the needle off the record.

"Well, it's getting late," she said, turning on a slide projector. "If we don't hurry, we'll never get through today's lesson."

I closed my eyes in an attempt to continue those whale songs inside me. But the breathless flutter of Mrs. Lawler's voice, the hum of the projector's fan and the metallic slap of each new slide clicking in defeated me, and I looked up at the screen. A large, simple building stood in the distance, with a long grassy roof supported by wooden pillars, and walls that rose only halfway up. Squinting at her notes, Mrs. Lawler said, "This is a Northwest Coast Indian shrine devoted to attracting whales."

I barely heard her. What I'd first thought were walls I now saw were people, standing stiffly shoulder to shoulder. Something about them seemed odd, but before I could really concentrate, my restless teacher clicked to the next slide.

We were just inside the shrine now, and I gaped at a new surprise: those people were actually life-size wooden statues, their torsos stiff, their hands and feet stumps. I imagined that their openmouthed, flat faces were shouting out a warning at the approach of trespassers.

"These are the wooden images of dead whale hunters," Mrs. Lawler announced. "The Indians held ceremonies in this shrine, and they sang songs that they believed would cause whales"—she paused and turned a page—"to drift close to shore, where they could then be caught."

Now another slide filled the screen: a close-up of maybe half a dozen statues, their identical, plaintive expressions so much like the three-holed faces of bowling balls, so much like my mother's own unhappy features that last terrible day. I blinked back tears at the thought, yet still I couldn't look away from that wall of faces. And then I knew why: they could just as easily be Mother's hidden characters. I longed to hear them sing out keening songs like the whales, songs filled with secrets that I would finally understand.

I raised my hand and waved it wildly, trying to think up a question that would keep Mrs. Lawler from the next slide. But she wasn't looking my way, and even if she were, I knew she'd say her usual, "Let's save our questions for later, okay?" I wouldn't let her do that to me. I dropped my thick science textbook on the floor, for a nice, solid *thump*.

As the class tittered I quietly dragged the book under my seat with my foot. Mrs. Lawler turned to us. "And who, may I ask, did that?"

Of course no one gave me away. "I'm waiting," Mrs. Lawler said. "We'll just sit here in the dark until the smart aleck confesses."

I knew from previous class disturbances that only a minute or two would pass before Mrs. Lawler lost her patience and made the kind of threat that usually drew a confession. So I imagined myself inside the shrine with the statues and I peered into their faces, I grasped the rough grain of their wooden shoulders and tried to draw out their voices, but no song rose above the hum of the projector.

"I'm waiting," Mrs. Lawler said, and I returned to my own nervous foot shuffling.

"I'm waiting," she repeated, and the terrible weariness just beneath the impatience in her voice belonged to someone I'd never noticed before: a teacher afraid of her students. *That's* why she rushed through the class lessons, leaving us breathless or bored behind her. Mrs. Lawler fiddled with the record player, examined a button on the slide projector, trying her best to pretend indifference, but I now knew that she was most wary of us during these moments of classroom tension.

I raised my hand and confessed. "I dropped the book, Mrs. Lawler." Then I added something I thought she needed to hear: "I dropped it so you wouldn't go to the next slide. I know you were in a hurry, but I wanted to look at this one a little longer. It really interests me. I'm sorry."

Her open mouth echoed the statues on the screen, and then she let out the long breath of an exhausted runner. "And have you seen enough now?" she finally asked.

I gave the statues one last regretful glance. They had no voices I could hear. "Yes, ma'am."

"Then let's go on, shall we?" But she stood for a long silent moment before clicking on the next slide.

I stood at my bedroom window that afternoon as the sky darkened in the distance, the twilight spreading into a deep underwater blue. Then the whales' haunting call-and-response rose up inside me, long, enticing songs that I could imagine flowed from the open mouths of those Indian statues. Yet however carefully I listened, their language remained elusive, and I pressed my forehead against the window, felt its cold seep into my skin until I heard Father announce from the kitchen that dinner was ready.

It was the usual hushed affair, bowls passed politely among us as we spoke softly, filling Father's silence with our reports of what we'd done in school: Laurie's math problems, Dan's recess.

"We listened to whale songs today," I offered.

"Good," Father said, nodding. "Good," he repeated, and somehow the subject was closed. I returned to the slab of meat loaf on my plate, chafing at Father's indifferent approval. It was the only intimacy he could give us, and it wasn't enough.

After the dishes were washed, Dan took off, despite the growing cold, for his evening wanderings up and down the block. Laurie and I spread out newspapers and sprawled on the living room floor with her art kit—our occasional quiet time together. Laurie preferred creating watercolor faces, filling in their primitive features with pink cheeks and red lips and wild dark eyes, while I worked at my own awkwardly rendered scenes: a house floating on still, deep-blue water; clouds nestling inside the back of a station wagon; a flock of birds asleep on a couch.

As usual, Father sat in a corner and hid behind his newspaper, and

I could see from the headlines that it was filled with tales of woe far worse than what our family had lived through. Perhaps reading such stories gave him bitter comfort, but tonight I wanted to tempt him away from that wall that held off the rest of the house. With a few indirect suggestions I managed to lure my sister into painting something that I thought might appeal to Father—a garden. Across the page she spread outlines of fat-petaled flowers on spindly stems, squiggly ferns, and trees that looked like giant lollipops. When it was time to fill them all in, Laurie's brush hesitated over the paint set's tiny trays of blue, green, brown, orange, yellow.

"Hey, Dad," I called out, "you're the expert on flowers. Laurie's got a whole garden here—what colors should she use?"

Without even a grunt of complaint, Father set the paper down and crouched beside us. "Well, green for the stem, of course. Here, honey." He guided Laurie's hand, and they filled in a few petals until she protested, "No, not all yellow, Daddy. I want blue and red too."

"Fine," he said, drawing his hand back. "Paint away. You kids seem to be doing fine without me." Then he stood and returned to his newspaper.

Her face scrunched in disappointment, Laurie began smearing jagged brushstrokes of color across her picture, a rainbow gone amuck. "Wait," I whispered, applying my brush, and I showed her how those flowers could be turned into flying saucers, their green stems an otherworldly exhaust.

Father shook the paper as he turned a page, a ripple like a wave, and again those beckoning whale calls seemed to speak inside me, messages breaking against the silence they swam in, the silence in our living room. Father was the real wall, I realized, not his newspaper. Perhaps this was what Mother had hurled herself against, shattering into too many people. Yet I knew she wasn't the only person who harbored others inside—even Mrs. Lawler hid something of herself from the class. So why should Father only be what he appeared to be? I had to somehow learn to read him, learn how to coax him out of himself.

I squirmed in my seat in the school auditorium, resigned to endure the annual holiday pageant, another nondenominational tribute to correct behavior for children. After a relentlessly cheery song sung in the ragged snippets of fifteen languages by the second grade chorus, our principal parked himself behind a podium and gave a nearly endless list of tips on how to avoid the flu. Then there was a long pause, punctuated by backstage scufflings. When the curtains opened again, we saw a stage set dominated by a long counter cluttered with toys.

Sets of shelves borrowed from the school library held even more toys. Behind the counter stood the shopkeeper, a chubby boy with a ridiculously thick mustache that wiggled too much as he sang out, "Toys, toys! The joy of all children! Oh, to be a kid again!"

Across from him stood a tall girl whose long maroon dress, string of pearls and wide-brimmed hat indicated she was a grown-up. Beside her, sucking on a lollipop and tugging at her skirt, was a classmate in a sailor suit and undersized cap: her son. She picked out a dollhouse—a present, I supposed, for the little brat's sister—and the shopkeeper carefully fit it into a cardboard box.

"Oh my," the mother said in an unconvincingly adult voice, "this package is much too heavy for me to carry by myself. Won't you please help me take it to the car?" She patted her hair and wiggled her hips, which set the audience hooting, for we all understood that her flirting was a spur-of-the-moment, subversive gesture aimed at the teachers.

The shopkeeper waited for the laughing to die down before he delivered his next line. "Why of course, madam! Nothing is too good for my customers!"

Then they trooped out, and for a moment the stage was strangely empty, but I ignored the whispered joshing and exaggerated yawns around me, because Laurie entered through the half-opened stage door. Why hadn't she told me she was in this skit?

"Hello, is anyone here?" Laurie asked, stepping cautiously inside. She swept her hands to her heart and sighed loudly. "If only I had enough money to buy one of these lovely toys!"

She tiptoed among the toy displays casually, as if hundreds of us weren't watching and waiting to see what she'd do. Laurie picked up a kaleidoscope and peered into it, then turned it toward the audience. She wasn't supposed to see *us*, of course, though a few clowns waved at her. But she *could* see us, and as Laurie slowly swung it along the length of the dark hall, I wondered what she thought of our multiplied, fragmented faces.

With a shudder, she placed the kaleidoscope back on its shelf. Then she noticed the doll.

It was the largest toy in the shop, a rag doll as big as a child, scrunched firmly on a rocker, its button-eyed face smiling contentedly. Its stuffed arms and legs, colored a bright pink, poked out from a crinkly dress. Laurie stood before the doll and she plucked at one of the frilly sleeves, stroked the thick yellow curls.

Laurie scanned the empty store, the open door. This, of course, was the moment of temptation. *Don't steal that*, I thought, *you'll never be able to sneak it down the street.*

She hesitated, then pulled at the doll's gloved hand.

"*Stop*," it said, "you haven't *paid* for me."

I think we all felt a thrill of surprise at the sound of a girl's voice, muffled and yet booming out of that doll's face. Some of the smaller children in the front rows cried out.

"But I am a poor girl, and you are *so* beautiful," Laurie said, unfazed by this suddenly animated doll, its arms and legs now waving excitedly.

"No excuse!" it shouted, one arm pointing to the ceiling.

The dramatic shock was over. The doll started yammering on about the importance of honesty, sharing, even politeness, and once again we were all crazy with boredom in our seats. The figures on the stage seemed disconnected from the scripted lecture, and I noticed that Laurie must have been given her part for technical reasons: she was tall for her age, and whoever played the doll must have been the shortest.

The doll finally wound up its long speech with the solemn question, "Now do you see how wrong you were?"

As Laurie nodded in agreement with the doll's virtuous logic, the stage light dimmed for her dramatic moment, and a spotlight found her face. The stark shadows turned her many years older. When she replied, "Yes, now I see what a terrible mistake I made," her voice was dark with regret and Mother's voice, her long gone voice, rose out of those words.

Still holding on to the doll's gloved hand, again Laurie said, "*Now I see what a terrible mistake I made*," and this repetition could not have been called for in the script, because she cut into the returning shopkeeper's entrance line—"Well, *that* wasn't heavy at all!"

Her tears weren't scripted either, and she looked so defeated it caused the shopkeeper to feebly improvise, "Why, little girl, you're not supposed to be crying."

She *wasn't* a little girl: she was Mother, asking forgiveness. I gladly gave it to her, I almost called out, but the curtain closed and cut the scene short. A miscue of any sort was welcome at these dreadful affairs, and already the audience whooped with delight. *I*, however, let tears flow in exquisite relief until the boy beside me started up with the dreaded "*Wussy.*" I smacked his head to the back of his seat.

Ordered to the bench outside the principal's office, I fairly sauntered down the halls, unconcerned and still basking in that strange moment Laurie had given me.

Dan was already there, warming his usual corner. He grinned at my unexpected presence.

"So," I said, affecting an older brother knowingness, "you got kicked out of the auditorium too?"

"*Huh,*" he grunted, "I punched Tommy Walters so I wouldn't even *have* to go."

He'd missed Laurie's skit. Instantly I felt a great wave of sympathy for Dan, and I gazed at his little tough guy face until he asked, "So, what did *you* do?"

"Knocked John Caligliano's head against his chair."

"How come?"

I hesitated, unable to find the words I needed to describe Laurie's brief reincarnation of Mother and that opportunity for forgiveness.

"Well," Dan muttered finally, "it doesn't matter if you had a good reason or not, Dad'll still get on you."

He was right. Father's usual silence would be tinged with disappointment—I had seen Dan suffer under it so often, forcing him to range about the neighborhood away from its bitter presence. Now I would feel it too. I'd lose my name for a day—I would be "*son,*" spoken as if that word couldn't be too short. Settling into the hard wood of the bench, I promised myself I would never allow this to happen again, for how could I draw close to my father if he held me off with his disapproval?

No Seeing Left for Us

Father lit another cigarette, exhaled, and lavender-gray smoke curled in the air. I'd taken to doing my homework across from my father in the living room, keeping watch for any break in his aloof front. I'd come to imagine that those twisting tendrils were billowing hieroglyphics, eloquent signals of all he hadn't said in the three years since Mother's death.

Yet the cigarette accomplished its steady immolation before any message could be translated, and after one last puff Father sighed and snuffed out the smoldering stub. As always I felt a wild surge of guilt that I had failed to decipher that elusive language. Perhaps those signals were *meant* to disappear.

So I was secretly relieved when Father reached for another cigarette, paused, and asked, "Summer vacation starts in about a week, doesn't it?"

"I can't wait," I said, closing my textbook.

"Well, you're fourteen now, old enough to learn about the value of a dollar. I think it's time you did a spot of work at the nursery."

I agreed happily, even to his condition that I put half my salary into a savings account. Though Father didn't raise the subject of my new job again, in the following days I plotted all the ways I would impress him with my industry: saving *more* than half my paycheck; refusing pay raises; working long hours of overtime or, better yet, working so late that *I'd* have to close up.

On the drive to work that first morning Father barely acknowledged me, though I sat beside him on the front seat. I almost believed he'd forgotten me until, his eyes glancing in the side mirror at a passing car, he finally spoke. "Remember, no special privileges."

"Privileges?" I asked, insulted he thought I might expect any.

"*Privileges.*" He cleared his throat, flipped a turn signal. "Once I park this car, you're not my son, you're my employee."

"Yes sir," I replied, suddenly curious what that difference might be.

When Father parked the car he turned to me and launched our new relationship with a cool gaze: his skeptical appraisal of a new employee.

Gerald's Garden Services was a long, one-story building with two attached greenhouses fronting acres of ordered trees and shrubs and potted flowers. Acknowledging the occasional wave of a worker with a flick of his hand, Father led me to the nearest greenhouse. Inside, we walked through the thick humid air, past drooping, broad-leafed plants to a skinny, sandy-haired man crouched over stacks of empty flower pots. He sprang up at the sight of us, as if somehow embarrassed, a coil of unruly hair dangling over his forehead.

Father introduced us with a studied informality. "Bob, give Michael here some work that'll keep him busy, and make sure he stays that way."

"Sure thing, Mr. Kirby, no problem at all," Bob replied, gulping and nodding, and I noticed an odd patch of stubble on his left cheek.

"Michael," Father said, "if you want to learn, you have to ask a lot of questions, and Bob's the one to answer them."

Now it was my turn to nod.

"Well, I'll come by later today to see how you're doing." The epitome of a man in charge, Father turned and walked off, his steps crisp against the slate tiles.

With a raspy little whistle, Bob motioned me through the door to the grounds. "You're a lucky boy to be working with your dad," he said with a wink, my presence at the nursery and his authority over me apparently amusing. "That man has more to teach than most people can learn. All he has to do is look at a tree's shadow and he can tell you what kind of tree it is. In any season. With or without leaves."

He offered a conspirator's smile and I understood that this praise was meant to make its way to Father. If I did my job as go-between, he and I would get along just fine. So I returned Bob's smile and discounted his hyperbole. Still, the possibility that Father possessed a secret ability intrigued me.

Fitted with gloves and gardening tools—my usual weekend yard-boy gear—I weeded along the borders of ornamental flower beds, then watered long rows of seedlings. Far from Father's critical eye, I worked well with only my own standards to follow. Bob occasionally skulked along a nearby gravel path, though never near enough to see if the boss's son actually worked. Resenting his assumption that I might be there to waste time and collect an easy paycheck, I bent down among the rows of flowers with even greater determination and searched out the slightest hint of any alien green shoot.

The hours passed, and the sun cast lengthening, multipetaled shadows along the paths. Yet however I stared at them, they resembled nothing more than dark swaying shapes. Could Father really read such indecipherable patches? I had to know. During my afternoon break I snuck off to the plot of trees with a clipper and furtively snipped branch after branch.

While Laurie and Dan helped clear the dinner table, I slipped away and pushed the living room chairs into a semicircle, with Father's upholstered recliner in the middle. Then, with a great show of secrecy, I cajoled my family into their arranged seats. Still refusing to answer any questions, I turned off the lamps, stood behind my audience and shone a bright circle on the wall with a flashlight.

"Shadow puppets?" Laurie asked.

"Not exactly," I said, my arm rustling around in a grocery bag. I teased out a leafy branch and held it before the light. Its shadow spread across the wall.

"Aaand now," I drawled with a ringmaster's aplomb, "the A-maazing . . . Dad!"

"Michael," Father said, "just what are you up to?"

Ignoring his question, I began my barker's patter: "The Amaaaaz-ing Dad has never seen this branch before, but he will now tell us, simply by looking at its shadow, exactly what sort of tree it came from."

Father laughed uncomfortably, and Laurie said, "Can you really, Dad?"

"I'll bet he can't!" Dan snorted.

"Oh you do, eh?" Father replied, spurred by the challenge. "That's an oak branch. Much too easy, Michael."

I groped about in the bag again and then aimed the light at a new branch, its leaves curled at the edges like potato chips.

Without hesitation Father announced, "Beech."

Determined to make the challenge harder, I shook the next branch a little to evoke its swaying in the breeze, but he immediately said, "Hickory." Laurie giggled at this feat, but Dan didn't join in, doggedly unimpressed.

Because I still didn't know much about trees, I couldn't discount the possibility that Father might be faking, so I dangled the first branch in front of the flashlight.

"Oak. What's the matter, run out already?"

"No sir," I answered, chastened. Then I continued through the rest of my collection and Father easily called out their names—fir, walnut, hemlock, spruce, elm and juniper.

"Is that the best you can do, young man?"

"No, there's more. But *first*," I said, returning to my ringmaster's patter, "a short refreshment break." I switched the lamp on, passed around a tray of cookies, and hurried to the bathroom with my gro-cery bag.

Hunched over the linoleum tiles, I pulled off every leaf or waxy needle from the branches. *Now* we'd see just now good he was.

When I resumed the show Father easily identified each naked, knobby branch, and Dan and Laurie clapped with each new feat. Father was a kind of wizard.

"The Amazing Dad!" I sang out.

He bowed—an unusual, graceful gesture. "Okay, time to clean up, kids."

I started hauling the chairs back in place. Dan and Laurie scrambled over to the bag of branches and leaves and quizzed each other. "No, that's not elm," Dan snorted. "Dad," he asked, leaves cupped in his hands, "what are these?"

Father was already behind his newspaper. He turned down a corner. "That's enough fun and games for tonight, Danny." The corner turned back up. "Isn't it almost bedtime?"

"No, it's not," Dan said, crumpling the leaves in his fist. Father said nothing, as if he hadn't heard.

The happy spell was broken. We drifted from the living room, leaving Father in his upholstered corner. I thought of that succession of leafy shadows and wondered how my father could have such eyes and be so blind. I hated to consider it, but maybe he had no seeing left for us.

I'd proven myself such a hard worker that Bob gave me more responsibility, each morning simply suggesting a list of jobs that would keep me busy. I'd take in his instructions and spend the day sterilizing soil by covering it with long sheets of clear plastic, hammering copper sheeting around planting beds to keep out slugs and snails, or molding cubes of soil for seedlings.

Overhearing the idle talk of other employees now and then, I learned that Father was considered exacting yet fair, though he didn't seem to inspire much affection in anyone. Once, while on my way to the greenhouse for my morning assignment, I noticed my father in conference with a new cashier, a greasy-haired young woman who kept pinching at her nose. I stopped and listened to Father's firm, patient voice explaining the key code step by step.

He turned to me, one raised eyebrow posing a silent question I understood, and I answered by continuing on to the greenhouse and my work. Yet I couldn't suppress an ache of resentment: he'd never spent as much as a minute with me since I'd started working.

Perhaps it wasn't entirely an accident when I sprayed the wrong bush with the wrong insecticide. Within an hour the leafy clusters were nothing more than dark, dangling burn victims. What would Father say when he discovered this devastated bush? I knelt before it and tried, without success, to imagine any excuse that might put me in a sympathetic light.

"Nasty, that's truly nasty," Bob whispered behind me.

A swift tremor rippled through me. "Hey, don't creep up on me like—"

"Don't worry." He grinned. "I won't tell a soul."

I could only shift my eyes from his face, not at all certain I should feel gratitude.

"Hey," he said, suddenly glancing at his watch, "it's time for lunch." He squinted at me, amused. "But I can't really say that you look hungry."

We settled down in the open shed behind one of the greenhouses. I sat there with a clear view of the long lush rows of ornamental shrubs, sandwich in hand yet unable to eat, my stomach as ruined as those leaves I'd sprayed.

"So what's up for the big weekend?" Bob asked, initiating what would become a ritual teasing about all my supposed girlfriends.

I considered eating my sandwich, anything to avoid responding.

"Oh, I bet the girls, they just love you," he chuckled, fueling my silent misery. He'd intuited a sore spot: a few girls at school *had* noticed me, but my damnable shyness always held them off. I forced myself to take a bite of the sandwich, the cheese and mustard sour in my mouth. I set it aside.

"Hey," Bob said, "I *told* you I won't say a word. You can bet on it."

At the end of lunch break we wandered over to the employee snack machines. Bob looked about and saw no one in sight. "I've got a secret for you, too," he said, and pulled from his shirt pocket a curiously twisted paper clip. He slipped it into the tiny circular lock on the side and the door popped open. Grabbing two candy bars, he clicked the door shut with a deft elbow.

Wagging a finger, he said, "Don't tell a soul." He unwrapped one of the bars, offered me the other. "How's about a nice dessert?"

"No," I muttered unhappily.

Bob rubbed at his stubbled chin as if contemplating my seemingly unusual reaction. "Suit yourself."

Bob ambled by to check on my progress with new racks of seedlings that afternoon, and before leaving he crinkled the candy wrappers in his pocket, a grating music meant to remind me of the pact he'd offered. Ignoring the seedlings, I made my way back to those destroyed leaves. They had revealed a different Bob to me, someone who gave off his own hint of ruin. And now this person held a secret over me.

I decided to confess. Across the lot Father was working his way down the rows of baby trees, inspecting the firmness of their burlap sacks. I waved, and he actually waved back. Emboldened, I motioned for him to come over.

With every step of my father's approach, I worried what revealing my mistake might now reveal of him. When he finally stood beside me I could only point to the crinkly leaves. He bent down and pressed one between his fingers. "What happened here?"

"I, I sprayed the wrong stuff on it."

Father crumpled the leaf. His face betrayed nothing.

"Guess I didn't know what I was, you know, doing. I should have ask—"

He sighed. "Follow me."

We walked past the flower beds to the main storeroom, where Father unlocked the door and flipped on a light. He pointed to a short bench in a corner. "Sit over there."

Afraid to ask why he'd brought me here, I waited while my father rummaged through a pile of papers. Then he sat down beside me with a chart of spraying applications, and he carefully taught me how to read the color-coded bars so I wouldn't make a similar mistake again. "See here?" he said. "Just match up the greens or blues and your troubles are over."

I managed to offer a handful of grateful *Uh-huhs* as he spoke, doing my best to follow the various correspondences he pointed out. Finally done dispensing advice, Father paused a moment, then rested his hand lightly on my shoulder. I almost eased into that absolving touch but restrained myself: this moment might turn into one of those special privileges he'd mentioned, and I wanted to obey him.

Over the next two years Father took me along on his end-of-the-day rounds. He taught me how to ease back a curl of birch bark in search of a feathery white mold; how flowers with similar needs should be grouped together when designing gardens; and why I should plant along curves and not straight lines, always considering the effects of sunlight. I pinched back marigolds and nicotianas to generate more blooms; I wiped my scissors with rubbing alcohol to avoid spreading plant diseases when cutting stems; I learned how to push a willow twig deep enough into the ground in autumn so that it would grow as a new tree in spring, its bright red shoots flaming like flowers.

The nursery offered a world of hidden pleasures I now had eyes to see. The crevices of chestnut tree bark—spiral swirls rising around the trunk like a tornado funnel to a cloudy crest of leaves—reminded me somehow of my father's tightly wound formality; at the base of certain spruce trunks hungry tree worms ate along the surface of the bark, elegant squiggles that looked like some foreign alphabet. "Worm words," Father called them, with what I thought was a false brusqueness, for he sometimes paused longer than was necessary to examine those strange marks.

Though I had entered into the intensity of Father's varied campaigns against mold and rot, weeds and insects and tree disease of all kinds, I hesitated spraying those worms: they'd made the bark into a kind of paper, and they themselves were squirming pens that wrote tales of their tiny blind lives.

I sprayed them anyway, regarding their writhing deaths as the eradication of my own continuing secret: overwhelmed by that long-ago, welcome moment of Father's sympathetic touch when I'd confessed to him, I'd simply forgotten to report Bob's larceny. Only the following morning, when I saw Bob puttering around in the greenhouse, a candy bar in his shirt pocket, did I realize I'd missed my chance.

He continued his petty pilferage—a package of seeds one week, a can of soda another, engineering me into a guilty bystander whenever he could. Yet each time I thought of denouncing Bob I imagined my father's disappointed face and the clipped rhythms of his sternest voice as he said, *Why didn't you tell me before?* The excuses I endlessly rehearsed ate little trails inside me.

Dan's latest angry antics overshadowed my own worries: he now fought almost every day at school, and once he was nearly expelled after shaking his fist at a teacher. For that crime Father threatened terrible, never-to-be-forgotten punishments that finally resulted in a simple month's grounding. Dan kept to his room, rereading his great stack of comic books. Occasionally I kept him company, admiring his tough-guy spunk even if I also felt I had to reproach him for his latest trouble.

"What am I supposed to *do*, Mike?" he asked. "If somebody wants to fight with me, I'm not going to disappoint him."

We returned to our separate comic books and the adventures of ordinary people who could suddenly change into creatures of power, bursting into flame without burning, twisting steel with no effort, flying without wings, or stretching their limbs like lariats. And these heroes fought such grotesque villains: half-metal mutants, or brutes covered with crater-like scabs, the exaggerated deformities of their barely human faces exposing a frightening inner ugliness. Who did my brother silently cheer on as they wrestled with each other's transformations? Perhaps both. Surrounding those titanic conflicts, bright balloons burst into jagged edges with the words KERBLAM! KABLOOM! FWEEEE-CRASH! SLAM! and POW! POW! POW!, and Dan quietly mouthed the captions to himself, lingering lovingly on each panel's mayhem as if he were his own private target range.

These battles quickly wearied me. I set my comic aside, and to the sound track of Dan's hushed explosions I paged through a book of mazes. Searching out the most intricate puzzles, with my finger I followed a slow, circuitous path through an insane tangle of industrial pipes or the weaving shadows on the face of a storm cloud. I could afford to be patient. These complexities, I knew, provided an exit. Yet while tracing my way through an unpromising path of corn stubble, I heard Laurie call me. Once, then twice.

"Coming," I answered. My sister's interest in drawing pictures had shifted to a teenager's fascination with the nuances of makeup, and she liked to display her latest application of eyeliner and blush. I walked to her room, determined to feign interest and not mention— wasn't she daring me to?—that her accumulation of faces reminded me of our mother.

I opened the door to Laurie's room and she turned from the vanity to face me. In startling contrast to her dark curly hair, harshly etched wrinkles radiated from her eyes and mouth and across her forehead.

"What do you think?" she asked in a withered voice, but I could only stare at those lines re-creating her face.

"I'm trying out for the grandmother in a play," she said, still in character. "Do you think I have a chance?"

"Only if you dye your hair gray," I said, attempting a light tone.

"Oh. Wait." She reached into her bureau drawer and then pulled a scarf over her head. "Now what do you think?"

I took a step back from the eerie sight of our reincarnated Nani, who'd died last year.

"I think you'll get the part."

My prediction came true. Laurie memorized her lines in a few hours, lounging on the sofa and speaking to invisible characters whose responses only she could hear as she clutched the xeroxed script. In the following days she went further, attempting the voices of other characters, one by one. Standing by the door to her room, I could hear her murmuring disjunct bits of half dialogue, questions that received no answers, or answers that replied to no questions, and I imagined an old woman, head bent and weaving through the clutter of Laurie's room, filled with the voices of a lifetime's memories.

Father shifted in his seat beside me, so ill at ease in the auditorium's competing murmurs and flapping of programs that I thought he might try to escape his own daughter's opening night performance. But soon enough the lights darkened, the curtain rose, and there on-stage sat a family at a dinner table: a foursome of high school kids pretending to be a mother, father, son and daughter. Behind them painted backdrops impersonated the walls of an apartment, with two windows offering views of a cramped city landscape. The actors picked at plastic food on their plates and raised empty forks to their mouths, they took great quaffs of nothing from tall glasses, and they projected loudly to the back rows a clumsy plot rundown of what had led up to this opening scene.

Already suppressing the urge to yawn, I told myself that sooner or later my sister was bound to make an entrance. Father seemed to have forgotten her entirely—he had eyes only for the window in a corner of the stage set: perhaps its painted panorama of skyscrapers offered a distraction from this poorly acted play.

Laurie finally appeared, at the edge of a crowd milling outside an old-fashioned barbershop. While the rest of the cast plainly marked time, their lips mumbling through the motions of "Rutabaga rutabaga," Laurie's character gazed out at the audience, a senile wandering over the darkened rows. The intensity of her eyes, somehow impossibly old, exerted a strange gravitational pull that reminded me so much of Nani. Father actually gasped. Then the barber finally stepped out to his storefront and Laurie turned away to join the crowd's rising murmurs.

For the remainder of the play, whenever Laurie appeared onstage Father averted his eyes, though she no longer looked our way. Instead she concentrated on her occasional lines, her ancient voice. By now I'd lost the thread of the plot, for Father's brooding discomfort kept distracting me: he shifted in his seat, he flicked his playbill impatiently, and increasingly he sought out that window on the painted wall.

After the final curtain calls and applause Father gruffly insisted on a backstage visit. We joined the throng of beaming parents and well-wishers and made our way across stage. While the crew lowered the klieg lights with a great show of professionalism, cast members began to appear, their costumes slung over an arm, a shoulder. Laurie approached us through the hubbub, a moist towel in hand. One side of her face was scrubbed clean of makeup, the other side was still old.

Father averted his gaze and once again took in the bustling activity. But when he finally turned to her his eyes were cold, his voice grim. "So *this* is why your grades have been going down?"

Laurie's divided face flinched, then quickly recovered. "Only a little, Daddy. I'm not Dan, you know."

At these words Father relented enough to actually offer grudging praise: "You spoke your lines . . . very well."

But he'd already done his damage, and Laurie returned to the rest of her makeup with that towel, scrubbing at her face as if she wanted to remove it.

Later that night I knocked on my sister's door and waited for her barely audible "Come in." Her eyes flickered with disappointment that I wasn't Father. With one cheek still pink from her rough usage, she looked as if she'd been slapped.

"Well, *I* thought you were terrific—"

"You thought I was scary. So did Dad."

"No, not scary, really. . . ." My voice trailed off at Laurie's sad eyes.

"It's all right, Michael, you don't have to worry. I washed off the makeup. I'm me again."

"Who said you weren't you?" I replied, afraid of where our words were taking us.

"Nobody *said* anything. Look, I'm not like Mom, I—"

"I know you're not—"

"I just want to understand *why*."

I gaped at her—in our separate ways, weren't we both trying to recover our parents? Laurie allowed herself an indulgent smile at my surprise. "Remember that Christmas play I was in, you know, the one with the doll?" she asked quietly.

I nodded.

"I never told anybody about this, Michael. Can I tell you?"

"Sure."

"I had a dream about Mom that night. I was with her in a department store, and we were standing in line, at the checkout counter. Mom was looking for something in her purse—I thought it was her wallet, but then she took out a slip of paper, like a really long fortune from a fortune cookie. It had words on it too, and I don't know why, but I just *knew* that it told a little story about one of her . . . people. The second I thought this the paper just burst into flame. But it didn't burn her fingers."

"Laurie," I said, but my sister spoke rapidly, cutting off any interruption: "She lifted another slip of paper out of her purse and when I decided to grab it Mom had the creepiest smile on her face, like she knew what I was going to do. So I touched it and it lit up, but my fingers didn't hurt, they only sort of *tingled* and then I . . ." Laurie held her hands out as if they gripped a strip of paper, and she mimed an incredulous reaction to whatever she silently read. The memory of this dream had become just another performance. She bowed to silent applause, she laughed when I left the room.

While Laurie kept her grades up so Father couldn't forbid her from acting in school plays, Dan discovered new opportunities for trouble in school and on the streets, and a quiet, sullen anger settled into the rooms of our house. Even I nurtured my own defiance of Father, I now suspected, for how could I have let Bob's petty dishonesty continue unless each filched can of soda or packet of cheese crackers somehow gave me a secret satisfaction?

The very possibility so disturbed me that, after much nervous deliberation, I spent one Saturday morning at work quietly tracking Bob. When I saw him making off for the snack machine during a break, I followed and caught him popping the door open with his makeshift key. Before he could hide the candy bar in his vest pocket I grabbed the door and held it open.

"Put that back."

Bob stood back and sized me up, trying to gauge the hazards of this unexpected confrontation. "Well," he said, his voice cautious, even a little weary, "sometimes a sweet tooth can get out of control, now can't it?"

"Back," I repeated, blushing at the tremor in my voice.

"It's nothing I haven't done before," he replied. "You know that."

I said nothing. Bob sighed, then slipped the candy bar back into its metal slot in the machine.

I closed the door, exhilarated by my victory. "Do it again, I'll tell my dad."

"Tell him what? I never took anything that wasn't mine, not even once. And your father wouldn't like to think that anybody ever saw me do otherwise, would he?" Bob managed a weak laugh, his best show of bravado, and without a glance back at me he retreated to the nearest greenhouse.

Father and Son

Perhaps it was inevitable that my brother would bring his trouble-making home. Over the course of a few short months toothbrushes and favorite drinking cups vanished, mysterious stains began to appear on the carpets, two of the dining room chairs' wicker seats suddenly developed frayed holes, an ugly scratch marred a kitchen cabinet. One day, returning home from my after-school hours at the nursery, I opened the door to my room and saw that my odd collection of discards had been swept from the shelves, and now a strange brew of styrofoam peanuts, buttons, tiny bones and dirty coins, glass shards, feathers and nail clippings was strewn across the floor. I'd long since lost interest in them, and so I decided to keep this latest example of Dan's vandalism to myself. Yet when I emptied that mess into my wastebasket, the sound of those incompatible pieces jostling against each other filled me with a peculiar sadness.

A week later the living room house plants all died at once, an inexplicable mass suicide. Of course Father blamed this latest disaster on Dan, who stood before him and declared his innocence in nearly convincing, stuttering frustration. "I, I didn't *do* it, why d-do you always blame *me?*"

"Why do I always blame *you?*" Father returned with mocking contempt. He swiveled his recliner away to face the wood paneling on the wall.

"*Why?* W-why do you . . ."

"That's enough, *son.*"

Again, Dan was nothing. Torment distorted his face, and he turned that bitter face on me—on *me*, who hadn't done anything!—before rushing from the room and the house.

Father's chair rocked back and forth while I stood by the window and watched Dan's unhappy figure striding down the block. He was surely off to seek revenge somewhere out in the neighborhood, revenge that would certainly invite further punishment. But couldn't this cycle be broken? I had to bring him back. Without a word to Father—who rocked and rocked and thought whatever thoughts he locked inside himself—I slipped out of the house.

My brother was already far off and walking a good imitation of a run, and I hurried to catch up, silently willing my brother to please cool down, please come back. Turning down one street, then another, Dan seemed to be following a well-worn path, each angry step habitual, and then I decided to follow, to see where he would lead me. I lagged behind, keeping a careful distance between us.

At the edge of our town's small business district Dan turned a sharp corner and when I reached the street he was gone, as if he'd been biding his time to lose me. Was he peering out through one of the shop windows, pleased with his little trick? No, I thought, he'd never once looked back at me: if my brother was inside one of these stores, he wasn't thinking about me. I paused—maybe Dan came downtown to shoplift. If so, I needed to find him quickly. My eyes scanned the street for the most likely store.

I tried the comic book shop and slowly stalked the aisles, prepared to come upon Dan paging through a new adventure, surrounded by racks of superheroes and monsters. But he hadn't sought refuge there and I hurried out, skipped a flower shop and the law office, then sped through the stationery store so swiftly the cashier seemed to suspect *me* of shoplifting.

The toy store farther down the block was another likely candidate.

Like some cartoon version of a detective, I stealthily edged along the storefront of the model train museum called Tomtown—devised by a Tom somebody, this sprawling little world was one of our town's few prides. I hadn't wandered in there for years, but at the sound of a tiny train's shrill whistle, I couldn't help glancing inside.

There was Dan, his back to me and so preoccupied that I easily snuck in and stood a few feet behind him. Three sets of trains rolled with restless energy through a miniature downtown much like the one I'd been sneaking through: fast-food restaurants, clothes stores, mom-and-pop shops, a church and travel agency. Those tiny trains must have turned in the same circles and tracks for decades, past the carefully sculpted hills and an abandoned factory, a drive-in movie and a fairground's tacky carnival. The thought of such relentless repetition made me queasy.

Dan hadn't moved or shifted his head once since I'd come in. Instead of following the trains, he was watching something in the miniature town, where nobody moved, no matter how pressing the business of those little plastic figures. A mother led her reluctant son to the barbershop, a drunkard hunched over in an alley, two kids peeked into a toy-store window, a dogcatcher reached out with his net for a mongrel, a hook and ladder crew hurried before a house engulfed by red-paper flames, and every action was locked in place. Which of these scenes held my brother's attention?

Then I noticed Tom himself standing quite still in a corner, an old, old man with alert, shifting eyes, enjoying us taking in his carefully constructed world. He began to shuffle down the aisle, ready to point out some little detail that we might have missed. But I didn't want Dan to discover me so I stepped backward, trying to keep out of his line of sight. Then I was out the door and down the steps, hurrying across the street to Young Miss Fashions—somewhere my brother would surely never go—where I'd wait for him to leave.

Unfortunately, the saleswoman seemed to think I had no business wandering in her shop. She dogged me down the aisles, interfering with my lookout on Tomtown's entrance and I had to feign interest in the racks of blouses and skirts. "I'm looking for something for my girlfriend," I offered as she hovered beside me, and she finally left me alone.

I still had no idea how to even ask a girl out for a date and doubted

I'd ever learn, yet I pretended the smooth, pleated skirt in my hands belonged to an actual girlfriend rather than someone I'd invented for the sake of a saleslady. Blushing at my terrible ignorance of the secret world offered by this store, I stroked the shoulder pads of a blouse, lightly touched a skirt's belt loop in an attempt to defeat my shyness. I discovered that skirt zippers were thin, almost delicate, and that blouse buttons buttoned on the wrong side—I felt flushed with clumsiness at the thought of my fingers ever undoing them. Relief flooded through me when I saw Dan march down the street and out of sight.

I didn't follow him. Instead, I returned to Tomtown and stood right where Dan had kept watch. Crouching slightly to reproduce his line of sight, I peered at the crowded downtown street of meticulously painted figures, searching for whatever had drawn my brother's attention.

I heard Tom's steps behind me and then his hand was on my shoulder. He coughed lightly and said, "You know that boy who just left here?"

Had Dan stolen something? Afraid of betraying myself, I shook my head *no* without turning around and lightly shrugged off his hand.

"You sure? You look a little alike I think. And that *was* you who came in a while ago, wasn't it?"

I nodded slowly, stalling for time. "Uh-huh . . . I, I remembered I had to post a letter for my dad."

"You always walk backwards out a door?"

Speaking quickly to distract him from my blushing, I said, "I do if I don't want to miss what the trains are doing. I haven't been here for a while and I'd forgotten what a great place this is."

Tom didn't reply, then sighed. "Well, too bad you don't know that boy. I'd ask a question or two about him if you did."

Afraid anything I might say would give me away, I didn't reply and continued my survey of the little figures: a mother and daughter holding their hats against the wind, a dog eyeing a fire hydrant, two old men taking it all in from a storefront bench.

"Y'know," Tom broke in, "he comes in here about once a week and he doesn't move from that spot you're standing in."

I nodded, straining for disinterested politeness, and peered at a tiny man slipping a coin in a parking meter.

"He can stand there for up to an hour, real interested in whatever it is you're looking at." Tom coughed. "Though perhaps you could move just a touch to the right."

While thankful for his advice, I didn't move, still not trusting Tom enough to give him satisfaction. Eventually he walked back to his captain's chair in the corner, and of course I shifted before he turned around.

At first I saw no difference: the barber staring out his window remained the same barber, and the young mother kept pushing a baby carriage past the same streetlamp. Then I noticed a tiny arm raised in the air, cut off by the sharp corner of a hardware store—*damn it*, I thought, I hadn't moved enough to the right. Tom was watching me now, so I took infinitesimally small, infinitesimally slow sideways steps until that upraised arm became a man leaning over a child, a little boy who crouched down and shielded himself from a coming blow.

They were father and son, two tiny figures that never moved, the father's threatening gesture always held in check. This terrible stalemate must be what drew Dan here week after week under Tom's watchful eye, a little sculpture of what he came home to every day after school, for weren't Father's angers and silences a kind of beating, inflicted without lifting a finger? I remembered his harsh words the opening night of Laurie's school play, remembered her later that evening, her cheek as raw and pink as if she'd been struck.

A train and its five little passenger cars chugged by, and I stepped away, ready to leave.

Tom called out, "Find anything?"

I had, and with his help, but this was nothing I could share. "Sorry," I managed, and ran outside.

Unable to bear the thought of returning home just yet, I took a detour through the park, passing beneath shade trees, and with a quick glance here and there at the shadows at my feet I easily tossed off *oak, maple, dogwood*. But while my abilities now approached Father's, they didn't nourish me in the same way.

I stopped and sat in the gnarled crook of an oak tree. The spreading branches above shook their leaves as if in rebuke, and beneath me, I knew, was a broad echoing skein of roots. I was locked in the middle of the tree's grasp, and I closed my eyes for an escape that offered no escape: the image of those two toy figures returned as if bestowing some unsettling secret. That little posed drama played inside me the same way I'd long stood by and watched my brother and father combat each other day after day.

I'd always been more than a mere spectator. From the look of fury Dan had trained on me today, it was clear *he* understood this. My silence supported Father, a price I'd been willing to pay. Yet what had I received in return? During my hours of transplanting and weeding at the nursery I would sometimes sit, transfixed, by a simple sight: a caterpillar chewing a leaf studded with holes, or a grub boring tunnels into a delicate stalk, and I'd despair of ever finding a way inside my father's private world.

If I was tired of silent green things, then perhaps it was time for my brother to work at the nursery: as an employee he would never be called "*son,*" Father would have to be fair with him, and I could oversee the transition in the next year before leaving for college. Already I let myself imagine Dan and Father murmuring protectively over sickly plants, trimming and pruning, planning the spacious curve of a garden.

Father's recliner still faced the wall when I returned home. Only a slight pause in the steady rocking acknowledged my entrance.

"Dad," I said. The rocking stopped. He was ready to listen to whatever I had to say, and so I said it. "Why not give Dan a job at the nursery? He's old enough."

Father swiveled around, his face guarded, surprisingly weary. "Why? So he can vandalize my business as well as my home?"

This wasn't, I realized, an outright rejection, so I continued. "I don't think he'll do that. Anyway, you know how he hates to stay indoors. He might even like a job out in the open—"

Father shook his head *no.*

"If he does mess up," I said, "you can just fire him." Suddenly inspired, I added, "And if he ruins anything, I'll pay for it, out of my own salary."

Father kept silent, as if we hadn't spoken. But his rocking eased to a relaxed rhythm, convincing me that soon he'd agree: this family matter had now become something more manageable, a business proposition.

Convincing Dan that evening was less easy. The mere suggestion set him flinging his comic books about the room, and their colored pages flailed eloquently in the air—briefly, magically animated—before falling to the carpet.

"Never. *Never*. No *way*—"

"No—wait, Dan. He's different at work."

"So?" he shouted, kicking through his collection.

"So, maybe—I don't know. Maybe you'll get along."

Dan laughed bitterly, but he stopped his rampage.

"He pays attention at work," I added, encouraged. "He *has* to, to teach you stuff."

Dan's lips trembled, and he knelt to gather up his comics. "What makes you think he would?" he whispered.

I sat beside my brother in the backseat of the car as Father drove us all to work without a comment, withholding the sort of advice he'd offered me on my first day. After parking he strode off alone without a glance back at us. Dan loitered by the car and pretended indifference, squinting at the reflected light of the greenhouses, while I struggled with my own sense of injury—Father was barely honoring the bargain we'd agreed to.

And he'd left me with the job of introducing Dan to Bob. We set off across the grounds, and I found Bob behind the main building, overseeing the stacking of plastic bags of peat moss and ornamental wood chips. He'd kept away from me since the end of his thieving days, and if we ever found ourselves working together he restricted himself to deferential smiles, faintly tinged with resentment. Now he set down his clipboard as we approached, that familiar smirk on his face, and I decided I wouldn't play the fiction that Dan was just another employee.

"Bob, this is my brother Dan. He'll be working here too now."

"I'm pleased to meet any relation of such a fine worker as Michael," he said, shaking Dan's hand.

Turning to my brother, I tried to assume Father's crisp authority. "You'll work under Bob today. He's the man to listen to."

Bob nodded with satisfaction. "That's what your father always says."

Unimpressed, Dan said nothing, and while he waited for his first orders I left for my own chores.

All morning I resisted the impulse to check on my brother, wishing I could have kept him close to me this first day. Half expecting his temper to erupt, once or twice I stopped, listened for any hint of trouble, then returned to my work.

During lunch break Dan brooded through every bite of his sandwich while Bob went on and on: "Oh, it looks like he'll fit in, it looks like he'll fit in fine, just fine."

When Bob snuck outside for a quick smoke, Dan muttered, "Jeez, what a creep. Wherever he is, he keeps *staring* at me. I think Dad said something to him."

I shook my nearly empty soda can and listened to the harmless sizzle of its fizz. "I don't think they talk much. Don't worry—just do your work and you'll be fine." I crumpled my lunch bag and tossed it at the trash can, hoping to impress Dan. It bounced against the rim, somehow dropping in, and I offered my brother a triumphant grin. He stared at the ground. "Hey," I said, "I have to check the sprinkler system. You want to come along?"

He groaned. "I can't. Bob said I gotta do some stuff with a bunch of seedlings."

Maintaining the sprinklers involved too much tightening and loosening, then tightening and loosening again with a wrench that nourished blisters. The metallic groan of each tug echoed my own discomfort and at one point echoed the distant shouting that carried across the nursery. It was Father's angry voice, then Dan's. *No, no*, I thought, dropping the wrench, and I tore through rows of potted juniper bushes, turned the corner past a tool shed and hurried toward the tight circle of my father, Dan and Bob.

"He—he did!" Dan cried out, his hands waving almost in supplication before Father's ominous stillness.

"Of course he did not."

"He *did*," Dan repeated, now turning to me. "Bob popped open the snack machine and just lifted a candy bar—"

"I never did such a thing," Bob insisted. "Michael here has worked with me for three years now. He knows I'm not like that. Isn't that right, Michael?" He turned to me a cruel little smile that revealed how badly I'd misjudged him. Petty thievery had never been the point, after all.

Father mistook my hesitation as a reluctance to condemn my brother, and he took a sharp step toward him. "Liar!" he cried, now actually shaking with rage, and Dan flinched before him. They both hesitated an instant before the terrible logic of what must follow, and before me was the scene my brother had stared at for months as if in preparation for this moment. I couldn't let it happen.

"Wait!" I shouted. "Wait! Dan's telling the truth. Bob . . . Bob's been filching stuff for years."

"That won't work!" Father barked. "You're protecting your brother."

"No! *I've* seen him do it too. Lots of times."

"Aw, now—" Bob protested, but Father cut him off with a flick of his hand. "Why didn't you tell me before?" he asked me, his voice hushed, trembling.

"I, I, I didn't . . ." I stuttered, remembering with despair when Father had rested his hand gently on my shoulder, how in the spell of that long-awaited moment I'd forgotten to report Bob's petty larceny. "You, you see . . ." I tried again, but the only explanation I had was in a language my father didn't speak—the language of family, not business.

"Bob, you're fired," Father announced without even bothering to glance at his shocked face. Instead, my father regarded me with the determined expression of an employer who is certain of what he must do. Yet there was regret, even tenderness in his voice—I'll always believe this, I have to believe this—when he said, softly, "And you're fired too."

My father never again uttered a word about that terrible afternoon. As for my brother, he sometimes offered me surreptitious, apologetic glances whenever he and Father discussed the nursery over dinner. I'd pretend to enjoy my meal, while Laurie gazed at a wall, silently rehearsing another school play.

"You think mulching is enough?" Dan might say, unable to hide his happiness. And why shouldn't he be happy? In an instant he'd

changed from bad son to good, a transformation as radical as anything in those comic books he loved. And my transformation was
just as complete: I'd become another false face, an unhappy surprise
like Mother. I was even haunted by the thought that now Father suspected *me* for Dan's brief run of domestic terrorism, but I didn't
dare deny something I hadn't been accused of, afraid any protest of
innocence might instantly brand me guilty.

The debacle at the nursery attuned Father to other possible betrayals. Increasingly he confronted Laurie about the Theater Club at
school—*he* knew where play acting could lead, and was more than
ready to revoke a host of household privileges if she didn't "stop all
this *pretending.*"

As if she'd been an understudy for Father's hurtful ways, Laurie
matched him, an insolence for every blustering threat, usually goad-
ing him into a theatrical bout of shouting. Then, with a smile of satisfaction, she'd walk away, and her bedroom door slammed so hard
Father would step up his raging again, laying down the law to living
room walls that wouldn't talk back, practicing his lines for the next
confrontation.

Unwilling to jeopardize his overnight favor, Dan used the occasion of these disputes to find an errand outside the house. But I refused to repeat my mistake of silence and served as Laurie's ally,
even if Father barely acknowledged my attempts. In the wake of one
particularly bitter quarrel, when Father and Laurie had howled at
each other in eerie harmony, I tried to calm him but he turned away
with a dismissive wave of his hand, a farewell more cutting than any
harsh words he might have said.

He left me alone in the living room. Longing for any hint of the
last bit of tenderness I'd heard in his voice that day he fired me, I
slumped onto the couch and stared at the furniture arrangements
that hadn't changed in years. Yet Father's silence had changed: it
now contained the refusal to forgive. Is this what Mother had hurled
herself against long ago? Even if this offered an explanation for my
parents' troubles, how could I ever discover what Mother had done
that Father wouldn't forgive? It was a story that would never be told.

I held my hands over my ears, as if this might stop my thoughts,
and then I rose from the couch and walked to my sister's door. I
knocked, a few quiet taps, but here was no answer. I entered anyway

and found her sitting before the mirror, examining her flushed face. She spoke in a voice made husky from all that screaming. "I appreciate what you're trying to do, Michael, but don't waste your time. Your word doesn't mean a thing to Dad any more."

She began working up her latest display of what eyeliner and blush could do, poking through her extensive makeup kit as if I weren't there, and I had to retort, "Whether he listens to me or not, you can't win, you know."

"Oh? Just watch me," she replied, so drawing out the dark tones of her ragged voice that I suspected she employed her arguments with Father for their hidden artistic opportunities. But Laurie had more parts to play than I could have predicted: when she was done with her elaborate application, she turned to me with a face that appeared absolutely plain, as free of makeup as one could imagine.

The following day my sister applied a similarly deceptive makeup: she set her face to Obedient Daughter and stopped arguing with Father. She even renounced her school's theater club, and this became her best role, one that established a false calm in our home. When Laurie waved good-bye with a demure flick of her hand and walked out the front door, she usually headed for her job at the local magic shop. There she gave makeup demonstrations and modeled wigs and costumes. Freed from scripted dialogue, she so effortlessly assumed the roles of an angel, witch, or vampire, even a pirate and a soldier of fortune, that her impromptu performances drew more than enough customers to constitute an audience.

I spent that final year at home waiting for my graduation and eventual escape to the state university. Yet sometimes I'd pass an early evening by my bedroom window, watching small flocks of birds navigate elegant geometries above their chosen tree before roosting for the night. I wanted to join them, imagining that those supple, weaving formations offered a hint of how to alter my family's separate trajectories, which were taking us farther and farther from each other.

PART THREE

The Butterfly Effect

"I have a hunch about you," Sylvia repeated, waiting for me to respond. But I was so unprepared for her words that I could only stare at that pillow she hid behind. What did she mean—that she needed to be saved the same way her father had saved her mother? If only I could, but I was such a poor choice—I'd never come close to saving anyone before.

I was silent too long. Sylvia pushed the pillow away, her eyes rich with regret. "Oh god, I'm so embarrassed I said that." She reached for her bra on the floor. "I've got to get dressed."

"Wait," I said, fueled by my own regret that I'd let such a moment pass by. "It's not that I—"

"Stop looking at me like that," Sylvia said, turning away. "I'll end up telling you my whole life."

"Please—don't leave."

She slipped on her panties. "I don't think you'll be surprised to hear that I'm very late for an appointment."

But I wouldn't let her escape so easily. "Sylvia, I want to know, I do—are you in some sort of trouble, do you need any help?"

Sylvia sighed. "Where to begin?"

"Wherever you'd like."

"I can't believe I'm . . . Look—you were right, I am a meteorologist—you know, on TV—a weather lady? I'm deeply hurt, by the way, that you still don't recognize me. I'm supposed to be a local personality. Though probably not for long." She paused, concentrating on her minute, elaborate adjustments as she tucked up her pantyhose, disappearing into her clothes before my eyes.

"So I guess you could say that meteorology is one of my troubles. I just don't believe in what I do any more. Pass me that skirt, please? Thanks. The problem is, on any given day, the odds aren't high enough for my getting the weather right: temperature, cloud cover, humidity, whatever. Did you know a rainstorm can pop up in less than an hour? It's depressing—I'm about as accurate as the horoscope. But forget about my prediction. Check the other channels, listen to any radio station, call up the weather number, read the paper. None of us says the same thing, even if the difference is only a matter of a couple of degrees."

"But a little variation doesn't seem—"

"This is supposed to be science, *it's supposed to be* exact. *Ha! Do you know what? One of my main competitors works part-time as a magician for children's parties. A* magician.

"Anyway, there's more than that," she said, buttoning her blouse. *"The Five Day Forecast . . . how much do you pay attention to the weather report? Not much, I'm sure, like everyone else. Well, almost every day my extended forecast changes. If there's anything I can guarantee, it's that what I predict on Wednesday about the weekend weather will be different from what I predict on Thursday and Friday about the weekend weather! Who checks, who cares, right? That's not the point. I'm a practitioner of bad science—just a smiling face in front of a satellite photo."*

"But aren't weather predictions getting more accurate?" I asked, groping for something soothing to say. *"Isn't there lots of research?"*

"Hey, every day I review the U.S. Weather Service reports, I work with satellite photos, radar, the works, and there are new supercomputer programs coming out in droves. I'd like to believe they'll do the job, but really, all of it can be undone by the flap of a wing. Ever hear of the Butterfly Effect?"

"I'm not sure. Is it—"

"It's part of chaos theory. Great name, huh? The best computer can make a very nicely detailed forecast, based on all the available data, but one minute later the tiniest atmospheric fluctuation that no computer can catch sets off a chain reaction that knocks the weather off-kilter. All because some butterfly flapped its wings." Sylvia laughed. "And to think I used to love butterflies—when I was a kid I cried whenever anybody caught one."

Sylvia slipped her feet into low-heeled shoes, once again a beautifully dressed woman. Still naked, I reached for my shirt, a white lump of underwear, but then stopped: my scattered clothes seemed like pieces of myself that might never fit properly again.

"Anyway," Sylvia went on, "all my doubts seem to be giving me away when I'm on the air—it's getting harder to drum up commercial sponsors for my segment. I'm not sure how much longer I'll be with the station." She sighed. "Well, time to go."

She headed for the door but I couldn't let her just leave, not yet. "Wait—what can I do, I mean, about this problem of yours? I'm no expert, but I could buy a net, round up all the butterflies I can find—"

"Look," she said, grinning, "why not just watch me on the tube, give me some tips?"

"I'll try. Can I call you—"

"At the station."

"Let me give you my number—"

"Not necessary. I have it memorized," she said, pointing to the night table. "Remember? Your phone was right in my field of vision for a while."

Her lips barely touched mine and then she was gone, leaving me to wonder if I'd just been given an elaborate brush-off. I wasn't sure, after all, if she'd told me her real name, or even if she actually was a meteorologist. Her quick footsteps echoed down the hallway, I heard my front door open and close, but I was long past pursuing anyone who didn't want to be pursued.

The Dream-Lit Room

Filled with the exacting contortions of percentages, I hurried from
my statistics class, once again questioning the wisdom of pursuing a
degree in business even if it did offer the possibility of a reconciliation with my father. Passing the quad—a mere corner of this vast
campus that even now, in my second year, seemed to sprawl in every
direction—I decided to bask in one of the last warm days of autumn
and stretch out on the grass. Here and there couples curled together
on the lawn, a Frisbee toss was underway with someone's dog
bounding after the whirling thing, and a few students with acoustic
guitars slowly worked up some out-of-tune folk music nostalgia.
Across from me stood one of the old oaks planted at the time of the
university's founding—its thick branches stretched over the lawn, a
canopy of leaves already tinged with purple and red.

A young woman, her delicate features clear even from a distance,
sat on the other side of that tree in her own circle of intensity, a large
notepad on her knees. Her blond hair framing her face, she stared up
at the branches, one hand ranging across the pad as if she didn't
need to see what she was doing. Then she examined what she'd

sketched, erased a trace of something here and there and sketched again. She worked from the crest down to the twists of exposed roots on the ground, and this last part gave her some trouble. She hesitated, erased again and looked up with such concentration that her gaze could easily have passed through the tree to me. I watched her so carefully I actually felt I was helping her draw.

Finally done, she set her pencil aside, tucked her blond hair back behind her ears, and my curiosity overcame my shyness. I found myself walking toward her, with each step shedding a bit more of my habitual restraint, and when my shadow passed over her notepad she looked up in surprise.

"Could I see?" I asked. "I hope you don't mind. . . ."

She held the notepad against her chest. Her forehead squinched in alarm, though something else in her face held me: a hint of smoke in those blue-gray eyes, the aftermath of some fire. Her lips moved slightly, silently, and I imagined she was calculating dangerous odds.

"Okay," she said, breathing out harshly. She set the pad back down on her lap.

Prepared to dispense polite praise that hid disappointment, I looked down at a tree reproduced in such detail I could almost see the autumn color in her penciled shadings. She knew the texture of bark and the odd symmetry of branches as well as anyone.

"My god, it's like a photograph. How can you do that?"

"Oh, it's all in the shadows." She laughed nervously. "What's there, and what's not."

Then I noticed that behind the tree sat one lone, distant figure on the lawn—*me*, though only half filled in: empty space where my arms folded across my chest, my face an outline with almost no detail, as if obscured by distance. "Oops, I moved. Sorry—I didn't know. Hey, I'll go back and you can finish."

She glanced down at her pad, clearly embarrassed. "No, that's all right. Anyway, I have to catch my next class."

She stood to leave, the slight flutter of her hand a wave good-bye, and she hurried across the lawn toward the fine arts building, taking with her that unfinished me.

*　　*　　*

My memory of her drawing's intricate details and empty spaces stayed with me for days. As I tried to take notes during lectures I couldn't complete a sentence. Sometimes, suddenly feeling watched, I'd look up and glance about, but no blue-gray eyes met mine. Soon enough I found myself wandering the halls of the fine arts building, shyness and longing rising and subsiding within me as I searched for someone whose name I didn't know.

I'd almost given up, when one afternoon I walked by the student union's plush study area and saw her ensconced on a couch, busy with her sketch pad. She radiated such concentration that I simply stood and stared. But if I waited for her to finish she might run off again, so I marched over to the couch and sat beside her.

She turned without surprise, as if expecting me—though I caught a momentary tenseness in the delicate line of her jaw—and then set her pencil down to let me look. She'd re-created a section of the Oriental rug at our feet—circles within circles of stylized flowers, like a garden from a dream.

Her eyes, so clear and yet tinged with elusive shadow, seemed to say, *Do you like it?*

"Of course," I blurted out, at once chagrined that I'd so openly answered a question she hadn't asked. Yet had I read her correctly?

Her lips parted, then suppressed whatever she was about to say, and I took in the lines of her drawing again. Each detail was shaded into a slight slant, making everything vibrate, even the blank spaces she hadn't yet filled in, and then I remembered why I'd searched for her. "You never finished me, y'know. Can't I give you another chance?"

She arched an eyebrow a notch, then tamped it down. "Well, I'm not very good at drawing people."

"Really? But that tree you drew was incredible."

"That's what I mean—I'm good at trees. Things. Not people."

We sat in silence until I blurted out, "I know something about trees too—I used to work at a nursery. I can tell you something a little unusual about that oak you drew."

Her attentive gaze invited me to continue, and I said, "Do you remember that bunch of fungus growing near the bottom of the trunk? Kind of wedge shaped?"

She nodded. "Uh-huh. It looked a little like . . . steps, from where I was sitting."

"Yeah, that's right. Beefsteak fungus—don't ask me where the name comes from. Well, it turns the wood under the bark a nice, dark brown, makes the tree more valuable when it's cut down."

Her eyes narrowed—a sign of pleasure, I would eventually discover. "That's very interesting, but I can't draw what's under the bark, can I?"

"Well, maybe not directly. But I think it gives the tree more personality, don't you? Wouldn't that affect the way you draw it?"

"Certainly. Anything else I should know?"

"Let me see . . . ever draw a tomato plant?"

"Not lately."

"Well, if you do, remember that the leaves are poisonous."

"I'll try. What can you tell me about this?" she asked, gesturing to those swirling yet stationary flowers on her drawing pad.

"Sorry, I don't know much about Oriental rugs."

We were back to silence again, so I struggled to discover something in those dazzling patterns that might be its own strange language, and then I recalled the curious designs left on bark by tree worms. "I can tell you an odd idea your drawing gives me," I ventured. "It looks like letters or words from an alphabet people can't read. I mean, if flowers could write, that's what a page from one of their books might look like."

Her hand lingered near a crescent of white petals. "That's nice," she said. She turned the page. "What about this?"

It was an illustration of a bicycle, the spokes of its wheels flaring in furious motion, though no one rode it. She might not have been able to draw people, but she made objects animate: alone on the page, that bicycle sped headlong down its own path, on some mysterious mission.

"Well," she said cautiously, "does this give you an odd idea too?"

"Yes, it does." I laughed. "Those two wheels—um, see the angle you give to the tires?—seem like they're trying to move toward each other. Impossible, but sweet."

She regarded her drawing as if with new eyes, though I couldn't tell if she agreed with my interpretation. She turned the page again. "And what about this?"

*   *   *

Her name was Kate Martin, and when I asked if I could see her again she tucked a wave of hair behind her ears and agreed in an offhand way that it would be nice if we bumped into each other again some-time. And suddenly I was alone on the couch, watching Kate making her way down the promenade, clutching her artist's folder like a shield.

What could I do in the face of such skittishness? I waited. Yet af-ter one long week that I could barely endure I finally allowed myself to look up her name in the student directory. Then I crossed the campus, repeating her address and room number like a mantra. Hoping to engineer a chance meeting, I loitered outside her dormi-tory, an old brick building with long rows of windows open to the im-probably mild air. Her room was on the third floor. I scanned each window carefully for a glimpse of her, and I found myself wondering how she might draw that curtain's idle fluttering up there, or the skewed reflection of the clouding sky on a pane of cracked glass. I only vaguely heard the dry crackling of steps through the fallen leaves behind me.

"Hello?"

I turned to see Kate precariously balancing a pile of art books that reached to her chin. If she'd caught me at my vigil, her face betrayed nothing.

"Oh, hi," I managed, astonished at my good luck. "Can I help you with those books?"

Kate glanced furtively toward the door of her dorm, then the hint of a smile surfaced on her lips. "You could've helped me a lot more," she said, "if you'd waited outside the library instead of here."

"I'll try to do better next time," I replied, blushing as I reached out for the books on top.

Having succeeded far beyond what I'd hoped for, I happily climbed one flight of stairs after another with Kate, though when we reached her door and she fumbled with the keys I expected her to politely send me on my way. The latch clicked. Kate pushed the door open with her foot and strode inside.

"You can put them on the floor," she said, affecting a light tone. "Doesn't matter where."

While she hung her jacket on a coat rack, I carried my load of books as far inside her room as I dared and eased them down on her desk. Setting my backpack on the floor, I glanced around her room: the usual ancient oak dresser, prison-regulation bed, and two chairs, one with worn cushions. Not so usual were the rows of drawings tacked to the white walls and gleaming in the afternoon sun: a dried leaf; a necklace of small, ridged shells; a drinking glass, its surface delicately patterned with condensation; a few coins, face down; a worn book, its spine a tattered flap; one single, magnified blade of grass.

A breeze swept through the open window. Those drawings shivered and swayed gently, alive somehow, their rustlings an odd whispering. "They're beautiful," I murmured to Kate, who'd settled in the cushioned chair. "You really should try to draw people."

"There's a reason I can't. . . ." she said, then stopped, her calm front gone.

Afraid she thought I was hinting for her to finish my portrait, I began, "It's okay, I didn't mean to . . ." But my words trailed off too. Kate's face seemed to struggle with itself, a private battle that I had to turn away from.

Why had I said that? Now she was preparing to ask me to leave. I scanned Kate's gallery for one more look and paused at the drawing of a drinking glass and its moist surface. Each delicate drop was a tiny world, its tracery of shadows hinting at the teeming life within. One bulging bead appeared so ready to burst that I waited for it to streak down the glass until I heard Kate's hesitant voice.

"Would you like to hear why I don't draw people?"

Exulting inside at my good fortune, I answered, "Yes, I would."

"Well, pull up a chair," she said, her words traced with an odd weariness.

I sat across from Kate, and her face, bathed in afternoon light, looked as ripe as those nearly trembling beads. She stared at her gallery of drawings a few moments, as if asking their permission before beginning.

"I guess I should first tell you," she finally said, "that I'm a transfer student. At my last college I took a lot of jobs freshman year, anything to get by and help pay for school. Once I even took a job as a model. An art class model."

Kate paused, stared hard into my face. "I'm telling this only to you. Only to you. Do you understand, Michael?"

Already my curiosity was tempered with a vague unease, but I replied as earnestly as possible, "Sure, this is as private as you want it."

Kate nodded, gulped nervously and continued. "I arrived a little early for that art class. The studio professor told me to make myself comfortable. *That* meant I had to undress behind a screen in the corner and put on a scratchy robe. So I did, and when I came out the studio was still empty. In front of the easels there was this riser with a small couch and stool, so I sat on the stool, and because the professor didn't say anything else I kept my robe on. When the students finally came in I checked to see if any of them were in my classes. None were, thank god, but this kept me so busy I forgot that I still hadn't taken off the robe."

Kate looked away and ran her fingers slowly through her hair. "This is really embarrassing. . . ."

"It's okay, you know, you can stop if—"

She shook her head, laughed. "No. I've gotten this far, haven't I?" She crossed her arms over her chest. "They all sat in front of their easels, arranging or sharpening pencils, but really, they were waiting for me. Finally the professor kind of coughed and reminded me that everyone was ready.

"If I'd undressed before they'd arrived, that would have been that. But now, with all those . . . *eyes* on me, I felt like I was about to do a striptease. I fumbled with the belt, my fingers were so . . . Anyway, I dropped the robe."

Kate turned her pale face to me and I blushed as if she'd caught me gawking, as if she'd just undressed before me and her white blouse and jeans and everything else were crumpled on the floor. But she simply said, "It's funny, but now that I've gotten started, every-thing's rushing back to me. I'm not usually so . . . talkative. I need a glass of water—my mouth is so dry."

"I'll get it for you," I offered, suddenly thirsty as well.

I knocked on the door of the corner bathroom and when no one answered I entered a room cluttered with towels dangling from shower rods. Shampoo bottles lined the edge of a bathtub, and toothbrushes, a nail clipper and makeup kits sprawled across the flat porcelain rims of a row of sinks. Drinking glasses of all shapes and sizes nestled together on a ledge above the water spigots, and then I recognized Kate's glass from her sketch. I filled it and gulped down cool water, then filled it again and waited for beads of condensation to appear on the glass's smooth, transparent surface, so I could see what she'd seen while drawing those beads of water.

But Kate was patiently waiting for me and I hurried back to her room. With a wan smile she took the glass. Head arched back, her throat rippled from swift little gulps and I sat across from her again, now with the growing suspicion that I was being seduced. Yet Kate, her face nearly drained of color, seemed the unlikeliest person in the world to attempt this.

"Thanks," she murmured, setting the glass down. "Well, nothing happened, I just stood there, all goose bumps. Then the professor asked, really very gently, if he could suggest a pose. All I could do was nod my head, so embarrassed that I was standing there like a stupid block, that the class *still* hadn't started.

"He asked me to just sit up on the stool with my back straight, and zombie that I was, I followed orders. Everyone started sketching away. It sounded like this faraway applause, and then I was goose bumps all over again. After a while the professor asked me to try something on my own for the second pose, so I kind of hunched my knees up and shook my hair over my shoulders, hiding whatever I could."

But the sweet curve of Kate's blouse did nothing to cover the breasts I imagined, and I shifted uneasily in the chair. Kate shifted too, an echoing that seemed to connect us, and she let out a long breath. "After another pose it was time for a break, so I slipped the robe back on, trying really hard not to look like I was in a big hurry. Nobody cared—they were still concentrating on finishing their sketches.

"The professor motioned for me to take a look if I liked, and I was surprised that, well, that I wanted to. I made sure I stood behind everyone, though—I wasn't interested in any small talk, no eye contact for me. It was really odd to look at parts of me that I normally never saw—my shoulder blades, the back of my thighs. But only a few of the sketches caught anything *I'd* draw if I had the chance to watch myself from a distance."

Kate paused, took one last sip from her glass. I stared at her feet, unable to stop imagining her long legs extending upward without jeans.

"But what I noticed most of all," she said, "was that the three sketches of any student were pretty different, as if three separate people had been modeling up there. At first I thought they just weren't any good at drawing, but then I realized that just by shifting my hips, or hunching my shoulders, I'd made them see me in a new way, that somehow *I* was in control. Even though this made the second half of the class much easier, I never posed again."

Kate sat back, and now that she'd finished I looked up at her, half expecting something—a little flick of her hair, her legs stretching just to the point of touching my own, a shifting of her hips—that would bring us together in a tangle of arms in the center of her room.

But Kate's gaze was steady, controlled, the gray in her eyes seeming to absorb the blue. She cleared her throat, sighed. "I thought my silly adventure was over, but a week later I was in the student union, getting a Coke, when I saw one of the art students walking down the hall. I remembered him because he'd gotten me all wrong: too much hip, not enough chest. I practically flattened myself against the soda machine when he passed by. But I couldn't help thinking that any of those art students could bump into me at any time. And then I'd be, well . . ."

Naked again, I thought as she paused.

"Anyway," Kate continued, "I couldn't go anywhere on campus without checking for art students, even if I couldn't quite remember all of them. That upset me the most, never knowing who might be beside me in the cafeteria or the bookstore, remembering my body. Sometimes I'd lie in bed at night and try filling in their faces. Then one day someone's stupid little laugh across the quad actually made me blush, and I decided it was time to leave.

"So I transferred here. But I couldn't shake the memory of that art studio, you know? So I signed up for a drawing course, and that first class, a young guy posed for us. He didn't seem nervous at all. He bent his knees and stretched his arms out together like they were pulling on an invisible rope. I tried to capture the strain on his arm muscles, and I knew right away that I was good at drawing. But I'd been a model too, and when I remembered how a model can control an artist's attention, I felt as if *I* was being pulled with that invisible rope.

"Well, I didn't want him to do that. So I started again and just drew the rope he was pretending to pull, with only a hint of his hands at one end. But what about the other end? I thought. After a few shadings something came to me and took shape like a dream: a lamp, bolted to a wall, two of its hinges coming loose from the strain on the rope.

"When I drew that lamp I actually felt something coming apart inside me. This wasn't a lamp at all—it was me, somehow. But my drawing had caught the moment in time, you see, so I couldn't be torn off the wall. I was safe. The professor came by and reminded me that this was a figure class, but when I told her, 'That's what I see,' she looked again. Now she lets me draw whatever comes out when a model poses, even if it's always an object."

I regarded Kate's drawings on the wall—they weren't still lifes at all, they were really self-portraits. The sketches fluttered again from a stray breeze, a trembling of shadow and light and the revelation of their true identity, and there I sat in that dream-lit room, holding on to the wooden arms of a chair.

"It was so peculiar," Kate said, her voice low and vaguely accusatory, "when I drew that tree and then there *you* were on the page, beside the tree and somehow part of—anyway, it was the first time that ever happened. And when you came over to talk to me, it was like you knew you'd appeared."

Strange, subtle emotions flickered over Kate's face that I couldn't quite read. I felt the strain of my own secret hinges and leaned toward her. Kate stared back at me, as if memorizing my face, and then she wrenched her gaze away. "I think I'd like to be alone now," she murmured.

"Alone?" I repeated, nearly breathless with disappointment. "But, um—tomorrow. Can I come by—"

"I'll be too busy tomorrow."

"Then the day af—"

She shook her head no.

I blushed. "Wait—wait. What do you mean?"

"I'm sorry, Michael," she replied, her face reddening, her mouth an embarrassed grimace. This wasn't easy for her to say, yet somehow she had to. She waved an arm awkwardly at her own words, perhaps an ineffectual attempt to erase all that she'd revealed, but it was too late for that. Hadn't Kate modeled another kind of naked-ness for me, a confession that was the beginning of this good-bye?

"You don't have to worry, you know," I said, still unwilling to give up. "I promise, I won't tell anyone."

"Thank you," she said quietly, her face hardened with resignation. "I know you won't."

I collected my backpack. Those pictures on the wall still shud-dered in the breeze, her secret self waving good-bye. I waved back, then offered the other Kate my stunned, false smile and left her room.

I hurried away from the dorm, filled with the bitter unfairness that I'd finally lost my shyness over someone even more wary of inti-macy than I ever was. I turned for one last look at her window, and I saw a dark figure, still as stonework, framed by the fluted curves of her curtains: Kate too wanted another glimpse. Then she slowly stepped back into the room's shadows and I realized she'd driven me away not because of my desire, but because of her own.

Later that evening I opened my backpack and discovered her sketch of the oak tree, me. Yet my incomplete likeness no longer held any interest, for now I knew that the twists and shadows of bark, the unerring way Kate found conflicting crevices flourishing within crevices, was the real portrait. Then I caught my breath—Kate must have slipped this farewell gift inside my pack when I left for her glass of water. She'd already known what she was going to do.

In the following months, even as the memory of Kate's drawings haunted me day after day after day, I tried my best to keep clear of her dormitory and the fine arts building. But I needn't have troubled myself—wasn't she avoiding me too, in the same way she'd dodged all those art students at her former college? I caught sight of Kate only once, as she walked along a path beneath a trellis of vines, un-aware of me and on her way to the student pub, her brilliant blond hair shining in the shafts of sunlight. A large portfolio was tucked be-neath Kate's arm and I felt the tug of something strange inside, for that artist's folder kept no secrets from me. I knew it surely held pages and pages of new self-portraits that looked nothing and every-thing like her.

A Form of Floating

I huddled over my class notes outside the economics building, certain that the first snap quiz of the semester waited inside. As I flipped through page after page of my suddenly alien handwriting, I heard footsteps on the steps: hesitant, then resolute, then hesitant again. They stopped a few feet away and, as I still sometimes did, I imagined that when I looked up Kate would be standing before me.

So I looked up. This time Kate *did* face me. She'd let her blond hair grow long, and now it was coiled into a knot at the back of her head, a few fringes loose and shining. Her face gleamed in the sun, and when she didn't turn away from my gaze, for one brief and weightless moment I almost believed that I'd actually conjured her up.

"Hello," Kate finally said, trying for a light tone to make the best of this awkward moment. She shifted her artist's portfolio from one arm to the other.

"Oh, hi," I offered, somehow able to echo her casual greeting.

Kate cleared her throat with a tight little cough and asked, "How are you?"

"Fine, I suppose—still suffering through my major. How are you doing?" I gathered up my books, waiting to see if she'd take this chance to escape from me and what I knew about her.

Shifting slightly to the side as if to block me, Kate said in a rush, "I'm going to be a cartoonist for the school paper."

She didn't try to hurry off. Instead, she tucked a few loose strands of hair behind her ears. But still I was wary: after so long, why suddenly this small talk?

Kate misunderstood my silence. "It's true. The art director is in one of my classes. He likes my work."

"That's . . . great," I ventured.

"The problem is, I don't have the best sense of humor. But how can I refuse?"

"You're right. A challenge is a challenge."

The bell rang inside and I glanced at the door of the economics building. I was going to be late. Kate pulled a sheet from her portfolio. "Do you see anything funny in this?" She handed me a sketch of a snail shell, its rounded spiral imbued with strange life: dark, edgy markings ran along its surface like the mysterious notations of electrocardiograms, recording my excitement as I held the page.

A little dizzy at what she'd done, I managed to say, "Well, it's not funny ha-ha. Funny *weird*."

"Weird?"

"It might help if you added a caption," I said, and again I examined this shell that now seemed to twirl madly in space. "How about something like . . . 'No more carnival rides for me!' "

Kate frowned slightly in concentration. "I *think* I get it."

"Well, I know it's not much. If I had more time I could probably come up with something better."

"You think you could?" Kate said, the waver in her voice an apology, a confession.

I gaped at her. This wasn't a chance meeting at all, Kate had sought me out. I forgave her, forgave her so easily because she needed me, or at least she needed my words to translate her self-portraits. "Absolutely," I replied. "Show me a drawing and I'll come up with two or three lines to choose from. Then we can pick out our favorite."

"Our?" she said, so softly I might have imagined it.

"Our," I said firmly—I knew all about business propositions. "We'll have to share the byline too, of course."

I've often wondered if I should have made Kate court me more, even at the risk of losing her, yet I never wanted to exact a punishment. I knew how it felt not to be forgiven. We never once mentioned that afternoon in her dormitory room, however its memory may have hovered over us, and instead we devoted ourselves in the following weeks to combining her uncanny drawings with my captions. A straight-backed chair, so alone on the page, said to itself, *I remember there was wind and rain, but where?* A half-eaten sandwich abandoned on a bench mused, *Why must I be denied digestion?* A flat stone, hurtling in mid-skip across a pond, declared above its echoing shadow, *If only I could float!*

We called our cartoon strip "True Confessions," though Kate always preferred her own suggestion, "Thing Thoughts." Conflating our names, we signed it "Mite," but no one on campus seemed particularly interested in uncovering our identities. At best, the strip was mildly popular among our small circle of friends. I suspected that the art director, an anxious sort of fellow who called Kate at all hours about each impending deadline, kept the strip running only because he was interested in far more than her drawings. Nearly every work session I'd have to answer the phone and field his halting attempts at nonchalance as he asked if my collaborator was there.

I was willing to double as Kate's bodyguard because the more we worked together the more it became clear that she and I were kindred spirits. Her desire to both hide and reveal herself made her objects come alive, and understanding this helped me add something of myself to the struggle seeping out of her precisely drawn lines. Kate always considered my captions with a sort of quizzical acceptance, as if my words had all along been her secret inspiration.

I loved to sit beside Kate and watch her draw. Her fingers barely held the pencil—a light touch for such clarity—and her careful movements became a form of floating, a sign language somehow caught on paper. One evening, as Kate was about to begin another illustration, I placed my hand next to her notepad.

"Draw my hand?"

"Michael. You know . . ."

"It's not a person," I said, "it's a hand. Quite an interesting piece of machinery, actually. C'mon, give it a try."

Kate closed her eyes, sighed, and then looked down at my patient hand. Slowly she began sketching the whorls of my knuckles, as if they were separate little whirlpools pulling her in. Next she drew those long-ridged bones that fanned from my wrist, and slowly the individual parts took hold of each other and grew fingers, took on the contours and shadows of flesh.

Finally she set down her pencil. My hand lay twinned before us. I gave her no time to choose between them: I turned mine over, palm up. "Draw it again?" I asked.

She did, first extending the particular curves and intersections of the lines of my palm, though no palm yet existed on the page. She continued that seemingly chaotic crosshatching until they led to my fingerprints, where she stopped. After a long pause, she drew the outline of my hand, then gave dimension to all the rounded slopes that circled the center of my palm. Again she hesitated, staring at those five fingers and their empty faces. Meticulously she gave expression to the delicate, echoing curves of my prints, adding slight shadows that hinted at sadness and anger, subdued joy, the possibility of laughter.

When she was done I stared at my hand and its image; indeed, both seemed filled with conflicting emotions.

"Now touch it?" I whispered. Kate hesitated, then laughed quietly with a hint of resignation. She slid one long-nailed finger along the lines of my palm, just lightly touching my skin: now *we* were pencil and page. But before she could finish tracing me, my fingers reached up and held her hand. Neither of us moved. I pulled her gently toward me. Her eyes narrowed with pleasure, then closed as we settled and twisted on the carpet, and I let her imagine a private sketch of what we did together.

And so we began our entry into sexual mysteries that were breathtaking for their very ordinariness: the borders between ticklish and arousing that we'd chart on each other's bodies; an unexpected stomach gurgling or surreptitious fart mingling with the cries and moans we were capable of; the shifting map of our sweaty scents as we accomplished exquisite unfurlings in each other's arms.

And before curling into sleep together we'd practice an intimate ritual. Kate would stretch with languid grace and pull a tissue from the box. "Want one?" she'd ask lazily. When I whispered *yes* she'd lift out another. Then Kate would sop up the excess sperm that dripped from her, while I dabbed her sweet moistness from my penis.

Kate always threw her tissues at the wastebasket in the corner, one by one, and I tossed mine too. We rarely made the target, and our failed shots—crumpled balls of sticky tissue—lay scattered on the floor. Yet in the morning, while on my way to open the bedroom curtains, I saw those little balls as flowers blooming out of the hardwood floor. I'd bend down to gather them up, always surprised how light they'd become overnight—our dried sex was now a delicate white crust, enfolded in the tissues' twists and curves.

At first Kate kept even our artistic collaboration a secret from her parents. "They wouldn't approve," she said simply, and even though they apparently disapproved of nearly everything, she was in no hurry to include me in that long list. As for me, during my periodic phone calls to remind my father that he had another son, I'd occasionally make a few cryptic comments that hinted at a girlfriend, but Father's terse telephone formality invited little more than another rundown of my latest courses and an estimation of future grades. And Kate was certainly in no rush for introductions. The few stories of my childhood that she could bear to hear made her draw such ugly pictures—the chipped face of a toppled doll, a stain on a rug that looked alive—that I held off from any further confidences.

Kate claimed her own childhood wasn't worth the telling. "I'm *glad* I don't have the kind of stories you do," she'd say, responding to my skepticism. Though even ordinary, daily details would have satisfied me, I didn't press her, suspecting that I loved Kate at least partly for her need for privacy—I wanted to embrace whatever was frightened inside her and make it mine. So I was startled, thrilled, and made more than a little anxious when Kate asked me to accompany her home for the Thanksgiving holiday.

Kate's parents met us at the front door, their mild faces so nondescript I couldn't quite grasp where her delicate, beautiful features came from. Her blond hair, though, was clearly a gift from her mother, even if Mrs. Martin's resembled a doll's wig that had been fussed with too much.

"Welcome, dear," her mother said with a brush of cheeks before stepping back and adding with a smile, "Oh, your hair will look so beautiful when you finally get a decent cut."

When Kate winced, I saw for one fleeting moment my sister flinching before Father's words after her school play. Then Kate's father reached out and without a word shook my hand, forcing me to introduce myself. We all stood together for a clumsy moment, none of us quite meeting the others' eyes.

"Well . . . ?" Kate murmured.

"Oh, of course," Mrs. Martin replied with a glance at her husband, and they led us into a home thick with upholstered furniture and yellow shag carpeting. Heavy living room curtains closed out the crisp blue autumn sky, yet even dull light couldn't hide the cold gleam of the porcelain figurines lined up in a curio cabinet: a little band of musical frogs, Jack and Jill lugging a pail together, a barefoot student asleep at his desk, a family of elephants, a quartet of drunks crooning beside a lamppost.

Kate vanished into the kitchen with her mother. I settled onto the couch across from Mr. Martin, who grunted as he fit into a chair, turning a bland gaze on me that I'd been warned was deceptive. Anticipating a fatherly grilling, I was especially nervous about any question touching on life after college—I was still marching through an array of business courses without a clear idea of what I'd ever do with my degree. What I most cared for at school was the comic strip Kate and I worked on together, but this was another of the many subjects that had to be kept secret.

I needn't have worried—Kate's father hoarded words as if they were in dangerously limited supply. He so efficiently parried whatever conversational gambit I came up with that I began to suspect this was his way of drawing me out, of making me give away something he wasn't supposed to know. Adding to my unease were the snippets of casual criticism I heard Kate's mother offer her in the kitchen: "Straighten your shoulders, dear . . . what do you have against lipstick, anyway?"

Finally Kate murmured an excuse and joined us in the living room. She tucked herself in a corner chair, but instead of speaking she simply joined her father's lingering silence. In the dim light Kate's face began to resemble her parents' bland features, her cheeks so smooth that I imagined her skin was as cold as those tiny figures in the curio cabinet. If only I could reach out and gently stroke life back into her face, her arms.

One slow minute after another passed, and Kate sat so still she might as well have been one of her own sketched objects, waiting for a caption. Afraid she was somehow sinking into her family's gravitational pull, I realized I had to offer her a way out—with words, words, any words I could think of, and I soon found myself in the middle of a slightly manic rundown of my current classes, piling one trivial detail onto another, from the relative weight of each course's textbooks to the statistical likelihood that at least one of my professors per semester would smoke a pipe.

At the sound of my voice Mrs. Martin came out of the kitchen and asked me to help set the table. Trying to hide my reluctance, I joined her with a hearty, "Of course!" Then I extended my living room monologue, loud enough so it would carry back to Kate, and commented on the tastefully arranged bowls and serving plates, the lovely blue-rimmed dishes, the impressively ancient silverware. Mrs. Martin moved gingerly from chair to chair beside me, hemming and hmming in vague disapproval until we completed the table's careful symmetries.

The carving of the turkey was a funereal event, Kate's father mournfully slicing soft white slabs of meat and setting them in even layers on a serving dish. Then the various bowls were passed back and forth with great solemnity and still Kate said nothing. Spooning cranberries onto my plate, and by now crazy with the urge to keep talking, I announced, "Oh, Cape Cod Bells! They're the most popular type of cranberries, you know."

Recalling that experimental corner of my father's nursery, I embarked on a disquisition on how the cranberry bush grows in sandy soil that has to be drained before the flowering season. Having given up on me as unacceptably chatty, Kate's parents answered with silent nods. Kate merely passed the bowl of stuffing yet still I rattled away, now in despair at my words struggling in such unpromising soil.

"But what does a cranberry bush look like, exactly?" Kate interrupted, finally joining in, accepting the escape I offered. She faced me, her eyes clear and curious.

"Well, it has small evergreen leaves," I replied happily. "They're pale underneath, if I remember correctly, and their edges roll back a bit."

Kate had heard enough of my nursery days to know something of my former skills, and now she lifted a forkful of sweet potato to her lips and asked, "What do the branches look like?"

"Um, they're thin, and connected to a woody stem that's kind of like a creeper. It stays low to the ground."

"And the flower, Michael? Is there such a thing as a cranberry flower?" she asked, eyes narrowing with pleasure, because of course she knew there was a flower and that I'd be able to describe it.

"It's light pink, only about a half inch or so across, I think—"

"So tiny."

"Yes, tiny—"

"What do the petals look like?"

"Well, they're . . . narrow, but they open out nicely."

By now released from the spell of her parents, Kate's eyes had almost closed, my words the model for what she limned within herself. Imagining from what strange angle she'd shadow in that flower, I tried to inspire her inner sketching: "Those little petals curl up in the wind, like . . . arms reaching out."

"And the stamens? What do they look like?"

Kate's parents took in our words with a raising of eyebrows that, in this household, was equivalent to assaulting pots with wooden spoons. But my Kate ignored them, and we continued entwining our words into an invisible, collaborative illustration.

On my lap lay a drawing of a coffee mug so enveloped in darkness it seemed to be melting. Yet the cup's shadowy edges also suggested a woman's profile—wasn't that a cheek, an ear, a wave of dark hair? Perhaps I was wrong. The more I stared, the more it switched from shadows to something like a face and then back again, a frustrating ambiguity that reminded me of that Thanksgiving months ago when I wasn't sure at first just whose side Kate was on. Yet even now, though we were living together and content beyond what I'd ever hoped for, sometimes Kate's eyes confounded me as I looked at her across the room or over a spread of pillows—were they blue with gray highlights, or gray with the brightest blue shining through?

Concentrating on Kate's drawing again, I tried to imagine something hot inside that cup—cappuccino, herbal tea, a tangy broth?— hoping this would help me guess my way into a caption. Then I heard footsteps on the stairs. Kate had effectively moved in since January, but those weren't her distinctive soft steps that stopped outside the door to my apartment, or any friend's that I could recall. With an unhappy lurch in my stomach, I wondered if one of her parents had finally decided to discover our secret.

The knocking on the door was strangely familiar—light, yet insistent. Before I could place its signature the door opened. There stood my sister in a dark rumpled skirt, her bright red blouse only half tucked in, her gaunt face forcing out a weak smile.

"Well, hello, Michael," she said in a small hoarse voice, and then she stepped inside.

Her sudden appearance so surprised me I could only produce a feeble "Laurie?"

She kissed me on the cheek and then collapsed on the couch, kicking her shoes off. "Oh, I want to hear something else—how about, 'Good Lord, dear sister, you look as if you've driven across three state lines without a wink of sleep!' "

"You have?"

"Mmm-hmm." Laurie plumped up a couch pillow. "Wake me up in time for dinner?" she whispered, almost instantly slipping into sleep, a curl of hair easing over her cheek as her breathing steadied and slowed.

I hadn't seen my sister, had barely spoken to her since she'd gone off to college last fall, so why had she come here, so obviously in some kind of trouble? I almost shook her shoulders to wake her up, but her calm face reminded me of our darkest days with Mother, when I sometimes checked on my brother and sister at night, always startled at how sleep could wipe the worry from their faces.

Laurie's profile, pressed against a dark pillow, eerily suggested that border of shadows on Kate's cup. I returned to my quiet struggle with the drawing. It *was* a woman's face, I decided. Or at least that's what *I* saw, and my caption would have to make a reader see it too. *I feel like my head is filled with hot coffee* was a possibility, but not much of one. Occasionally I glanced at Laurie as she shifted an arm or leg in her sleep, hoping for inspiration, and then Kate returned, huffing through the door with two brimming bags of groceries.

Her smile dissolved at the sight of a young woman asleep on the couch. "Who's *that?*"

"Laurie."

She stared without a sign of recognition and I had to add, "My sister."

"Your sister?" Her voice rose. "Why didn't you tell me she was—"

"Kate," I whispered, "I didn't know. She just appeared."

"Why is she here?"

"I don't know that either. She came in and fell asleep like *that,*" I said, snapping my fingers. "We'll have to wait until she wakes up."

Kate nodded, her mouth a grim line, and I could see that my sister's sudden appearance conjured up what few stories I'd told of my family—and the specter of those I hadn't. Shifting the bags in her arms, Kate left for the kitchen.

I followed and helped her unpack the groceries. With growing frustration, Kate couldn't seem to remember where to put the cans of soup, the cookies, the brown rice. "The cereal, where's the cereal shelf?" she groused, waving a box of cornflakes.

"Hey, calm down." I touched Kate's arm lightly, lingering on the sweaty crook of her elbow. She turned and held me, and over her shoulder I saw Laurie stirring on the couch. "My sister needs some rest," I whispered into Kate's ear. "She drove a long way to get here."

Kate pulled away. "Something must be wrong," she said, her face crumpling at the possibility of a new and gruesome tale.

"No. Not at all." Unconvinced by my own words and afraid that Kate might draw me into her fears, I returned to the cans of corn and frozen orange juice, assorted fresh vegetables and the tub of butter cluttering the counter. "Look, let me put the rest of this stuff away. Why don't you try to relax, maybe hit the books? I'll cook."

I cleared out the bags while Kate settled at the desk in the living room, her back to Laurie. As I worked up a sizzling concoction of chopped meat and onions, tomatoes and diced eggplant, I tried convincing myself that no emergency lurked behind my sister's sudden appearance. After all, wasn't it just like Laurie to make a dramatic entrance? Wasn't she happy, now that she was far from home and Father's strictures? I silently repeated these questions until they slowly became assertions, sturdy facts above dispute. Then, above the sweetly dissonant bubbling of dinner on the stove, I heard the murmur of Kate and Laurie's voices in the living room.

I stood in the doorway. Sitting side by side on the couch, together they turned their faces to me. *So, you're living with a girlfriend,* my sister's amused gaze said clearly, while Kate's eyes pleaded silently for rescue.

"You woke up just in time," I announced. "Dinner is almost ready."

We sat at the three place settings I'd squeezed on the tiny kitchen table and filled our plates. If my sister's visit had been spurred by trouble, there was little sign of it: she punctuated mouthfuls of my culinary offering with animated patter about her wild, nocturnal roommate, her decrepit dorm, the ratio of bars to churches in the nearby town and, most of all, the ins and outs of her college theater program.

"So in spite of everything, *I* got the lead, can you believe it? My first try! I guess there's just something about me that takes to dark little dramas. Anyway, there was more than one jealous thing in the cast who hoped I'd . . . I don't know, drop *dead* during rehearsals." Laurie waved her fork like a flag and added airily, "But I'm alive to tell the tale, alive to report that the campus newspaper gave me a rave review."

Except for the punctuation of a few appreciative comments I added little to the conversation, depressed that I'd never heard any of these stories before. My family was losing even the casual intimacy of shared history. Worse, Laurie's bright, anxious eyes didn't match her gleeful monologues, and I was sure Kate noticed this too: she sat silently, waiting for my sister to finally announce a tale of woe.

With the meal finished, we all helped clean up, getting in each other's awkward way. "Hey, how about a round of Scrabble?" I suggested, thinking that with each of us limited to whatever words seven letters might produce, we might find ourselves on more equal conversational footing.

Kate and I *did* speak more, even if we commented mainly on the double and triple values of words and letters, bemoaned a dearth or abundance of consonants, or challenged the occasional suspicious spelling. Meanwhile Laurie rattled away, at one point reciting a monologue from her recent theatrical triumph. Yet when we finally tallied up the spoils of our competing vocabularies, it was Kate who eked out a win.

Blushing a little, she accepted our congratulations, then murmured "Excuse me," and padded off to the bathroom. Once the door closed I scooted my chair closer to my sister. "Well, what do you think of Kate?"

Laurie flashed a too precisely casual smile. "Oh, she's nice."

I sat back, hurt. "Just *nice?*"

Unfazed, Laurie arranged another polite smile. "And she's pretty—"

"I *know* how she looks."

She sighed, then leaned over and whispered, "Well, she's just not *onstage.*"

"What do you mean?" I asked too loudly, ready to defend Kate's quiet ways, yet also, I vaguely understood, to bully down my own doubts.

"Just what I said," Laurie returned. "She doesn't . . . project out to the audience. And if she's not where she is, then where *is* she?"

I said nothing, remembering how sometimes during lovemaking, when Kate's ecstatic eyes narrowed to slits, I wondered if she shut out more of the world than she took in.

"By the way, Michael, does she know about Mom?"

"Of course she does."

Laurie raised a eyebrow. "And?"

"And nothing. We just don't talk about it much."

"Oh." Laurie paused and glanced about the room, stopping at Kate's drawings taped on the walls. She took them in for a few moments and then asked, her voice slightly dreamy, "Well, what *do* you talk about?"

I heard the distant whoosh of the toilet and said, "Let's leave this for later, okay?" Yet as I listened to the faint sounds of Kate washing her hands, I couldn't help thinking she was about to make an entrance onstage, with my sister and I a secret audience awaiting her performance. Just as the door opened, Laurie whispered in my ear, "So tell me this—which dwarf is she?"

Though furious at my sister for asking such a question, I nodded earnestly, pretending she'd confided something important, because Kate stood in the doorway. She lingered there, hesitant, afraid to interrupt a moment of family intimacy, and I loved her for this, loved her for being *present* and gracious and proving my sister wrong.

"It's okay, sweets," I said, and when she sat beside me I hugged her with perhaps too much fervor.

"Michael . . . ?" she whispered, gently shrugging away.

"So, what do you do, Kate?" Laurie asked, clearly relishing our little struggle.

"You mean my major? Art."

My sister leaned forward, projecting great interest, but I jumped in, gesturing at the sketches on the walls with a foolish flourish. "We collaborate on a daily strip in the school paper. Kate does the illustrations—"

"Those, really?" Laurie said. "They're so . . . beautiful."

I fetched Kate's latest from a bookshelf and handed it to Laurie. "And I write the captions. I was trying to come up with something for this when you came in."

My sister examined the mysterious cup as though it were some script she needed to memorize, and I tried to imagine it through her eyes: a shadowy face, perhaps, staring off at its own world?

Laurie looked up from the page and said, "If my lips touched this cup, they might never speak again."

Kate quickly glanced at me, and I forced out a tiny laugh. "Funny, that sounds like one of my captions."

"Well, we *are* brother and sister."

Kate reached out for her drawing, offering no response to Laurie's interpretation. Instead she stretched and yawned. "Please, you guys, don't mind me, but I've got a nine o'clock class tomorrow. Anyway," she added, turning to my sister, "let me get you settled on the couch before I go off."

While she gathered bedding from the closet, waving away Laurie's offer of help, I watched Kate's nervous hospitality and wondered, which dwarf *was* she? Her own, perhaps, one with a secret name still waiting to be discovered.

Kate kissed me, wished us good night and closed the bedroom door. I turned to my sister, now slumped in her chair and uncharacteristically quiet. Was she already lost in whatever troubles she'd managed to briefly banish? I didn't want Kate to overhear them, so I tugged at Laurie's elbow. "Let's take a walk."

She blinked at me without recognition for a moment, then recovered and grinned. "Sure, why not?"

I led us across the sprawling campus, waiting for Laurie to begin her unhappy tale. Instead, we walked and walked without a word until she finally said, "Dad doesn't know you're living with her, does he?"

"No, but if he cared enough to ask about my life, I'd tell him. I really don't know if he'd be upset."

"You're not sure what upsets dear Dad? How lucky for you!"

"So that's it," I said, stopping short. "You had another fight? Why am I not surprised you still can't get along—"

Laurie frowned. "Oh, the only way Dad wants to get along is to be left alone, no complications. Why do you think it was so easy for him to fire you?"

I grimaced at her cruelly casual words. Laurie stopped and answered her own question in a kinder tone: "Because you asked too much of him."

"That's not why. I failed him—"

"Oh, have it your way, Michael." She turned away, suddenly interested in a hedge bordering the engineering building, and I couldn't stop myself from saying, "Then tell me this—why do Dan and Dad get along so well?"

Laurie laughed a bitter laugh that sounded too much like Mother's. "*Those* two. They'll murder each other one of these days, I'm sure of it."

I reached out and held her arm. "Hey, no jokes—what are you saying?"

At the sight of my anxious face Laurie giggled. "Oh, not *that* kind of murder! Well, something worse, actually—no slit throats, but they're killing each other, just the same. The more Dan tries to be like Dad, the more Dad hardens that awful front of his that Dan's trying to imitate. Before you know it, they'll be the Zombie Twins."

We continued across the quad and I couldn't speak, suddenly filled with the memory of Dan coming home from the nursery, shaking with frustration over some minor difficulty ordering spring bulbs. Father calmed him down with a soothing, insistent patience until they both sat in shared silence on the living room couch. *The Zombie Twins.* Even though bringing my brother and father together had been disastrous for me, I'd never considered it might be so for them, too.

"Is that what you came to talk about?"

"Oh Michael, nothing so selfless! I'm here for *me.*"

We stood among a grove of trees leading to the observatory. "So tell me," I said, as softly as the rustling of the dark leaves swaying above us.

My sister watched me so carefully I believed she knew how afraid I was of what she had to say. She shook her head and pulled back a step. "It's . . . it's about me and Dad. When my first semester's grades were sent home he saw I was taking theater classes. So we've had our share of . . . telephone chats. It's bad enough that I'm still pretending, but he *really* can't stand it that I'm doing better in theater than anything else. Last night's call was just too much, Michael—he said if I take theater again my sophomore year he won't pay for school."

"Laurie, you know why he's worried—"

"I don't care! When he says I have to drop theater, he's saying that what I *care* about doesn't matter, or worse, that *I* really don't matter." She shuddered. "He's trying to erase me! Rub me out! Just like he did Mom. Well, he'll never get another chance, not one more. I don't need a degree to wait on tables, and that's what I'll be doing until my big break. So why not quit school?"

"Now *there's* a wonderful solution! Come on, Laurie, that's nuts—"

"I *have* to be an actress, Michael. I just have to. Did you ever hear of St. Vitus' Dance?"

"No, what's that?"

"Ha—there's what a business major will get you! St. Vitus' Dance, dear brother, was a very weird epidemic in the Middle Ages."

"So why don't you major in hist—"

"Let me *finish*. People started dancing like crazy, whole towns sometimes. They danced all day and night, bopped until they dropped, and when they woke up, they danced again. It was like a plague."

I stopped walking and knelt down, filled with the sudden, ridiculous desire to tighten the laces of my shoes. "You seem perfectly normal to me. No tap dancing at the moment, that I can see."

"Not here," Laurie said, wiggling a foot. She pointed to her head. "In *here*."

I held my sister, placed my ear against her hair. "Nope, I don't think so," I said. "I can't hear a single dance step."

She pushed me away. "C'mon, Michael, get real. It's *acting* I've got inside. And it goes way back, back to when we were kids and things were so crazy. I just hated it when Mom and Dad had those arguments alone in their room, working so hard to keep things quiet. They were playing out scenes we couldn't see—the most important ones, the ones that changed our lives."

"So?" I managed, my voice alarmingly tiny.

Laurie eyed me coldly, then said quietly, "So now, if I'm not in a play, I make up my own. When anyone leaves a room or goes off for a walk, I can't help it, I want to know what they're doing—who they meet and what they say. Dialogue, speeches, *scenes* just start pouring out inside me. I can't stop it."

"C'mon, Laurie," I said, unable to contain the tremor that rippled through my words, "what are you talking about?"

"Dad's got it all wrong! He thinks that if I become an actress, I'll become like Mom. He's wrong. If I *don't* become an actress, *then* it's time to worry."

"Look, don't you think—" I began in protest, but Laurie suddenly ran ahead and leapt in the air, her legs extended like a ballet dancer's. Then she twirled wildly along the path, her dark skirt rippling, her arms sweeping away imaginary branches.

"Hey, Laurie, come back," I called, but instead her entire body shivered as she improvised light, complicated steps to some frantic music I couldn't hear. A few students coming from the pub paused to gape at Laurie and I hurried after her. "Will you *stop?*" I hissed.

She shook her head *no*, turning her reply into part of that impetuous dance, her body swirling around and around. Then, after a series of skittering steps, she dashed up a steep path behind one of the dorms. I followed, beset by an unsettling echo of my long-ago scramble up the roof after Mother, and then I realized I'd have to play along with Laurie's performance.

"Bravo!" I called out, clapping heartily.

Laurie bowed briefly, but still she wouldn't stop and twirled away. So I huffed along after her, improvising a review: "Last night . . . across the campus of the state university . . . Laura Kirby, a young visiting artist, gave a stunning display of physical endurance . . . dancing all night before the smallest of audiences. . . ."

She ran ahead of my praise, her arms waving in uncanny concert with her steps. I could have caught my sister and forced her to stop, but I was afraid to touch her, afraid she actually was host to something contagious.

What was left for me to do? "Look," I finally asked, "do you want my advice?"

Laurie stopped, her skirt swaying about her legs. Chest heaving, she gasped, "Quick . . . thinking . . . big brother. Why . . . do you think I . . . came here?"

We sat together on the steps to the library, and Laurie's gulps of air aptly echoed my own inner breathlessness. Why was she asking me, and what should I possibly say? A terrible fear took hold of me: all my past good intentions had only brought on disasters—finally exposing Mother's cast of characters, bringing Dan to the nursery. "I don't know," I began hesitantly, "I'm afraid you might become like Mom."

"Mom made up her own stories. That's what I *don't* want to do. I want to memorize scripts, move where the director points me. That'll keep me safe."

"Great. You want to follow orders."

"No, Michael, *no*. I'll be *acting*. And I'll be *accountable*—to the audience, the other actors, even the stagehands. *I* won't leave anybody behind. Can't you see that?"

She spoke so fervently that I wanted to believe her, I wanted to believe that this was what she needed to do. But when I tried to speak no words came out, and I heard Laurie's own words from long ago, calling up to Mother on the roof: *Come down, please, please.*

I had to speak. I turned to my sister and almost flinched at the sight of her expectant eyes. "You have to consider, consider how Mom got swallowed up. I'm really worried about you, Laurie, worried that you're making a mistake."

"That's your advice?"

I nodded uneasily.

Her mouth curled to an oddly satisfied pout. "Well, I'll think about it." She stood, smoothed out her skirt. "Can we go back now?"

We retraced our path across campus in silence. My sister had asked for my support and thought I hadn't given it. With each step I reconsidered my words, wondered if I should reverse them. I sighed, walked on—perhaps I'd see more clearly by tomorrow morning.

When we approached the apartment, Laurie pointed to a battered import. "Here's my car." She opened the door and slipped behind the steering wheel. "Time to go."

"Hey, wha—"

"I got my nap, Michael. And I got your advice. Now I'm going to drive back to school."

"Laurie—"

She offered a farewell wave and drove off in her rusting hulk, the sorry remains of the muffler sputtering gruffly into the night air. When her car disappeared in the distance, I concentrated on that faint, distinctive mechanical grumbling, idiotically hoping to hear it all the miles she'd be driving. But quickly enough it faded into the background purr of traffic.

I turned away from my apartment and returned to campus. If Laurie was imagining me in a scene without her now, she might be surprised to discover that I liked to wander past the university greenhouses. I sometimes stopped and peered inside at a vibrant world of leaves and tendrils, wishing myself inside and breathing in the warm damp air, my hands moist with loamy soil.

One of the greenhouses tonight was brightly lit, a glass beacon that drew me, and already from a distance I could see the tropical palms and orchids, the thick stands of bamboo that seemed to shine from within. A shadow passed overhead and I looked up at a streak of wings lit by the greenhouse. What sort of bird would be out so late?

With another glance at the creature's swooping return, I recognized the shivering wings of a bat. It hovered in the night air, switching suddenly to a swift dive, and then the bat rose up, floating briefly before plunging down again. I stood and watched its quirky arcs and spirals until I finally realized they were a kind of hungry skywriting: this creature preyed on whatever flying insects were drawn to the light of the greenhouse. I turned away from the acrobatic display— so unpredictable and yet so inevitable—and walked off at a quick pace until I was almost running by the time I reached home.

Kate was already asleep, her body bathed by the gray glow of a half-moon shining through the bedroom window. I undressed and curled beside her, listening to the steady rise and fall of her breath. I touched her eyelids lightly with my finger. Her lashes trembled—she was dreaming. I imagined the moist inner walls of those lids were another kind of sketch pad, where Kate created scene after scene, a star on a stage of her own making.

I was the one offstage. But perhaps I could join her. Leaning over, I kissed Kate on the ear, a few strands of her hair tickling my lips, and her hand swept up sleepily, shooing away this disturbance. I kissed her again, first on the border of fine down at her temple, then her warm cheek. My legs slid against hers until our toes touched, the first cautious steps of a slow motion twining of limbs. Kate murmured at this budding pleasure, and however distant I might be from the intricacies of her dream, I was approaching, surely approaching.

Chiming Glasses

A postcard's gaudy colors showed through the slits of our apartment mailbox, and though I should have been rushing off to an economics lecture, I stopped and pulled out a view of a cityscape with an impressive backdrop of mountains. I turned it over to read my first news of Laurie since she'd quit school months ago: "I'm absolutely flourishing with a bit part here and there, and waiting—on tables, for my big break."

No return address. I sighed and slipped the card into my backpack. My sister had done the opposite of what I'd advised, yet I couldn't help envying her brave escape, even if her refuge was a bit part or some measly two line walk-on. All the hard work I poured into my lackluster slate of business courses gave me nothing in return, except the sort of grades my father would be proud of, if only he'd notice.

When I arrived in class the professor was already striding back and forth across the lecture hall's stage, flaunting his usual conservative agenda. I flipped open my notebook and jotted down his opinions, knowing they were more important than his charts and fact sheets.

Then he paused to pass out a few copies of what he labeled "a sterling example of overregulation": a government booklet on consumer safety that listed thousands of accidents involving ordinary household objects.

His narrow, well-tailored frame entirely still under the crisp glow of fluorescent lights, the professor asked, "What good could such a pamphlet possibly do for the economy?" He paused as if waiting for a reply, but no one spoke up. We all knew this question was rhetorical.

"None at all," he resumed with a satisfied chuckle. "Unless one considers the increase on insurance policy premiums across the country a salubrious effect."

One of the booklets finally came my way, and I paged through the suspect report idly at first, then with more care. I read that over eight thousand accidents a year were caused by tie racks, and that dishwashers, toothpicks, and household scissors were responsible for the same number. Improbably enough, twice as many accidents were caused by vacuum cleaners. Even more by wastebaskets. The list went on and on. Yet these mishaps weren't minor: the safety commission came by its figures from the records of hospital emergency wards across the country.

Frustrated that the booklet included no details of these mysterious accidents, I found myself imagining a light bulb shattering into slivers while being unscrewed; an electric blanket shorting out in the middle of someone's peaceful dream; a teakettle melting onto the stove after its whistle failed. Whether insurance premiums rose or not, what could be wrong with protecting people from such domestic betrayals?

"Hey buddy," the fellow closest to me hissed, "you gonna keep that? Pass it *over*."

"It's yours," I muttered, tossing it but sorry to see it go. I returned to my notebook, trying to follow the lecture but unable to shake the thought of a toaster shorting into flames; or one of Kate's drawings loosening from the wall, then drifting to the floor and the path of an unsuspecting foot.

After class I hurried back to the apartment and tugged gently at Kate's pictures, making sure each was firmly taped. But as I made my way across her gallery, the oddly vibrant shadings of the sketches themselves hinted at hidden trouble. The sheen she'd given a leather couch might well be seething with secret fury; that glistening drinking glass could easily be delicate enough to crack in one's hand, given a little pressure; and her close detail of a water fountain suggested something clinical, ominous: its gray metallic curves offered a space where a face could effectively, forcefully be fit.

Unwilling to take in another picture, I sat down, unnerved that such possibilities might be in Kate's work. They *were* self-portraits, after all, and what of the childhood she wouldn't tell me about—couldn't at least some secret memories have found their way into these unsettling details? I wished Kate were beside me, assuring me that what I now saw wasn't actually there.

As if she'd somehow heard me, there she stood framed in the doorway, keys in hand, taking in my pallid face with one of her sideways glances that I always loved: Kate trying me on at a different angle. But then she said, "Michael?" in such a tiny, concerned voice that my name sounded tentative, a word that didn't necessarily fit me.

"Oh, I'm just a little tired," I replied, afraid to voice my fears. With a troubled look, Kate kissed me lightly on the forehead. Then she set down her books and made her way to the kitchen, humming a quiet melody meant to dispel my dark mood. Ashamed that I hadn't spoken, I looked up at Kate's drawings again—she'd always let me give words to what she couldn't. Perhaps if I tested the limits of what we might express together, then Kate would finally reveal more of her past.

That evening she offered me her new drawing—an ordinary paring knife, the beautiful convolutions of its wooden handle's grain a twisted world unto itself. But the gleam of its sharp edge appeared almost deliberately menacing, and I let my caption reflect a darker vision, letting the blade murmur, *Stare out that kitchen window, forget you're using me.*

Kate accepted these words without complaint, but her silence only urged me on. The next week, when she presented me with a sketch of a can of hairspray, I could imagine it spreading a mist over waves of hair, encrusting what was wild into place. Instead I let that can whisper, *Set me down by the radiator, please.* I searched Kate's face as she read my caption, but caught nothing more than a slight quivering of her eyelids. So the following week I pushed further and made a shining paper clip croon, *Come here, baby, swallow me.*

"Oh, Michael," she murmured. Kate's questioning eyes met mine, and I said nothing, hoping to draw more from her, hoping she'd come out of herself to a new and more intimate level, the same way she had at her parents' home. But she merely set her drawing aside on the table and turned away.

The next evening, during our preparations for a quick meal, Kate washed the rice while I took on the job of chopping the vegetables. But I couldn't find any knife whose blade wasn't hopelessly blunt.

I said nothing and struggled away with a butter knife, thinking about that paring knife Kate had recently drawn and that I'd so darkly captioned. Where had it disappeared to? Yet instead of searching for the knife after dinner, on a hunch I checked my desk drawer and discovered that my little box of paper clips was gone. I explored further, through all the other drawers, the bookshelves, even piles of paper, then in all the other rooms. There wasn't a single stray clip anywhere in the apartment. I hadn't expected to find any: Kate must have removed the things whose hidden danger had been broached.

My recent captions had affected her more than I'd suspected. I stretched out on our ratty couch, weary with budding remorse, for didn't my words reveal as much about me as her? Those captions had become my own kind of domestic betrayal—I'd unfairly tried to provoke confessions from someone I loved.

Kate's next drawing was the gentlest of rebukes: a cotton ball's white haze. I resisted the impulse to find a secret threat in this most innocuous of objects, and instead presented her with a caption that was also an apology: *If only I were weightless, I'd float to whoever needed me.*

The candle on our table cast flickers of orange light across Kate's face as we sat together in a spaghetti shop. Waiting for our meal to arrive, we indulged in our little game of sharing a single glass of white wine, alternating sip after sip. Whenever a trace of wine seeped onto my tongue with a warming tingle, I savored it even more, knowing that when Kate lifted the glass to her lips she'd enjoy the same sensation.

Approaching the bottom of the glass, we took smaller sips, hoping to let the game linger, each trying to allow the other the last languid drop. With only a tiny cone of wine swirling at the bottom, I tilted the glass for a faint touch, leaving just enough for Kate.

"Yours," I said.

With an appreciative nod she emptied the glass, then examined its surface, cloudy from the touch of our lips, our fingerprints. If she was planning a sketch I already had a caption: *How many more lips will I meet?*

Our eggplant parmesans finally arrived, steaming and gooey with cheese. We ate and spoke of our classes, of a rock concert coming to the local amphitheater, of the glories of Indian summer in this otherwise chilly autumn, and we avoided any talk of what awaited us at the end of the next spring semester—graduation. I knew Kate wanted to someday exhibit her work, but we rarely spoke of this, or my plans, and perhaps our shyness hid a far more tender subject. What would *we* do, together, once school was done?

Before long we were quiet, with nothing and everything left to say. Wouldn't one of us ever begin? I watched Kate cut her meal into careful squares, watched her mouth deftly take in each neat piece, and the sight filled me with so much love and somehow sadness that I found myself saying, "You know, we've never talked, or talked much, about graduation, I mean, what are you, um, are you still . . ."

Kate paused, fork in hand, her eyes alert to the territory I'd just opened. "The art world awaits," she said with a cautious laugh, protecting her ambition by making light of it. "In the meantime, some dull dull dull commercial illustration job should see me through. I guess I should start sending out my résumé," she added. "What about you?"

I sat back in my chair and glanced away. Ever since paging through that government booklet on accidents, I'd been reading up on the subject of insurance—homeowner and life policies, major medical and collision coverage. The whole idea seemed so *ordinary*, even faintly foolish, but it was all I had to offer, and so I mumbled, "Maybe insurance." I looked down at my plate and the dregs of tomato sauce.

"Insurance?"

"You know, as a . . . career," I said, now watching for any sign of amusement on her face. Instead, her eyes took on a faraway look, as if contemplating unexpectedly ample vistas.

"Why not? You're a kind of poet."

"Me?" I said, blushing with pleasure at Kate's compliment—was that how she saw me?

"Sure."

I thought of the strange, airy feeling that sometimes swept through me, frightening and exhilarating both, when I found words for her drawings. Was this poetry, somehow? "But," I said, confused, "what's that got to do with—"

"Oh, poets, composers, they like to do that sort of thing."

"Who? Do what?"

"Oh, Wallace Stevens. Charles Ives . . . uh, Kafka, too. They all worked for insurance companies."

"Really?" I said, but when she explained further, I realized with disappointment that their jobs had been merely the source of a paycheck. Still, I remembered reading a few poems by Stevens in an English class, how they flowed with a kind of liquid music that made me go back to them again and again. If I *were* somehow a poet, wouldn't it be possible—even if right now I hadn't the faintest idea how to go about it—to make a kind of poetry *with* insurance?

The check arrived, yet we lingered at our table, perhaps needing time to broach the still unspoken subject of *us*. Outside, people sauntered by and the steady stream of couples hand in hand, arm in arm on their way to somewhere else in town, seemed to pull us from our seats, as if, in joining them, we might find a destination too.

So we ambled down the sidewalks, and the reflection of our faces in the storefront windows hovered over kitchenware, antiques, floral arrangements—all of them domestic scenes, cluttered interiors that seemed to welcome us, but we passed them by. Then, at the corner before an intersection, Kate stopped at an art store display: sets of colored pencils arranged in circles like a series of pinwheels. She lingered there so long I felt forgotten.

"Kate?" I asked, tugging lightly at her elbow.

"Okay," she said, but didn't move, not yet ready to leave.

What held her so? I looked at the art display again and saw Kate's entranced, nearly transparent features in the window. She seemed to me a spirit, floating over those instruments of her inspiration. Then

I saw the reflection of two cars behind us, hurtling across the intersection at each other, across the reflection of my own shocked face.

Tires squealed, followed by a horrible, grating crunch of metal. We turned to see the two cars twisted at odd angles, steam rising from their mangled hoods, a dark splotch against one of the shattered windshields. A door groaned open and a woman lurched out, clutching a purse, her blond hair already puddled in blood. Dark streams rippled from her mouth, which was somehow loose, and a long scream gurgled out. She fell, and her purse emptied onto the pavement.

"Do, what do we do?" Kate asked, her voice raw with horror. I gulped, and gulped again, unable to answer.

The woman lay there so still, her face hidden by a red mop of hair. I approached but was afraid to touch her, so I knelt before her possessions strewn like litter across the road: a lipstick tube, a paperback mystery novel, a rectangular, lime-colored eraser, a foil condom packet, a hairbrush, a tattered train schedule, a small plastic bag of pistachio nuts, all of it ordinary evidence of a life now in danger. This scattering seemed so wrong, so terribly wrong, and I couldn't help myself, I began grabbing without looking, sweeping it all back into her purse and then snapping the clasp shut, as if that would somehow help her.

Kate stood beside me, sobbing, "My god my god my god," and I managed to say, "We have to, to, to call an ambulance."

A crowd had gathered by now and a man repeated, "Call an ambulance!" A grim-faced young woman, her short hair already streaked with gray, shouldered her way through the gawkers and began administering some sort of first aid.

Kate pulled me away, and we huddled together on the sidewalk across the street, listening to the drawn-out wail of approaching sirens. Less than a minute's difference, I thought: if I'd managed to lure Kate from the shop window we might have walked into that accident. But what if I'd lazed in bed a little longer this morning, trying to remember a dream; what if we'd dawdled longer at the restaurant—couldn't any slight change have altered our fate as easily?

My gaze raked over the pale, conflicted faces of the crowd milling about the crushed cars, imagining that they too were tallying the day's events and what might have been. Perhaps we'd all walk home haunted by the fear that every day was a gauntlet of possible disasters.

By now paramedics rushed about and police directed traffic. The ambulance strobe lights cast an eerie, skittish dance of light and shadow over the intersection, reminding me of that bat's shivering wings on its predatory flight, how it swooped down again and again without warning. I held Kate, as she held me, and I kept repeating, "Don't worry, it's going to be all right, all right." She turned her gaunt face to me, her eyes softening with the need to believe this, and at that moment I glimpsed a secret that the jargon of insurance texts had promised and yet disguised: we all longed for refuge, for a private sanctuary. Was this something of the poetry I hoped to discover? If so, I wanted to always bestow this sort of comfort on Kate, and not only on her, but on myself as well, and every frightened face around us.

Kate and I sat stiffly at the center of a curved dais, facing the round tables of guests, a long table piled with presents, an open bar, and I couldn't help thinking of our farewell cartoon in the student newspaper: her drawing of a wedding gown and tuxedo hanging together in a closet, with my caption, *Someday we'll dance, we'll unbutton, we'll slip to the floor*. While a quartet of potbellied rockers cluttered the small bandstand and checked their sound system, Kate picked daintily at the catered plate of roast beef and sculpted mashed potatoes. I hadn't yet touched a knife or fork, hadn't even placed the cloth napkin on my lap, still amazed that merely a month after graduation we were married and about to begin a new life. Already the vows we'd exchanged in a nearby church, my nervously tapping my shoe during the minister's short homily, her father's chronic coughing in the front pew, Kate's hand trembling as I awkwardly slipped on the ring, all of it seemed like the surprisingly intense memories of some distant event.

A delicate clinking now began. Spoons tapping against half-filled champagne glasses, the guests invoked us to stand and display our now official union with a kiss. Kate and I obeyed, bending our faces gently to each other, lips touching lightly, so much like that first, stunningly familiar kiss at the end of the wedding ceremony.

This time Kate whispered, "I love you, Michael," intimate words that were rarely easy for her to offer. I accepted them with a goofy grin of joy at what I felt was the first golden moment of our marriage, and our audience clapped with real warmth, as if they understood just what my wife and I had exchanged.

We sat down, and the tables settled back into their individual circles of chatter, with the exception of one pocket of mutual unease—the table just below us, where Father and Dan sat together with Kate's parents. I couldn't imagine her father or mother had much to say beyond their already voiced disapproval over my upcoming job as an independent insurance agent in a minor, distant city, or Kate's too modest starting salary at an ad agency just a little too small in that same minor, distant city. Their eyes kept to the table of presents—quietly counting, perhaps, or imagining what disappointing gifts lay hidden within.

Next to them sat Father, stiff and stoical, a sentinel with knife and fork before the meal on his plate. Beside him sat Dan, who had indeed taken on more of Father's restraint—having already disposed of the main course he seemed to hope, with a cautious glance here and there at passing waiters, for the arrival of seconds. I found it hard to believe that this grown brother of mine now worked full-time at the nursery and still lived at the same home where, so many years ago, he used to shake the rungs of the banister like prison bars.

The chiming of glasses started again. Kate and I dutifully stood and kissed, and when with patient smiles we ended our clinch, I saw Laurie framed in the faraway double doorway. I couldn't believe she'd actually appeared. Fresh from a world of low-rent theater productions, she'd certainly prepared for a dramatic entrance, with a long, dark dress and brightly patterned shawl, and her hair dyed a shocking red. Her eyes searched the room, and then with determined steps she made her way through the maze of tables toward Father and Dan.

But it wasn't her table. Much woe had passed between Father and me about this. Still furious at Laurie's quitting school mid-semester, he'd declared she wasn't to sit with him. He wouldn't attend the wedding otherwise, and out of one last, ignoble hope of healing my own rift with him, I'd finally given in, sure that Laurie would never show up anyway.

Before I could rise and head her off, try to explain, Dan stood to greet her. Laurie grinned flamboyantly, certainly aware of the stares from the nearby tables as she approached. But Father gazed past his own daughter, as if she wore a disguise he refused to see through. He actually leaned over to my new mother-in-law and attempted a bit of chat, managing to elicit a few monosyllables from that tight-lipped woman. Laurie stood across from them, her face for a moment surprisingly defeated. But that unguarded look hardened when, with a quick glance, she saw that there was no place for her at the table.

Dan's face at least filled with shame, surely mirroring my own, and I waited for Laurie to make a scene. Instead she accepted Dan's offered arm and he led her to a remote table featuring an aging Aunt Myrna and a clutch of Kate's distant cousins. I turned to Kate, relieved that I'd kept the misery of these table arrangements a secret from her. She stopped picking at her scalloped potatoes, looked up at me and smiled, unaware of the family drama below.

Settled at her table, Laurie drained her champagne glass and waved for a refill, exuding a sharp sadness that I knew too well. She wouldn't look my way, and why should she? My sister knew that she couldn't have been banished without my compliance.

The glasses began clinking, and once more Kate and I stood and kissed. We'd barely sat down before that insistent tinkling began again. With a weary sigh, Kate rose to embrace me.

"Don't worry," I murmured in her ear, "dinner'll be over soon. Then we'll all be dancing."

But every minute or two that silly ritual repeated. The requests became a giddy, collective joke, much enjoyed by our college friends who, rowdy with drink, couldn't resist the impulse to tease us. With each clinch Kate grew increasingly grim-faced, until finally she turned her back to the crowd. I peered over her shoulder at the tables and saw my sister beaming drunkenly. Our eyes met, and with a flourish of her spoon Laurie tapped her glass, starting up another round of chiming. At once I knew she'd been the ringleader of this stale prank, that this was her revenge: she was trying to goad my wife to finally come out onstage and reveal herself.

When Kate and I kissed again, I tasted tears on her lips and understood that for her my tuxedo and her bridal gown might as well have been invisible—we were naked to everyone's eyes. Yet the temptation was mine—I couldn't help searching Kate's face for whatever stood poised within her, any hint I might find of what she still kept hidden. But her moist eyes remained a blue sky obscured by strange gray clouds and she shuddered at the sight of my probing face, the opportunism of my tenderness.

Once again Laurie didn't allow us to sit down, and our guests' celebratory glasses echoed through the room, a tinkling that now resembled the sound of shattering. I bent to kiss Kate but she crumpled into my embrace. Chastened, I stroked her back, tried to maneuver her weeping face away from our audience. Everyone lapsed into an embarrassed silence, the room so still that they might have heard me whispering urgently what I wanted my wife so much to believe, that everything was all right, all right, and that I would always, always protect her. But Kate pulled away from these reassurances, and my reflection in her wide eyes seemed so small, as if, having run far away, she'd turned back, briefly, to regard me.

PART FOUR

Matching Faces

The next morning I made a few calls from my office and discovered that Sylvia actually was a meteorologist. As I wrote down what local station she worked for and what time she presented her weather report, I told myself that this wasn't chasing, it was merely concern for a woman who'd asked for help.

That evening I turned on the local news and sat impatiently through the usual local snippets: a scandal in the state capital, the fire department's new mascot, a community charity drive. And then there was Sylvia, once again dressed in a primly tailored suit, now with a microphone clipped to her lapel.

Yet she seemed different, hesitant even as she introduced the motto of the evening's sponsor: "Nothing's too tough for McDuff . . . Hardware." Then, on a screen behind her, a computer-generated jet stream appeared, a curving line of little flashing white arrows. Wagging a pointer at a cold front, Sylvia reeled off temperature highs and lows much too quickly, as though afraid she might be interrupted and contradicted.

I remembered Sylvia saying that hardly anyone paid much attention to a weather report, and it was true that I'd never really noticed the special effects. The various states on the map changed suddenly to blue or red, depending on whether it would be warmer or colder than usual the next day; little icons—a smiling, shiny sun, a frowning cloud with rain pouring from it—flashed off and on across the map like a fireworks display; and thick, wavy bands of color changed patterns, showing temperature distribution, then precipitation averages. Cloud patterns lurched across a convex map projection that stretched across North America to the rim of the earth and Sylvia dwarfed it all, looking down on the sweep of the globe like a god. Yet she was also just a tiny figure on the TV screen, stuck in a little box while thousands of us watched her stiff shoulders and the awkward, arrhythmic tap-tap of her pointer.

"I think there's only a slight chance of showers tomorrow," she announced, "so maybe this cold front will pass us by." The doubt in her wavering voice made me strangely anxious, and I imagined rain clouds, storms, lightning.

When the camera panned in for a close-up I knelt in front of the television, my face inches from the screen, and tiny crackles of electricity rose from the surface. For a moment Sylvia's face matched mine, dots of electronic energy spreading across her features. "C'mon," I whispered, my charged lips pulsing against hers on the screen, "relax a little."

But she was signing off. "May your weather always be happy," Sylvia said, presenting a strained smile. The camera quickly cut to the well-groomed sportscaster, who promised high school basketball scores right after the station break.

I sat back in my chair and kept hearing Chance of, maybe—hedgings that seemed so familiar . . . like the ambiguous language of the daily horoscope. I didn't know much about meteorology, but I'd certainly learned something from those days when I'd been addicted to the stars' and planets' equivocal pronouncements: precision wasn't the point. Whether she liked it or not, Sylvia was more than a talking head in front of that overexcited weather map—she was a high priestess of a technological oracle.

"And that's it for tonight," the news anchor finally announced. While the credits rolled down the screen I hurried to the phone and punched in the station's number, hoping I'd catch Sylvia before she left.

The receptionist put me on hold and I fought a growing urge to hang up—what if my idea was too off-the-wall, what if Sylvia didn't want to hear it whether it was or not?

"Hello?" Her voice, wonderfully intimate against my ear, was still faintly laced with doubt from her weather roundup.

"Hello?" she repeated.

"Hi. This is, ah, Michael."

"You . . . you actually called?"

"Yeah—I just saw you on the news, and I've got a suggestion about this . . . dilemma of yours. Could we meet, maybe tomorrow?"

I waited for her reply, and through the receiver I could just make out the television crew's faraway chatter, a distant world that I really knew nothing about. Unnerved by her silence, I said, "I'm not trying to pester you, Sylvia. If you want, just hang up. I promise I won't call again."

Little Explosions

My first year as an independent insurance agent was less than mildly promising. My ads in the local paper found no takers, and each daily telephone sweep of possible clients met only put-upon silence, my every unwanted word leading to the inevitable "No thanks, we're not interested," or worse. All those faceless voices seemed vastly indifferent to my ambitions, yet what *were* those ambitions, exactly? Whatever hope I had of uncovering any hidden poetry of my profession was inevitably lost in my volleys of feigned camaraderie over the phone. Again and again I went over my checklist: was my throat tense, my voice shrill or too loud, had I employed enough variety in the pace and timing of my delivery?

To meet our bills, Kate took on side jobs. After a long day at the commercial graphics firm, she kept to her small upstairs study in the evenings and turned out black-and-white renderings of canned groceries for a local supermarket flyer, the cartoonish mug of a bulldog mascot for a high school's fund-raising drive, whatever came her way.

I'd wash the dinner dishes alone and then, after an hour or so of brooding over how I hated the hard sell, I'd climb the stairs and peek in at my wife's progress. One evening I found her at her drawing table, quite still and staring without pleasure at the challenge of a blank sheet. I recalled with a pang those days when we'd create an object's radiant world, and I wished we could collaborate again, if only for our own private portfolio.

On the gray carpeted floor, beside a pile of art books, was a phone whose old-fashioned rotary dial might tease out her imagination. So I set it on her work table and asked, "Think you might try your hand with this? I could probably come up with loads of captions."

As Kate quietly regarded the phone's black plastic sheen, it seemed to sit there as silently and reproachfully as the modern one in my rented office. Then she turned a weary face to me and her eyes, glinting from the overhead light, divided the tiny image of her husband standing before her. "Oh, Michael," she replied in a half-whisper, "I'm just not inspired."

"Well, maybe some other time," I murmured, clearing the phone from the drawing table. In my disappointment I set it back down too harshly. The bell inside pinged in protest, and once again I was standing with Kate before our wedding guests, surrounded by the tinkling champagne glasses of all those toasts.

Now I glanced at Kate—did she too hear this unhappy echo and remember when celebratory clinking mimicked the sound of shattering? But she simply sat at her table, regarding an empty corner of the room, her eyes so clear with concentration that I knew she *was* drawing, but without the aid of any pen or paper. I waited for Kate to complete whatever design inside herself she needed to complete, waited patiently for her to return from wherever she was. Perhaps one day she'd share with me her backlog of secret images. Hadn't she come back to me once before?

The following morning I returned to my office and an image of my own that I hadn't shared with Kate. A batch of old *Life* magazines had been left behind by a previous tenant, and I'd often page through them in between the disappointments of my phone call sweeps. That's how I discovered a photo that had been taken during the Depression, though it could have come from any time of trouble: a black-and-white close-up of a girl standing before a shack, her face streaked with dirt, her eyes holding in a starved childhood and shat-

tered innocence. As far as I could see, this young grim face held nothing else. Perhaps this was why I kept staring at it, for even in my deepest unhappiness as a boy, I knew I'd managed to find brief solace in a
book of mazes or some goofy cartoon stunt on TV. Sadness and illog-
ical joy would flicker through me at any moment: despair could indeed contain its own escape.

This was just what seemed absent in the photo of that girl—it
didn't begin to hint at the hundred little contradictory births that
percolate on a real face. All of us have more than one face—we just
don't give them names, as my mother did. How many had there
been? Margaret, who hated cooking; Tamara the Magnificent, who
juggled; Rosario, the nurse; Valerie, a photographer; Tina, a dancer;
Daisy, the furious artist; and many more whose names I'd forgotten.
All of those women, I now knew, were hands reaching up out of
something dark and roiling inside Mother, hands searching for a firm
hold.

Then I knew what I had to do. Skillful listening might be a watch-
word of the insurance business, but words aren't all that one can listen to. So, suppressing what pride I had left, I called an old classmate
who'd already become a successful local broker and I begged for a
lead, anything that would bring me face to face with a potential
client. With a head-shaking pity clear to me even over the phone, he
offered me a tip. He said it couldn't miss.

The next day I sat across from a young couple in their living room
cramped with upholstered furniture and, in one corner, a baby
bassinet. In the brief pause after our introductions, Pete plucked at
his shirt collar, coughed, and announced, "Well, I suppose it's time
to talk about buying some life insurance."

"Because of our daughter," Judy added. "She'll be a month old
next Tuesday."

"Well, congratulations," I said, opening my briefcase while the
couple waited with a hint of skeptical silence—I didn't exactly project an air of authority, fumbling through a small stack of policy lit-
erature. Contact, make some personal contact, I thought, and so I
said, "This sure is a nice house you have here."

They nodded and shifted in their seats, now even more ill at ease, for they knew as well as I that their home wasn't much more than a square little box painted dull green. I tried to recover from my mistake but my voice rose nervously with each word as I asked, "Is this your first home?"

A gurgling arose, then a tiny groan and a shifting in the bassinet. Judy hurried across the small room and leaned over, her hands gently plucking and soothing. I said nothing, ashamed that I'd disturbed their baby, and then I stood, with no sense of why I'd done so. I offered an apologetic smile. Pete's hand rose and tried to hide his frown.

Suddenly afraid that he was about to ask me to leave, I padded over to the bassinet—how could he possibly throw me out while I gazed at his child? I saw little wisps of brown hair, delicate eyelids closed in sleep and tiny puckered lips echoing the tuck of the blanket. This was a face that knew no trouble, and I found myself at the center of a vast stillness.

"My wife and I don't have children yet," I said quietly. "I wish we did."

Such a thought, so unasked for, surprised me, and I tried to push it away and hide it. But returning to my seat I saw that Pete and Judy had heard the sincerity in my voice—I'd confessed something, offered a secret part of myself. Now they sat back together on the couch and served up their own secret: they were afraid they could barely afford the right policy.

I had a number of options to offer and I spoke softly, careful not to disturb their daughter again. Pete and Judy had to lean forward to catch my words, and as they did I searched for the tiny, revealing changes that rose up in their faces. The faint wrinkling of Pete's brow, and Judy's pursed lips easing, then slightly crimping, helped me understand just what they were willing to sacrifice, just what level of coverage made them feel secure.

My first success generated another, then another. Soon I began receiving calls, and my days were filled with house calls and office visits. As my clients spoke, I listened and watched and tried to understand the vague unease on their faces and match it with the right policy, because I was always more concerned with their comfort than their money. Sometimes business picked up when a disaster dominated the news, whether it was a national park eaten up by huge fires or a Midwestern trailer park mauled by a tornado; before making my recommendations I probed any averted glances, sudden sighs or brittle chumminess. I knew all of this masked my clients' secret fears that hidden within them was their own flood or conflagration, their own condemned building or quarantined sick ward.

I shouldn't have revealed to Kate that reading others was the source of my recent success, for now her blue eyes rarely met mine, and when I watched her smallest movements about the house she tried to keep my unrequited curiosity at bay by living in a dream of neatness: no piece of paper could be out of order, no pristine surface was ever dusted too often, no carpet long left unvacuumed.

Kate still worked in her study in the evenings. I paced through our house, and though it had more fire insurance than we needed, I was easily seized by a gripping chill at the thought of a frayed wire, a stray spark. One evening, as I passed our bedroom doorway, I stopped and watched Kate kneeling before her dresser, arranging her shoes in straight rows. What sort of carefully constructed barricade was this? Then she crawled over to my adjacent wardrobe and did the same for my shoes, after first tying their laces into neat bows.

With a little grunt of satisfaction she stood, and when she saw me a tremor of surprise ran through her. I waited for Kate to speak. She said nothing, her gaze so studiously casual I almost cried out in alarm, but then she smiled and her fingers unbuttoned her blouse down to her waist. Then she tugged at her skirt until it fell to the floor. In another moment she was naked and beckoned to me with a flip of her hair. "Oh my love," I whispered, and Kate murmured encouragement as my hands gently traveled tender trails.

Later, with Kate breathing gently beside me, I lay too long on the edge of sleep. My eyes closed, a black field of barely defined shapes and colors drifting before me, only slowly blending into the face of a client considering replacement cost insurance, squinting and struggling to account for the contents of his house as I helped him recall his objects, one by one. Then another face rose up, a woman whose circled lips produced a wheezing intake of breath at the mention of accident liability for her car. Again and again my clients' expressive changes appeared, now superimposed over a pale floating disk that I eventually realized was Kate's face. The swift play of their features became a terrible flickering of shadows over that eerily calm expression that Kate had first offered me in our bedroom, a gaze as smooth as the contours of her skin.

I bolted up in bed and scattered those ghostly faces, my hands clutching at the blanket. Kate stirred briefly, then settled, and I looked down at her dark outline, a fear slowly growing within me that even her body was just another line of defense. Had those sweet paths we'd traveled been nothing more than a series of dead ends?

I slipped quietly from bed and hurried downstairs in the dark as if being stalked. It was true, true—no matter how many disasters appear in the form of car collisions or flooded basements, they more often arrive from some secret place inside us. I circled through the rooms, passing the dark outlines of our furniture without touching a single hard edge, walking like some stunned sleepwalker until it seemed I might actually disappear into the darkness. Exhausted, I simply slumped on a couch, longing to vanish, yet all the while hoping that somehow Kate would come downstairs and find me before I could.

Kate indeed searched for me: I heard her voice whispering my name, "Michael, Michael?" Then, in a gray light, her face peered into mine.

"Michael, silly, you fell asleep down here."

"Oh Kate," I managed, in a rush of surprise. "I feel so . . ."

I stopped. The sun already streamed through the slats of the blinds, casting bright bars on the rug, and Kate wore a skirt, a blouse, earrings. It was morning, and she'd actually showered and dressed before coming downstairs. What had she thought at the sight of my half of the bed, empty and cold?

I was ready to speak openly. "Kate, we need to—"

"Look at the bolsters, the pillows," she broke in, "they're almost as rumpled as you are." Kate made a great show of tidying, as if the real disorder was our living room. When she finished with the imaginary mess she said, "I'm so hungry, aren't you?" and set off for the kitchen. I listened to the busy clatter of her breakfast extravaganza and imagined it drowned out the words she couldn't bring herself to say to me: "Poor dear, you're working too hard," perhaps, or "Please don't stay away from our bedroom again," or "Why do you have to bring up our troubles?"

When I finally entered the kitchen the morning paper was opened invitingly by my place setting. I sat down and swiftly paged through it—I had no interest in examining the unhappy headlines. But when I arrived at Dear Abby I paused, half-considering writing her a letter:

> *Dear Abby,*
>   *My wife is hiding inside herself, and even though she's stand-ing before me right now, organizing the largest breakfast I'll probably ever eat, I don't think I can succeed in ever finding her. Abby, sometimes I wonder if she's been hiding so long that she's lost, and even if she wanted to break out of herself she wouldn't know where to begin. Why, just this morning—*

But what was there to say? This wasn't the style of letter Abby usually reprinted. I hadn't been insulted by a sister-in-law during a holiday dinner, I hadn't received an embarrassing gift from a co-worker, my dog hadn't chewed a resentful neighbor's newly planted shrubs, and I had no minister to consult. Certainly there must be a special trash bin for letters like mine.

I glanced down to the Daily Horoscope—maybe the mysterious con-junctions of the stars and planets would do better than a syndicated busybody. Though I knew it was a foolish indulgence, I laughed grimly to myself and scanned the prediction for my day: *The advan-tages regarding an ambitious endeavor you are presently involved in can be forcefully expanded at this time.*

Of course—I should shout or cry, sit Kate down for a blunt assess-ment of our miseries. Not bad advice at all. But there was more, so I read on: *It's best to keep your decisions to yourself, however, until you understand how you want to use them.* The horoscope was right— straight talk would only make her shrink further away. No, I had to intuit polite, unwritten rules for an invisible playing field.

Kate stood before me, holding a tray brimming with breakfast. "Time to eat."

"Good," I said, reaching for my fork and knife. "I'm so hungry."

*   *   *

The horoscope became my morning ritual. *If you concentrate too much on a needless detail, you may find disappointment in a joint venture,* I read. Was this business or personal news, or both? I knew which possibility was most important to me, but the horoscope never distinguished between the trivial and the significant. *Should, if, may, could* and *perhaps* were words that tantalized, quietly urging me to interpret and act, and I delved into second guessing, hampered by my desire to make the prediction come true or not. Of course I knew there weren't only twelve types of people in the world, marching individually through twelve singular fates. But none of my skepticism was truly conscious, and I continued to read strategies in those ambiguous sentences. Though there were times when I found no connection, that didn't stop me from trying the next day. I needed to believe.

Caution, my horoscope consistently counseled: *You might give in to an urge to test your will against the will of those with whom you'll be involved today.* I remembered those words that evening as Kate and I ate dinner at a local steakhouse, our table lit by the artificial glow from the dining room's fireplace.

"Another, sir?" the waiter asked, deftly gathering up my empty wineglass.

"No, thanks," I replied, forgoing a third, knowing it would make me too loud and Kate even more quiet. The waiter continued on to the next table, and though Kate said nothing, an appreciative smile spread across her face in the flickering light.

Another morning I read, *You might have trouble today realizing when victory is within your grasp,* and I was grateful for the warning. I looked for clues all day in every gesture Kate made, some hint that she'd tired of hiding. But I found nothing, and as I lay in bed beside her I thought of her sudden coughing fit earlier in the evening when we washed the dishes—did part of her want to speak plainly, while another part tried to prevent this?

Suddenly Kate awoke in a grip of a nightmare, words bursting from her as she bolted up—"Oh! No!"

I reached for her hand, found it under the blanket, and then she was oddly calm.

"Michael?"

"Yes, dear, I'm here. You were having a nightmare."

"A nightmare," she repeated, as if the word held no special meaning. "I . . ."

"Yes," I said, "tell me what happened."

She remained quiet for a moment before burrowing under the covers again. "I can't remember."

"Try," I whispered, but she was already breathing deeply in sleep, or pretending to, and I knew the moment the horoscope had warned me of had passed. If only I hadn't asked, she might have told me on her own.

Were my new designs against her resistance the source of her nightmare? She *did* seem preoccupied, staying up late and working with an almost alarming intensity at the new project she'd taken on for the local university: detailed drawings of the latest potsherds and artifacts some archaeology professors had uncovered. While Kate carefully sketched under her desk lamp's circle of light, sometimes I lingered over her portfolio and stared at those bits and pieces of something larger that was now lost. Each page boasted a single sherd, as if hurtled alone through the air after some explosion. Kate shadowed in the jagged edges in a way that tantalizingly suggested what was missing, yet leaving it a mystery, and I remembered that drawing she'd made of me years ago when we first met—maybe it hadn't been incomplete after all, but only as much as she'd wanted of my distant, curious gaze.

Today may bring you a mutual understanding you've long sought, but you must take advantage of an unusual offering. I looked across at Kate, lost in concentration over her butter knife and English muffin. Soon she would politely offer me half, and I would accept, thanking her politely—nothing unusual there. What could the horoscope possibly mean? I scanned the rest of the page and discovered an announcement for a traveling carnival, in its second day of a weeklong appearance. Yes, this was a perfect excursion for a Saturday evening and, since Kate and I had never been to a carnival together, perfectly unusual. By this time, though, I made no move without consulting her sign too: *A greater understanding of what is best for you and your family can be accomplished today.* Bingo.

"Hon, when was the last time you were on a roller coaster?" I asked, passing her the paper.

Her eyes swept over the ad. "A carnival? But Michael, that's for children."

"All of them accompanied by adults," I replied, "who're *easily* having just as much fun."

We drove to the fairgrounds in the late afternoon, the sky heavy with darkening clouds. "Rain?" Kate asked.

"Oh, I think it'll pass over. Let's take the chance," I said, knowing the horoscope's prediction wouldn't be in effect tomorrow.

Kate gave in with a sigh. Her blond hair looped across her face from the air rushing through the open window, those light strands a shifting form of camouflage, though of course a sudden gust of wind could just as easily sweep it away.

We paid the entrance fee and parked, then bought a book of tickets for all those rides that cluttered the fairgrounds: the spider ride, its passenger cabs like the thick footpads of an enormous insect; the distant, crackling sparks of the bumper cars; a fun house, its entrance lined with wavy mirrors, the recorded laughter of a clown booming from a speaker; a double Ferris wheel, the two circles twirling over and under each other like a giant, untethered figure 8. Soon the lights would turn on and then the magic of the place would take hold. But now it all looked shabby under the gray sky, and a steady drizzle soon made it worse. Before long, thick ominous drops splattered about us, and then it was pouring. Kate and I ran to the nearest shelter—the carousel.

We stood among the still herd of horses and watched as the dirt paths winding through the fairgrounds turned into long stretches of mud. There was much Kate could have said about this sight, but she leaned against me quietly, her damp hair flat against the back of her blouse, and I matched her silence gratefully. Perhaps this little disaster was just what we needed—at least it was unusual.

A long-haired attendant wove his way toward us through the horses, his Guns 'n' Roses T-shirt rolled up at the sleeves. His smile a bit wary, he hesitated before asking, "Tickets?"

Kate glanced at me doubtfully, but I said, "Sure, how many do you need?"

He grinned. "Two apiece—not bad for a roof over your head, eh?"

"Quite a bargain," I said, tearing the tickets from the book. He walked off, whistling, and I turned to Kate. "Why not, honey? That's what we're here for, right?"

She managed to smile and nodded. I picked a nice brown horse with a rearing head, fit my shoe into a stirrup and pulled myself up. Kate settled on the palomino in front of me.

The carousel lurched forward with a mechanical grunt and the calliope music burst into a dizzy, extended melody. I slapped the fiberglass rump of my horse and shouted "*Yee ha*," hoping to coax Kate into the spirit of the ride.

"Giddyap," she offered. The carousel turned and turned, and soon the muddy fairgrounds, the skeet-shooting booths and the food stalls advertising corn dogs and elephant ears seemed to spin around us.

"Not too bad, huh?" I called to Kate, but the music was now so loud she didn't hear me. I hoped for a sight of her profile, a sign of what she felt, but she kept staring forward, as if she were actually leading that horse somewhere.

The rain never let up: we were still stranded together on a tiny, circling island, so at the end of the ride I tore more tickets from our booklet for the attendant. Kate sat patiently, waiting for the carousel to start again, and I waited in vain for her to turn around and say something, to join in the carnival spirit.

Two, three more times I paid our fare and we wheeled about to the cheery, slightly mad music. And still Kate kept to herself. Why wouldn't she give in to this minor pleasure, why not turn and smile? But her knuckles were white from gripping the iron pole so tightly: as always, she fled from me.

What about that "greater understanding" the horoscope had promised? I'll make her turn around, I thought, I'll make her see how much I want her. Holding my arm out over the rim of the carousel and into the downpour, I cupped my hand until I had a puddle of rain. I flung it at Kate, streaking her dress. Her back arched in surprise, and she turned a terrified face to me.

Then I knew what she saw, what she thought: I was right behind her and always would be, and she'd never manage to put any more distance between us. No wonder she didn't turn around—how horrible to see me in such relentless pursuit. And what did my face tell her: that she had finally revealed herself to me, and that I was frightened by what I saw? We raced in place, in endless circles, and I'd never be able to draw closer.

Slowly the storm eased into a misty drizzle. I swung down from my horse. "That's more than enough," I said. Kate stepped down too, murmuring something I couldn't make out.

Water dripped from the soaked canvas canopies of the various stalls. "Game of chance?" we heard. "Try your luck?" But we were done—there was little to stay for. We stepped carefully past dark puddles, the last, stray drops of rain falling into them like little explosions, and our reflections shimmered and shook to pieces all the way to the parking lot.

Who's Next

Trying to deny what happened at the carousel, Kate and I made furious and exhausting love that night. She wrapped her legs around mine and held me inside but even as I shook and shook, Kate's hidden self stared out through narrowed eyes, determined that I would never truly enter, and we battered ourselves against each other, the equal pressure keeping an invisible door between us closed.

Finally we lay on our backs, panting in cross rhythms that slowly eased into silence, and then Kate pulled one tissue after another from the cardboard box. I winced at the harsh, rasping sound, which ran through me like the cry of some creature roaming through the neighborhood backyards, avoiding the sudden sweep of a flashlight. We wiped ourselves off as if sopping up damning evidence. Then we flung it away.

Listening to Kate yawn and settle above the damp sheets, I turned to her in the darkness. The warmth of her body almost touching me, I could hear the slow pulse of her breathing, feel its faintly moist draft. I inhaled deeply, trying to catch what had just coursed through her lungs and nostrils, and I held that breath inside as long as I could while it mingled with mine. Finally I released it in the moment just before her own intake of breath, and I continued this secret exchange over and over, hoping it could somehow hold us together.

Yet when I woke the next morning and padded over to the blinds, I stopped and knelt down in the dim light. Scattered across the carpet were last night's tissues. But they no longer resembled flowers. I reached out for one of the little twisted balls and held in my hand its convoluted, unpredictable angles. When I flicked at one of its folds, a dried crust flaked away.

The desire to insure anyone or anything began to seep away from me. Instead, the sound of a police siren, a fire alarm gave me an intense, momentary joy. *Let* disaster come, I thought. One day I visited a prospective client who wanted extensive coverage on his recycling center. The owner—a Mr. Bianci—was proud of his business and gave me a tour through skyscrapered stacks of old newspapers. But I couldn't exult in this environmentally sound enterprise and instead struggled to hide my horror at the countless discarded things. All the people who'd read about the latest property tax increase or inner city murder, or laughed at Dagwood's morning dash out the door, all those people had let these newspapers go and then went on with their lives. What was left was emptiness—ragged towers of ink-stained wood pulp waiting to be crushed and reconstituted. I knew at once I wouldn't agree to extend the slightest amount of coverage to this man's business—let him find it elsewhere; I'd much prefer that those huge paper stacks go up in flames.

The following morning's horoscope, as if in reproach, offered advice that I couldn't help reading over and over again: *Do not be afraid to find value in what has been abandoned.* So when I drove to work and noticed a YARD SALE sign tacked to a telephone pole, I followed the printed arrow. I parked before a scruffy front lawn and wandered through an array of card tables loaded with junk: toys that children had wearied of, framed pictures no longer worthy of a wall, shoes outgrown, half-read paperback books, appliances worn from overuse.

I poked through this discarded bric-a-brac with little pleasure, until I held a rusted toy truck: the letters on its cab were so faded that they seemed to be sinking into the surface, and I found myself imagining how Kate might have captured this with her subtle, penciled hues. Then I picked up an ancient blender, turned it this way and that and could almost see Kate's version—the plastic jar's faded scratches artfully heightened so that it seemed to dream of its own lost swirling.

I began searching out yard sales and pretending that Kate was beside me, our old collaboration finally reclaimed. I examined objects for hints of anything that might inspire her, even if that meant pacing through a musty house during an estate sale, as I found myself doing one Saturday morning. Wearily watching antique dealers appraise each piece of furniture, I wandered into the kitchen. There, on the bare formica counter, sat a white plastic ashtray similar to the one I'd used as a boy to hold stray buttons. Around the curving, outer rim of this ashtray, however, was an ordered line of burn marks. I picked it up and examined its odd disfigurement—a necklace of dark, circular scars.

A wrinkled hand plucked it away. Startled, I turned to a woman whose lined, pale face was clearly embarrassed by her abrupt action, yet she spoke with clear determination. "This isn't for sale."

"Excuse me . . ." I managed, "I didn't mean to . . . It just reminded me of an ashtray that I once had."

Her face seemed to collapse for a moment, then she fingered the plastic rim. "This?" she replied grimly. "This is like no other ashtray."

She made no move to leave, and because she stared at the ashtray with eyes that somehow gave it life, I said, "I think I understand."

She flinched at my words. "You think you do? I'd say not. This has its . . . its own tragedy."

"Mine did too," I murmured, recalling my ashtray of buttons, my entire collection of discards' ineffectual magic against my mother's spiraling troubles.

The woman must have caught the truth of what I'd just said because she hesitated, examining my face haunted by my own faraway memories. Sighing, she began to speak quietly, almost as if I weren't beside her. "It was one of my son's favorite things when he was a little boy. All those expensive toys we bought, but this—this he loved to wear on his head like a crown, pretending he was a king."

She regarded the ashtray with suddenly uncomprehending eyes, as if it had now become alien. "He was a wonderful child. He could have become whatever he wanted. But he died in that Vietnam war."

I offered faltering sympathy until she cut me off. "And this . . . I don't even know why . . . why I'm telling you this, but—don't you move away, you listen—this, this is worse: every year after that, on our son's birthday, my husband would drink too much and put out one of his cigarettes right here, on the rim. 'Jewels in the crown,' he called them."

The woman stood so still I didn't dare speak, but when she turned to me again she must have recognized, just like my clients, my willingness to listen further, for she said simply, "Now they're both dead."

Again, she had little patience with my polite words of condolence. "All that's over now, over," she said and then stopped, surprised at her own words. "Yes, that's right, isn't it? Why should I ever want to see this thing again?" She held out the ashtray, her voice now edged with a terrible resolve. "You want this? You can have it."

"No, really, that's all right—"

"Take it." She shoved the ashtray in my hands. "*Take* it."

"Th-thank you," I said, the ridge of burn marks rough against my hands. "What what should I . . ."

But this unhappy woman was no longer aware of me—she stared out the kitchen window, her lips moving slightly, silently, and I wondered who she spoke to now: her son, her husband?

I left her to that private conversation. Lingering in the living room among the milling groups of buyers, I prepared myself to return the ashtray if she changed her mind, though I hoped I wouldn't have to: my hands gently cupped that wavering line of blackened craters, each little circle a mouth offering eloquent secrets. After an hour, when she still hadn't appeared, I finally walked to my car, understanding that what I held was much more than a simple ashtray. And now I was its caretaker.

So once again I became a collector. What I sought out, though, was a different variety of archaeology from the sort Kate practiced at her drawing desk in the evenings: I recovered what wasn't yet buried. I haunted yard sales and estate sales, attended auctions and listened to the caller's rapid urgent voice coaxing the price higher. Over the following weeks I managed to find a sugar bowl, a pencil holder, a shoehorn, a stepstool and even the single plastic arm of a doll, each containing its own story, for I discovered that if I inspected an object carefully enough, someone might stand beside me, prepared to reveal its secret.

Sometimes I stared into my bathroom mirror and searched my ordinary features for whatever drew such yard sale confessions. Did those strangers sense what I needed and therefore tried to give me what might help? I thought of Kate, how I longed for her approach, and realized that pursuit had all along been my mistake: she had to come to me. So I collected more objects and placed them strategically around the rooms of our house. They were my own silent singing, like the statues of Indian whale hunters that I'd learned about in school so long ago. One day Kate might actually be moved to capture the intricacies of one of these objects and then, instead of offering a caption, I'd confess to her its hidden life.

"What's this?" she asked once, her hand gently sweeping over a doily I'd arranged on an endtable. Its snowflake pattern had once belonged to a newly blinded child: for a time it was her own personal Braille and late-night solace.

I looked up from my book at Kate and this was the moment I'd been hoping for, the sweet possibility of a return to another time. Yet caution ruled my casual reply. "Oh, just something I picked up. An interesting texture, don't you think?"

Kate's fingers played at a delicate corner, testing its complex weave. I waited for her reply. A subtle gleam of recognition surfaced in her eyes and her lips moved slightly, as if struggling to speak. Her hand continued stroking the doily until a nail caught at the nubby pattern. She hesitated, finally pulling it free with a sigh of lingering regret, and then her face became its own veil, in the shape of her familiar features. She only allowed herself a polite nod of appreciation and stepped from the room.

If my wife ever drew one of my objects I never knew it. Before long my anticipation hardened into a proprietary pride—at least those presences spoke to me. There were evenings when, as Kate watched a crime drama or paged through a magazine beside me, I scanned the room and silently savored my objects' stories one by one, inevitably leading to the tale of the wooden stepstool that now rested before our bookshelves. It once belonged to an elderly man who stood on it when his memories threatened to overwhelm him, who reached up and let his palms press against the ceiling as if the rigid pressure in his arms held something unspeakable in place. I could feel my own arms tremble from that imagined exertion. And so slowly, before I understood how much I relied on these private moments, each of my objects became a secret I kept from Kate.

A postcard from my sister arrived one day, her first message since the day of my wedding: "Hi. I'm in my third month of *Who's Next?*, a comedy/mystery: it's a mystery why anyone thinks it's a comedy, and it's a laughable mystery. Cheers, your sib."

How dare she write to me so casually after what she'd done? Yet her words were at odds with her handwriting: each narrow loop and slash evoked Laurie's wild, improvised dancing years ago, and I stared at those edgy lines until I heard Kate's footsteps.

"Did the mail come?" she asked.

"Uh-huh. Nothing interesting," I replied, hiding my sister's postcard behind a clutch of junk mail, turning it into another secret.

Over the next few days Laurie's dashed-off scrawl grew inside me, but now its subversive, infectious energy reminded me of her terrible grin as she'd led the wedding guests in those rounds of tapping champagne glasses, and once again I could hear the delicate chiming that altered my marriage before it had even begun. Yet if Laurie had known how to make Kate curl inside herself, then maybe she also knew of some way to unfurl her.

I bought a plane ticket to the small city where Laurie was performing and concocted an excuse for Kate about some pressing business. Soon I was soaring above the airport, glancing out my window at the patchy clouds, and the drifting shadows they cast on the ground below: long stretches of dark ovals sailed over farmland like a pod of whales, while other shapes suggested the slow geologic drift of undiscovered continents. A single huge, shadowy crescent might have been the jaws of some indefinable creature sneaking up on an unsuspecting town, just as I was traveling toward this sister of mine

I hadn't forgiven. I almost believed that *I* cast those shadows below: a panoply of my own dark wraiths.

I settled into a hotel far from the theater, to avoid any chance meeting with Laurie before the show. I wanted to see my sister performing on an evening that was no more out of the ordinary than any other night. I made it to the theater with enough time to study the playbill and discovered that *Who's Next?* allowed the audience to choose the ending. Flipping to the back pages, I then read Laurie's bio entry: she'd appeared in small-town versions of popular plays and musicals all across the country. No hint of a relationship that might keep her from traveling. I turned to the cast of characters and saw that Laurie played a maid, and when the curtain finally rose, there she stood onstage before the gaudy interior of a mansion, dusting antique furniture. If I hadn't known my sister's role, I might not have recognized her from this distance, with her curly hair now straightened and black.

"Millicent!" an older man's offstage voice called out.

"Coming," Laurie replied brightly, her stagy voice an odd version of the one I knew. She walked briskly across the set, just as two suspiciously quiet characters—a well-dressed young man and, of course, a butler—entered from the opposite side.

As the play progressed, Laurie served the other characters with a dutiful efficiency, yet her square-cut uniform and air of innocence was undermined by stiletto high heels. She was, I thought, a prime suspect, and by the final scene Laurie was the only surviving staff member of the large mansion. Legs firmly planted between the recently deceased bodies of the butler and the cook, she stood at the front of the stage while a disembodied voice declared over the p.a. that the time had come to vote.

Though I suspected the young fellow whose parents had been disinherited might be the culprit—if I remembered correctly, only he was present when each victim flopped to the floor, gasping for breath—I joined the applause for Laurie. I clapped and clapped and clapped, and even after the smattering of others in the audience had stopped, still I went on. I wanted Laurie to be guilty, guilty, I wanted to see her confess before being hustled offstage to prison.

But the audience's nod went to Walter, the hunched and frail grandfather and head of the family, who, he reluctantly revealed, had shot tiny dissolving darts of slow-acting poison from the footrest of his wheelchair, aiming under the dinner table to kill his only slightly less wrinkled younger brother Harold.

"But I kept *missing*," the old man moaned, wheeling his chair in circles as the other actors ducked. "I had nothing against Raymond—he was the finest butler in a hundred miles. And Jacques, who could rival his goose liver tarts? I was even sad to see cousin Sophie die, conniving bitch that she was. . . ."

"So why *did* you try to kill your own brother?" the hapless, greasy-haired detective asked, pointing to Harold, who cowered behind a suit of armor.

"He was trying to blackmail me." Parking his wheelchair center stage, the old man's voice cracked with emotion as he continued: "He threatened to expose my relationship with Millicent!"

All eyes turned to Laurie, who shed her modest demeanor with one piercing cry as she rushed to Walter's side. She ripped the top buttons from her uniform, revealing a sexy black teddy. "It's true, we love each other so!" she proclaimed huskily. "Every wrinkle, every liver spot makes me *seethe* with passion!" Laurie wriggled in elaborate ecstasy, both hands kneading the old man's chest and shoulders.

"All you want is the family fortune!" Harold howled, brandishing the suit of armor's gilded sword. Before anyone could stop him, he impaled his older brother and crowed triumphantly, "But now it's too late."

"Too late for *you*," Laurie glowered, her erotic glow now cooling to a cruel smile. "His will leaves everything to me. *You*," she hissed to the detective, "arrest the guilty party, clear away the bodies, and leave my house."

The stage erupted in conflicting, angry voices, and within minutes, after every remaining plot complication had been tidily disposed of, all the characters—both the survivors and the resurrected—stood at the edge of the stage and bowed again and again as they received our applause. But even from my distant seat, Laurie's brittle smile betrayed little pleasure at the evening's success.

I made my way backstage and almost immediately saw her conferring with a stagehand—an unfriendly exchange, certainly, from the way her hand cut the air into brisk little slices. I was able to approach without Laurie noticing. Close up, she appeared even less like my sister than when I'd sat in the audience—her dark-lined eyes and heavily powdered face were a caricature designed to reach the farthest seats. And then she turned that foreign face to me.

"Michael?" She puckered her lips and whistled two long notes of surprise. Quickly recovering, she announced to the stagehand in a singsong voice, "My brother—once he was lost, but now is found."

The man nodded, unimpressed, and Laurie waved good-bye to him. "Well, David, I release you—for the moment."

He strode off with a shake of his head, and my sister and I attempted an awkward embrace—tentative prelude, perhaps, to confessions and apologies that might lead to reconciliation.

"Now I'm *really* annoyed I wasn't picked tonight—my ending's the best. But tonight, apparently, I failed to connect with my audience." Her face twisted in mock anguish. "If I'd known you were here, I would have tried to look as suspicious as possible."

Some cast members had already disguised themselves in street clothes and were on their way out. Laurie pulled me along toward the butler—now a middle-aged man in jeans—who regarded her with barely veiled impatience as she introduced me with the mannerisms of a southern belle.

With each new introduction Laurie added or shed accents: first a naive little schoolgirl, then some hardened dame, then a shy woman who could barely manage the words of greeting. Who's next indeed? I thought. Where was Laurie in this shifting landscape? Her obvious relish for this backstage performance clearly wasn't shared by her fellow cast members. Ignoring her patter, each one searched my face intently for something more than family resemblance: perhaps some clue to my sister's behavior?

Finally she took my arm in hers, declaring, "To the dressing room!"

"Well, everyone seems quite friendly," I said, embarrassed that I had nothing more to offer than this dishonest chitchat.

She shook her head and confided, sotto voce, "Ah, but I've gone through them all. There's not much that interests me in this bunch any more."

Opening the door to the now deserted dressing room, Laurie gestured to the many chairs facing a long mirror bordered with tucked-in photos, handwritten notes and review clippings. She sat down before her section of mirror—bare of any memorabilia—and said with a flourish, "Here you are, Michael: my few square inches of stardom's real estate."

Laurie dabbed at her made-up face with a cotton ball. "So, what are you here for?" she asked, finally offering me a voice without practiced inflections.

Uncertain whether to trust this opening, I said, "Well, I was in town, so I decided to catch—"

"C'mon, Michael, I know that what I do makes your skin crawl," she said, now imitating Mother's taxicab bravado. She dipped her fingers into a jar of facial cream, rubbed some onto her cheeks, and asked in an eerily chipper voice, "Or have you had a change of heart?"

"Look, I enjoyed the show, Laurie."

She had nothing to say to this. After a few moments of silence she asked, "So, how've *you* been all these years?"

"Fine. Business has never been better, actually, despite a weakness in the economy . . ." and I continued to speak in a tone I *never* used with my clients, chatting up the latest policies, the different levels of deductibles. Laurie kept scrubbing away and seemed not to notice my insurance agent performance. When she was done with her face she stood and without a word deftly slipped the straps of her teddy off her shoulders. It fell to her waist, exposing her breasts. *If you're going to pretend we're not brother and sister,* she seemed to say, nonchalantly tugging the sleek fabric down to her hips, *then let's see how far this will go.*

I turned away and listened to the rustling of her clothes. Tacked onto a bulletin board was a list of Dressing Room Do's and Don't's, beginning with, "Private property is just that, even if it's not locked up." I read them one by one until, quickly glancing over at Laurie, I saw her neatly fitted into jeans and a blouse, combing her hair.

She turned to me, all innocence. "My mind must have wandered. Were you saying something?"

"Nothing worth repeating," I replied, and Laurie laughed with full-throated pleasure.

Still wary, I hesitated, then said, "I came here to, well, to talk. We have a lot to talk about."

Laurie nodded, willing to accept this without a smart remark, her scrubbed face now her own. "So, let's talk. Here's something I've always wanted to tell you. Remember when we were kids and we'd draw pictures together?"

I nodded. I could see Laurie kneeling beside me, her fingers smeared with the colors of her paint kit, her eyes sometimes far away before adding another brushstroke to her tablet.

"You know how I only used to like drawing faces? I'll tell you why. After bedtime I'd lie awake and make up stories about the people I drew."

"Stories? I never knew you did that."

Laurie laughed. "Well, I never told you. I gave them their own lives and then I tried them on, pretending each character was really me, just like Mom had done. Actually, I liked those stories better than anything we ever drew. But then—do you remember this?—you convinced me to try drawing other things, and I realized I could make up stories about being a flower, a train, a lion, or anything else in the world. Mom only became other people, but I could do her one better! I could become anything! That's when I first realized I wanted to act."

My sister's revelations were laced with so many bitter ironies that at first I couldn't speak. "So," I finally said, "*I'm* the one who got you started?"

The misery in my voice wasn't lost on Laurie. She turned her cold gaze away from me and followed the long line of the mirror, the empty chairs of her fellow actors. "Oh, you've been my inspiration in *so* many ways, Michael. That night I visited you at college, remember? Why *was* I there, anyway? Well, for your advice, so I could do the exact opposite of whatever you said. I had *that* low an opinion of your track record."

"What are you talking about?"

"What I mean is, you were such a screw-up, if you'd encouraged me to be an actress I would've stayed in school."

"Oh, get off it. You would've become an actress no matter what I said."

"You're right," she said, head tilted archly, her voice brightening with the need to convince. "And you know why? Because I *like* doing this. It makes my life snappy, playing all these different characters.

Safety in numbers, I always say. And I don't have any husband or kids to fuck up."

"You make living alone sound so attractive."

"Who's alone? Every cast is one big happy family."

"Like this one? I thought you were already bored with them all."

I'd exposed the imperfect surface of her artifice. "You think I'm not happy?" she hissed, her face hardening into a grimacing mask. "You think I'm *not happy?*"

"I don't know," I said, my voice barely a murmur. "*Are* you?"

She picked up a prop from the table, an ink bottle, and pulled off its glass cap. "Of course you don't know! When have *you* ever known about *anything*, Mr. *In-the-Dark!*"

I flinched, hands up to protect myself, but Laurie spun away and shook the open bottle at the mirror again and again, covering my reflection with a dark blotch.

Facing me again, she said, "Here's something else you never knew. *I'm* the one who broke all those things in the house. All the things *Dan* got blamed for."

I could only gape at her. "What—you?"

"Me. *Me.* I did it to spite Dad for ignoring us all the time, the stupid shit. But when Dan got blamed and I saw the way Dad got to him, I was too afraid to admit it was me. Now *that* made me angry, *really* angry, so I kept it up. I wanted to see how far it would go, even though I was sure that sooner or later the bastard would catch me. When you got Dan that job, you got me off the hook. But then Dad cooked *your* goose, didn't he?"

Laurie sobbed into her hands, her shoulders trembling as she squeezed out, "Oh god, oh god! I'm sorry, I'm, I'm sorry, Michael, I really am."

"Laurie, please," I began, turning her toward me.

Her face dry, her eyes carefully appraised my shock at her performance. Had her entire story been an impromptu script, a star vehicle designed to torment me? I pulled away to leave, then heard her voice, now feigning concern, ask, "By the way, how are you and Kate?"

She'd been softening me up for the kill, but it was long past the time that I'd offer this woman any more grist for her soap opera mill—instead, I'd display my own performance skills. Hadn't I practiced my own face of patience with Kate for so many months now? I turned, my eyes filled with gratitude that Laurie had finally broached a topic that brought me happiness, and I easily said the words I knew would foil her: "Kate and I are fine, really fine."

Suicide Songs

Wandering among the trickle of browsers through a yard sale's unpromising array of cluttered card tables, I paused to watch two young girls leaping and tumbling on a mattress their father had just bought.

"C'mon, kids, stop," he complained halfheartedly, proudly watching their manic twirls and twists in the air.

Turning from their welcome diversion for a moment, I picked up a small, battered tape recorder and noticed a cassette inside. This little surprise intrigued me, and I pressed the *Play* button. Immediately a man's voice mumbled something too low for me to make out, so I turned up the volume. He spoke slowly in a strange, foreign language, his voice strained, hesitant.

A middle-aged woman, her summer shorts tight against the bulge of her hips, hurried over and fiddled with the control buttons. "My god, I didn't know *this* was in there!" She turned it off, and when she muttered, "Hoo boy, I can't believe I tried to get rid of it this way," I knew this was something I wanted.

"Is that a language tape?"

She laughed strangely. "Oh no, far from it."

"Can I buy it?"

She pointed at the tape recorder. "Uh, sure. Isn't there a price marked on it?"

"Yes," I said, speaking softly, "but I'd like the cassette too."

"You want the . . ." Her eyes searched my face in a way I'd long grown accustomed to these past few months: a questioning look that seemed to imagine I was an answer. "You know what's *on* that tape?"

"I'd like to know."

"Suicide songs. Yeah, that's right," she said to my startled face. "Unhappy lovers sing them before they . . ."

"But he's not singing."

"He's trying not to."

"Why?"

She glanced around at the idle bargain hunters in her backyard, then examined my face again. "I'm sorry . . . look, just how interested in this are you?"

"Very. Please, tell me whatever you'd like."

She wiped the back of her hand across her forehead and sighed. "Well, I'll need a beer first. It's so hot today. *Joey*," she called out to a man standing by the garage, "could you take over the cash box?"

He nodded, and the woman stepped up the stairs to the back door and waved me along. "C'mon in. By the way, my name is Jill Harnick."

I shook her hand. "Michael Kirby. Pleased to meet you."

We sat at the kitchen table. Jill took a sip from her bottle, preparing herself for whatever she had to say. Her finger scratched at the edge of the label and I avoided the impulse to make small talk.

"Well," she finally began, "this goes back over ten years, back to when I was a Peace Corps volunteer. In the Philippines. I taught English in a small town, on one of the more remote islands. One of the teachers at the school was a Filipino man who spoke English beautifully. Agustin."

Jill paused and set her bottle down almost absentmindedly, and I imagined she could hear his words again on that cassette. "Agustin had been born in the area but he was educated in Manila," she continued. "Because Manila was like another world to the people in town, he was a bit of an outsider, and I suppose that's why we became friends. Sometimes after school we'd sit on my veranda and talk teaching strategy and more than once he invited me over for dinner with his family. His wife was very sweet, and a little wary of me, even though my friendship with Agustin was extremely formal and polite.

"One afternoon, when I was in the second year of my tour, he came to my veranda, very upset. It was later than usual—most people were at home eating dinner. He told me that a young woman, someone he barely knew, had fallen in love with him. But he was married, and in the local culture of that island, adultery is simply . . . well, unthinkable. So this girl was wandering the streets hopelessly at night, singing traditional songs that celebrated love. But they were actually a warm-up to suicide."

Jill pulled back from her chair and walked to the screen window. "*Joey*, how are you doing with change, need any more?"

"Got more than enough," I heard him call back, but she lingered there at the window, as if she didn't want to believe him. She returned to the table, avoiding my glance. "I'm sorry, where was I, anyway? Yeah—when Agustin told me all this, I remembered hearing a very eerie song a few nights before—a faraway voice that kept me up half the night—and I knew that was her.

"Agustin was incredibly upset, and even though I had no decent advice to give him, he was happy just to be able to talk with me—he couldn't speak about this to anyone else in town, since the custom was, no one could admit being the subject of the songs.

"Well, that girl finally killed herself, and for a week afterward he visited me every afternoon, grateful that he could let out his misery. By this time I was *so* curious about those songs, I wanted to understand why they were so powerful. I considered myself something of a student of the local culture—I was in my second year there by then. I'm sorry, did I mention that?"

"Yes," I said, nodding, "you did."

"Anyway, I asked . . . for something I shouldn't have. I asked Agustin to sing the songs for me, and help me translate them. He absolutely refused—he was really quite fierce about it. But the next day I managed to convince him just to speak the words of the songs into my tape recorder."

Jill covered her face with her hands for a moment, then stared straight at me, her eyes dark little disks. "Stupid, *stupid* mistake. Those damned songs were so powerful that even he wasn't immune. He recited the words and fell in love with me, and before he was done he knew he was a dead man. Because he was married, and in his culture adultery is unthinkable."

Jill regarded me carefully. "I don't suppose you need to hear any more."

"No," I said softly, "I understand." We sat there a while in silence, and I was surprised to hear the girls still jumping and whooping on the mattress outside. Finally I asked, "Are you sure you want to sell this?"

Jill managed to wince out a smile. "Hey, today's our special summer clearance." She pushed the tape recorder across the table, then tossed me the cassette. "Buy one, get one free."

I played that tape in my office, between phone calls and appointments. The man had a remarkable voice. He spoke so carefully, trying to avoid breaking into song, and in the course of ten short minutes I heard the gradual discovery of love and then the reluctant acceptance of death. I began to memorize his inflections, almost believing that I understood the language. As he spoke I examined Kate's photo on my desk: her eyes a bit distracted above the most cautious of smiles.

Kate had actually been quite happy these past few months. After dinner we sat quietly together in the living room with our newly compatible secret lives, making no demands on each other, and even if these evenings seemed uncomfortably close to what my father and Dan had become, locked in their own circle of silence, I didn't know how to break the pattern. And if I really loved my wife, why would I want to disturb her? As that sad man's intense voice continued, his foreign words lulled me into acceptance—perhaps it *was* possible for me to stay with Kate, even if staying with her might be for me a form of suicide. But before I could decide, I had to know if my wife heard what I heard in that voice.

That evening Kate sat across from me in the living room, paging through one of her home decorating magazines with such intensity I wondered if she longed to live in those meticulously appointed rooms where no other people could be found, where a fire in a fire-place tended itself; where a book on a coffee table lay open, read by no one; where neatly tucked-away toys never encountered a child's disruptive energy. Or maybe she imagined me there beside her in one of those rooms, a man content with whatever small intimacies she was able to offer.

The tape recorder lay beside me on the couch, and I slowly notched up the volume, so that at first Kate would barely hear those foreign words, so she might grow accustomed to them. With each tiny turn of the dial, I waited for some subtle sign of recognition.

Finally, Kate's eyes flickered slightly as she turned another page, and she lifted her head. "Michael, what *is* that?"

The man's voice fluttered a moment when I held up the tape recorder.

Her face recoiled at the sight. "How can you possibly listen to that?"

"Don't worry, dear," I said sadly, pressing the *off* button, "I won't ever listen to it again."

Kate stared at me, puzzled. She didn't yet know that she had saved my life.

Curled beside Kate on that last night that we would ever lie to-gether side by side, I listened to the even, breathy rhythm of her sleep, I watched her breasts and belly rise and fall, and I wondered why we'd never had a child. This was another subject Kate and I hadn't talked about, though we sometimes made love without thought of contraception. All our friends who were busy with chil-dren often commented how much more we'd learn about each other once we became parents. *You can't help but be surprised,* they'd say. Kate and I would nod politely, pretending those innocent remarks weren't central to our secret troubles. Now, shifting uncom-fortably in bed, I wondered if those words weren't also a clue to our infertility. Maybe each of Kate's eggs fisted itself up when my sperm approached, each little wriggling creature a question mark that shouldn't be acknowledged. Or perhaps my sperm purposely lost themselves in her moist, inner folds, unwilling to open what waited in that distant, mysterious egg.

In the morning, after opening the blinds, I sat on Kate's side of the bed and waited for her eyes to open to the early light. She stirred under the blanket, then her hand rose up suddenly, blocking the unexpected sight of me so close, so soon.

"Michael?"

I took her hand and held it, admiring the delicate bones, remembering the time she'd drawn an image of my own hand. Then I set it down on the blanket, terribly aware that no tender tracing could rewrite what I had to say.

"I'm so sorry, Kate."

"Sorry?"

I nodded. "I want a divorce."

Her voice unusually calm, she asked me to repeat what I'd just said.

"I want a—"

"But we're so happy," she interrupted, with a voice that held no such conviction.

I said nothing. Then Kate's body seemed to ease under the covers, her legs languidly stretching out and releasing this happy marriage.

Kate felt certain that if we sold the house and each moved elsewhere, then our new towns and homes and jobs would allow us to rebuild our lives as soon as possible. Barely able to hide her pleasure at our ending, she became positively voluble as she outlined the benefits of this plan, and I finally agreed, if only to curtail any more such painful discussions.

When the time came, Kate packed her half of our dividing house with a light touch, filling each box almost tenderly before taping the cardboard flap shut. I worked more slowly, noticing that she took special care not to pack any objects I'd collected—did she somehow understand that they held secrets, like the illustrations she kept inside herself?

Yet there was something of my collection that I wanted her to have, a secret gift that would be my rueful farewell: a long brown bootlace that once belonged to a young woman whose lush blond hair, I'd been told, was her own halo. While resting one afternoon in a park, she'd caught sight of a friend she secretly loved, unexpectedly approaching along one of the cobblestone paths. Though caught off guard, she quickly untied the lace of one of her boots and used it to tie back her hair. She greeted him as he walked by, and when he stopped to chat she casually reached back and loosened the knot, her hair tumbling undone for this man who now, suddenly, had nowhere else to go.

While Kate continued her meticulous, patient packing, I climbed the stairs to our nearly empty bedroom and searched in her closet for her slim leather boots, hoping she hadn't yet packed them. There they were, in a dark corner beneath a line of dresses, one boot lying sadly on its side. I picked it up and examined the lace—it was nearly the same color and only slightly thicker than the one I held in my hand.

I quickly exchanged them, my fingers fumbling at the button hooks, satisfied with this small presence I was bestowing on Kate. Each autumn through winter she'd wear these boots, tightening them in the mornings and then going about her day, but in the evenings she'd unloose those laces, and the subtle energy of the one I'd just given her might make her pause for a moment, as if she heard someone speaking from far off, not yet recognizing that stirring within as the urge to finally let herself go. And one day, as all laces do, this lace would snap, perhaps finally breaking the spell of her own inner knot.

While reestablishing my insurance business in a new town, I once again traveled from one yard sale to another, or I checked the local paper for an announcement of any new auction, longing for the sound of a caller's swift and keening voice. I quickly added to my collection, and in my new home I allowed every object its own perspective and tiny pull of gravity, so that it might radiate out to every other object in invisible, kaleidoscopic associations. My objects were always willing to silently retell their tales, and I was their rapt audience as I wandered through the house. On my dining room huntboard sat a gravy bowl that was once a young girl's magic lamp; on the living room mantelpiece stood the candlestick holder an elderly man had thrown out his window the day before he died; in a corner of the foyer stood a plant stand, owned by a woman who never dared grow anything and kept it empty. On my desk rested a petrified wood paperweight and its many stories: one woman had carried it with her everywhere, an unlikely balm for her too-tender heart; then her twin sister, jealous of anything that couldn't be shared, managed to steal it; and finally their brother, weary of the bickering that always seemed to exclude him, sold it to me.

In a wooden bowl on the kitchen counter lay the soiled, bent arm of a doll. It once belonged to a timid child who held it before her whenever she had to venture down the basement for a family chore: one quick wave of that tiny arm somehow warded off all imagined dangers. Sometimes I felt the need to hold it myself, snug in my jacket pocket, and take a long, aimless walk through this new town I was still learning. My little plastic talisman always seemed to lead me somewhere I needed to be: to a parade ground where the marching band of the local college blared out fearlessly uplifting music; to a small stream in the middle of a park, its gliding waters clear down to the smooth stones; to a late-night mall and its wonderful crush of teenaged kids flirting with each other up and down the aisles.

One evening during one of those walks I found myself hungry and standing before a diner, so I settled into a booth inside and ordered a greasy burger. While waiting for my meal I noticed a woman in the booth ahead of me, who brushed one graying strand after another from her face as she stared and stared at the small jukebox propped against the window. Occasionally she forgot her wayward hair and reached toward the buttons, her fingers poised but never willing to push.

Her quarters surely lay inside the machine, but she wasn't ready to spend them just yet, and again and again she nearly punched in the numbers before drawing back her hand. What song was she afraid to release, and why—some song lyric that might offer advice she was afraid to hear, a melody that would call up an old love or the memory of a child now grown and gone?

The quiet drama unfolding within that woman affected me as well, and I reached into my pocket and held that little hidden arm in an anxious grip. Then a surprising thought ran through me: Why not give this bit of toy away? It had helped someone once before. It had helped soothe my entry into a new life. It might, if I told this woman its story, help her too.

I shook my head ruefully, wishing my hamburger could arrive right at this moment and release me from the familiar impulse to save others. I'd make a fool of myself, wouldn't I, with my sudden appearance before this woman and the fantastic story I'd try to tell? Squeezing the soft plastic arm again, I felt little fingers cup into a budding, reassuring grasp, the gift of just enough courage to help me slide across my seat to the diner's aisle. My sudden movement drew the woman's gaze, her eyes so thick and dull with unhappiness that I felt sure she might be willing to try anything, even waving a tiny toy arm against whatever the world threatened. I smiled awkwardly, and stepped forward.

PART FIVE

No Rain Today

Sylvia sat across from me in the booth, and like last night's broadcast her face was once again in close-up. But now her eyes reflected the excitement of this Saturday lunch crowd's bustle—mostly young families heady with the morning's shopping at the nearby mall. I thought how uncanny it was that Sylvia had chosen to meet here: this very same diner where I'd given away a doll's arm to that sad woman. Almost two years ago. I'd given away so many objects since then.

Surely, I thought, this must be an auspicious coincidence. Yet we avoided each other's gaze, embarrassed by the irony that this was our first real date, and we let the steady, easy chatter of our neighbors serve as our conversation. Sylvia hid behind her outspread menu while I turned the dial of our table's jukebox, searching for the country tune that woman had wanted to listen to. I could still recall the singer's plaintive voice, even a bit of the lyrics—how sometimes it seems that God's own angels just can't help a girl help herself.

I flipped through the circular song file once more, but the song must have been replaced long ago. I returned to my menu.

"The chili is great here," Sylvia offered.

I nodded. "So's the peanut butter pie."

Our eyes met a moment— Yes, we both knew this place.

After we placed our orders, Sylvia said, "Well, tell me your grand plan. I'm dying to hear it."

"Oh, it's not so grand. My advice may sound pretty strange, actually, but bear with me—it's really not much stranger than butterflies terrorizing meteorologists. First, though, I have to be honest with you. I'm divorced. Nearly three years, though sometimes I still feel like damaged goods—"

Sylvia's face flinched and she murmured sympathy, but I waved it off lightly. "Thanks, but I don't mean to get maudlin. My point is, what helped me through a lot of the harder times was, well . . . the horoscope."

"The horoscope," she repeated, her voice suddenly stiff with politeness.

"Well, yeah," I said slowly, realizing I'd have to speak with some care. "It was a strange time. I can't say I actually believed in the thing, but then I didn't really disbelieve, either. It's just that . . . I found it comforting to think a few words might help me influence what happened the next day, especially since every day was so sad and dreary. Obviously, the horoscope didn't work. For a while, though, it gave me something to grab on to. I think that's its main attraction for a lot of people."

"Wait a moment, Michael, I think I see where this is going." She reached for her water glass, then stopped and rested her hand on the place mat, her fingers tapping nervously. "You know, I'm not about to do star charts for my audience. There is no such thing as Sagittarian or Aquarian weather—"

"Hey, don't judge too quickly. Remember, you yourself mentioned you're as accurate as the horoscope. That's actually truer than you think. I've thought about what you said, about the weather predictions being so imprecise. And I realized that even if today's prediction is completely wrong, people will still listen to tomorrow's weather report. Why? Because we want to believe. If it's wrong now and then, well, we forgive without really thinking about it. Like I used to forgive the horoscope."

"You're serious. You want me to be the Jeane Dixon of weather reporting."

"No, not at all." I laughed nervously. "Just emphasize accuracy less, oracle more. Forget the science—give your best guess. I'll bet most people in your audience aren't expecting perfection. They mostly want assurance, and maybe that's enough. Give them that, and they'll remember your concern, not your prediction."

"Well, I'll certainly mull this over," Sylvia said, her voice laced with a disappointment she couldn't hide.

The waitress brought our meal and we reverted to strained small talk about the co-anchors at her station, until Sylvia glanced out the window at the blue sky, the wispy streaks of clouds. "Well, at least I was right about today—there's no chance of rain."

"You're right," I said, "it's a beautiful day."

Sylvia smiled wanly at my appreciation. She dabbed at her lips with her paper napkin, then set it down on the table. I could just make out the faint lipsticked image—a disembodied, slightly open mouth, perhaps about to speak.

Her own lips remained pursed, silent, and already I could see us after lunch offering apologetic good-byes and then driving away in our separate cars.

When our desserts arrived I reached out for the jukebox again, then stopped myself—I needed far more than some song's pointed message. Again I recalled that desolate woman in the booth beside mine two years ago and how she'd whispered, "I hear voices." For too long they'd risen up from her whole life: her mother's efficient criticisms delivered with a giggle; a brother's telephoned wheedling and whining; a high school teacher's sarcasm; the dismissive monosyllables of her teenage children. All those voices had so multiplied that they hemmed her in wherever she went, making even the simplest decisions impossibly difficult. Yet she'd gladly accepted the doll's hand that I offered. Small as it was, it reached out to pull her from her own drowning.

Now I tried to imagine a similar rescue for myself—I'd even welcome the whisperings of inner voices. I closed my eyes and listened, but all I could hear were the tangled, overlapping words of strangers in the crowded booths around me.

Stitching Wounds

I slumped in my chair at the airport lounge and waited for my boarding call, weary after a three-day conference of independent insurance
agents. My mind still filled with too much business talk—such-and-
such coverage for such-and-such an occasion, the newest payment
schedules and benefit packages—I watched the people rushing along
the terminal hallway or loitering at a nearby newsstand, and I was alert
to the grim-faced, the haunted. *Here* was the true poetry of my profession, a version of insurance I'd been practicing for months now: I
searched those passing faces for any absence that might fit with one
of my secret objects.

My flight number was called, and as I gathered up my briefcase,
I noticed a neatly tailored man with well-kept gray hair hurrying by.
One of his arms rose with a slight, warding-off gesture, though no
one walked near him—what was he shooing away? Something I
couldn't see, perhaps something he couldn't even remember, because when he swiped at empty air again I understood he wasn't
trying to protect his expensive suit. I imagined that gesture was
from his childhood: his own young self inside him, a boy's now for-

gotten fear and sorrow rising up in nervous motion. He was defending himself still, after so many years, from troubles he might never escape.

I could offer him a small comfort, even if I had to miss my flight. I followed him through the crowd and waited nearby while he lined up at his departure gate's check-in counter. When he stopped at a sports bar I sat on the stool beside him. I ordered scotch too, but he didn't notice this or the three video screens above us filled with baseball, basketball, boxing. Under all that furious motion he stirred his ice cubes in clangy circles.

Because he might kick back that drink in seconds and hop off the stool for his flight, I didn't have time for his edgy movements to tell me what I needed to know. So I took a chance.

"Mutual funds?"

He stopped that stirring, turned to me a bored, I-don't-need-this smile. "Excuse me?"

I'd made a mistake, perhaps, so I offered a broad, self-deprecating grin and said, "No, I'm not selling, just asking. I thought that might be your field."

His face was flat: he wanted to frown, didn't want it to show. He didn't like being guessed.

So I decided not to try, and instead confessed: "Me, I'm a collector."

Something flared briefly in his eyes, a sudden interest he wanted to hide. I took a sip of my drink, making a good show of enjoying it, and waited. If the conversation was over I'd simply catch my flight.

"What do you collect?" he finally said, his question not quite idly asked, and to emphasize his seeming disinterest he glanced away at one of the three television screens, where a leaping shortstop made a catch.

"Oh, everyday objects, really. But only those that have stories."

"Stories?" Though he still stared at the screen, I knew he wasn't really watching the pitcher and manager confer on the mound. He was waiting for my reply.

"I'm interested," I said, "in things, objects, that once shared a secret with their owners."

This was something he wanted to hear about, because as he faced me I might as well have been another screen, offering a particularly absorbing show. There went his hand again, averting something invisible. But it seemed gentler now, almost a sign of healing. If every conversation is a kind of dream, as I had come to believe, then now he had found the place inside himself where I fit.

I coughed lightly, hesitated. "Before saying any more, I should tell you that I followed you here. You see, I noticed this."

I swung my arm in a tight, nervous arc: a passable imitation of his gesture, and the man drew back a bit on his stool, as if I had suddenly become unclean.

"I had a feeling," I quickly continued, "that your gesture is the symptom of a condition that might benefit from something I have with me."

He nodded, his eyes weary. He was going to have to hear out this pest. He set his drink down on the bar and I looked down at the lacquered surface, at the little trough of uncollected tips by the beer taps. The coins' tiny faces there glistened in the light, but what sort of speaking had ever come from those lips, those eyes? Each face in profile stared toward the edge of its circular world, unaware of us. As for paper bills, Lincoln, Hamilton and Jackson gaze out in three-quarter view, as if there's something much more interesting to see right behind our shoulders. At least George Washington regards us from his little oval window, his eyes half closed, his mouth a tight line. Yet they all seem unwilling to reveal anything of their mysterious travels or who has held them in their previous lives. That's the power of money—its indifference to us. But also its great emptiness. Certainly what I had to offer would speak to this man in ways his prosperity could not. Money hadn't yet warded off whatever chased him. It never would.

So I set down between us an oval stone: polished dark gray, with a deep nick across it the length of a fingernail. Its smooth surface flickered as if alive from the reflected, shifting images of the television screens.

His hard face told me that he was considering leaving, so I said, "Most people are accustomed to seeing value in objects. I hope you'll grant me that some objects, at least, have value for their stories. Just watch this stone while I speak, then decide if this is a joke."

He shifted in his seat, not quite the beginning of an exit, and I added, "You think I'm wasting your time? Why would I waste my own?" I took my ticket from my jacket pocket. "I've missed my flight, sitting here talking to you."

"So you'd like me to miss mine as well?"

"Your choice. My small misfortune creates no obligation on your part."

"Of course not." He sat down and motioned to the bartender for a refill.

I showed no satisfaction, merely nodded my head and gestured to the stone. "It's not particularly important how I came by this stone. What's more important is the man it once belonged to. Years ago he lived alone, in one boarding house after another. He only took part-time jobs, because they gave him just enough money to live on and more than enough time to collect rocks. Every day after work he'd find an old lot or a bit of woods, and he'd get down to his true work—loading stones into a box he'd collected from a liquor store or somewhere else.

"When he was done, he'd haul that box to his tiny apartment. Slowly he filled up the rooms, with more boxes stuffed with rocks and stones until there was room for no one but himself: boxes up to the ceiling, with only a narrow path leading from the door to his bed and hot plate, and from there another narrow path to the toilet and sink. Those boxes once held canned foods, quarts of paint, bottles of wine, power tools, books, small appliances, and their logos must have faced him along those narrow paths, images of the world he was trying to crowd out.

"He stayed in an apartment for only as long as it took him to fill it up. Then, somehow dissatisfied, he abandoned what he'd built, leaving behind a bewildered and angry landlord. He found a new town, a new part-time job, and settled in again, and over a few years he traveled a zigzag up California. I sometimes think of that path he took as stitches over an enormous wound."

My companion's hand flickered beside his untouched drink. He seemed about to speak, but then thought better of it, and I continued, "Whenever I think of this man's story, I always wonder: When he first moved in, did he feel the emptiness of the rooms opening inside him, so he had to fill them up? And what was worse for him: an apartment with all that space, or one with almost none? Well, whatever he felt, I often think how methodical his strange life was: stone by stone, box by box, apartment by apartment. But one day the floor by his bed gave way under all those heavy boxes. Fortunately, no one was home in the apartment below. He was gone, too, at a day job washing dishes. But when he returned, more than just the curious were waiting for him.

"This stone here, the man kept it with him for all the years he was institutionalized, working it over in his hand, trying to split it down the middle with his fingernail, until he died. But what's most interesting to me is its mystery: I look at the stone, with its scar from his fingernail and its polish from his handling, and what I see is an unfinished battle between anger and forgiveness.

"It's yours now if you'd like it. You can start up where he left off—continue the groove until you cut the stone in two. Or you can rub it until it's even glossier."

"So," he said, as interested as I knew he would be, "now we negotiate a price."

"No problem there. I give away objects to anyone who needs them."

He shook his head in disbelief. "What?"

"It's yours. No obligation," I replied, but he'd gone somewhere inside himself. I watched a few volleys across the net on one of the screens above us, and I waited for him to return. Quickly enough his eyes fixed on me again, now with an odd mixture of bitterness and amusement.

"All right. I accept your stone, Mr. Storyteller. I have a lot of reasons for my interest, though they really all boil down to just one. And now, if you'll indulge me, I have a story for you."

I nodded, pleased with this unexpected bargain—the telling of a secret I'd never otherwise hear.

"It's about a woman who hated men most of her life, and from what I know she had good cause," he began. "She deserted her first husband when she discovered she was pregnant, and when the child turned out to be a boy, she gave him away. She refused to ever remarry, though she couldn't entirely keep away from the company of men. But whenever she became pregnant she dismissed her latest man, and if her child was a boy, she sent him away too. She did, however, raise two girls. Most people would say her behavior was unaccountable, and leave it at that. But I can't afford that particular luxury. That woman was my mother."

He stopped, reading more than surprise on my face, and said, "You like that little twist? Well, I can tell a story too.

"My father was the first husband, the one who started it all. He somehow found out about me when I was six. He took me out of the orphanage and then took me along to where my mother lived. I didn't know this man—'Daddy' was a word I didn't know what to do with at the time. I watched him while he drove, watched him talk to me, watched one side of his mouth moving. He talked about this Mother I was about to meet, all the shame she was going to feel, and his voice grew more and more bitter.

"I wanted him to stop talking. In fact, I wanted him to stop driving, too. Just pull off to the side of the road and look at me. Give me a friendly grin, extend a hand, touch my shoulder, squeeze it. Or maybe I didn't wish it at the time, maybe that's something I wished for later, much later. He wasn't the sort of man who dished out large helpings of love—far from it. But in his favor I'll say that the way he treated me drove me to excel in the world in ways that he never could."

I set my drink down on the bar, shook my head. I'd seen far more in this man's nervous gesture than I at first realized. He paused, not especially surprised at the effect of his words, and then continued. "My father drove for hours and hours until he stopped in a little town, on a street filled with whitewashed, boxy houses. Whenever I see a house like that now, I still think of my mother. Hers had a small open porch, with bright white curtains in the windows. While my father stood at the door, not quite ready to knock, I stood at one of those windows, and when I looked in through a crack between the curtains I saw a woman dressed rather formally—high collar, dark hair pinned up—sitting in a cushioned chair and doing nothing but watching a little girl toddle around the floor."

The man's voice was low, I could barely hear him above the noise of the bar, and I leaned in slightly to listen.

"I was certain that woman was my mother, and the little girl her daughter, and I couldn't help wondering why wasn't *I* inside there too? Then I noticed the girl held something—a comfort rag I sometimes think, but it also could have been a doll, or a child's white cup. But it was white, I do remember that. The girl—my half-sister, of course—walked unsteadily, and my mother's arms reached out, ready to balance her. Or to hold her. I'll never know, because my father's fist was pounding the door.

"I hurried to his side and heard steps approach the door. It opened and there she was, her face a strange version of mine—older and much harder, even as she smiled at this man in the moment before she recognized him. Then she started shouting, and because my father's anger easily matched her own, I could barely make out what they said.

"She moved out onto the porch, the little girl now nowhere in sight. My mother turned to me—my identity had been screamed out at her in the rush of words—and her eyes turned suddenly deep and dark. She, too, must have been struck by the resemblance. Then her mouth turned tight and her arms stretched out—but not to hold me! She pounced at me, slapping and slapping and I raised my arms to protect my face. Then my father began hitting her, and her hands were like little walls that he slowly broke down. No one heard me wail except the neighbors, and soon enough they crowded on the porch and pulled him away from Mother and her bloody face.

"He would do that to me for years later—make my face bloody. Yet whenever I closed my eyes and tried to wave him away, I always saw my mother's terrible face instead of his."

The man reached for his drink. Downing the last of it, he set the glass lightly on the bar. "So, you like my little story?"

I nodded, my own mother's collection of faces swirling before me, and now I understood that all their promises of secret transformations lurked behind the faces of everyone I'd ever met.

He motioned to the bartender for another drink, then turned to me. "Well, I gather that you have many more 'objects,' as you call them, in stock somewhere. My name is Preston McCandles, by the way, and I have a business proposition to offer you."

The Gallery

In the center of Preston's gallery I turned in a slow, tight circle, taking in the convulsive black brushstrokes of the tall Oriental canvases that lined startlingly white brick walls. I closed my eyes, imagining I was an explosion, then opened them and faced the aftermath: the seething energy of those paintings. But what was it inside me that wanted to explode?

A gaunt young woman peered in through the gallery window, her face all stark angles above a black turtleneck sweater. She tried the locked door and then tapped on the glass pane, arching an eyebrow at Preston, who'd just returned from his office in the back, fresh drink in hand. He shook his head *no*. This was a private showing. She gave him the finger and walked off on the dark street.

Stepping beside me, he gestured to the silk wall hangings. "So tell me, what do you think?"

"I like them . . . very much," I offered cautiously, not yet prepared to reveal their effect on me. "Are these Chinese—"

"Japanese. A collection of their newest, their best calligraphers. Notice how each painting is a single character—a single word—from a cursive Japanese script. But in these artists' versions, each character becomes more than just a word, more than pictorial—it becomes a map of, well . . . a human mystery? You of all people should appreciate that. By the way, are you sure you wouldn't like a drink?"

"No thanks."

I drew near the wall to read the printed titles, to examine the paintings more closely. *Calm*, far from serene, was a figure-eight so deformed and slashed by a swift and agitated brush that it might be the hunched outline of someone standing before an empty, oval mirror. Another, labeled *Faint*, appeared to be two hands cupped to meet each other, the dark ink applied so thickly it bled beyond the borders of the brushstrokes into a misty haze. *Forgive* could be a face hovering between weeping and laughter. The black strokes of *Yes* were a knot straining to unravel itself. Surrounded by the oddly familiar landscapes of this foreign vocabulary, I felt my own inner loosening.

Dream, applied in thick yet graceful brushstrokes, resembled a dancer, the wavery lines implying swinging arms, and I lingered long before this figure. It seemed to rush away and yet rush toward me as well, the skittish ink about to release itself from the canvas. I had to fight the urge to reach out and either catch that hurtling figure or prevent its escape.

Preston's footsteps approached on the polished wooden floor. "This particular work intrigues you?"

I nodded.

He stood beside me, regarding the canvas, then sighed. "I think I see how it might."

I didn't think it wise to reply, knowing where this was leading. He wanted to display my objects, sell them to any interested customers. I'd laughed at the idea back at the airport, laughed when he'd said I owed him the professional courtesy of hearing him out at his gallery. Yet here I was.

Preston shook the ice cubes in his glass, then slipped the smooth stone from his jacket pocket. "Up till now, Michael, our exchange has been unfair. We've matched stories, but now it's time for me to offer a gift, of equal value to this stone. This painting, *Dream*? It's yours. Whether or not you choose to show your collection here."

Alarmed by this generosity I didn't trust, I said, "I really can't accept this—"

"Of course you can. As far as I'm concerned, you already have. There's no obligation," he said, cunningly echoing my words.

I laughed bitterly, waiting for the rest of his pitch. If he understood just what moved me the most in this room, then perhaps he'd also located some hidden part of me that wanted to set loose all my objects and release the burden of their stories, their sad, sad stories.

"Are you still upset at misreading me at the airport?" Preston asked, chuckling with the satisfaction of someone who'd managed to escape detection. "Your mistake was understandable. And yet . . . never mistake a gallery owner for the art he or she displays. Of course I'm a businessman, though I like to think there's more to me than that. I have a secret too, like this wonderful stone, like this lovely Japanese calligraphy. Whenever I open a new show, I imagine I'm actually redecorating my mother's house, the one I wasn't allowed to enter. My gallery isn't only public space, Michael, it's private space as well."

"Of course," I murmured, and as I scanned the room again a strange dizziness overtook me: those surrounding canvases could just as well be my own mother's daily dramas, or Kate's hidden self, or any number of other languages I had yet to discover.

"I choose my shows carefully," Preston continued, "always mindful of the money, of course, but once that's taken care of, I look for work that helps me reinvent someone I never knew. You see, I'm an idealist of sorts—why else would I have given you the time of day at the airport? But I'm also always calculating my self-interest, and I'm telling you this because I know you like to hear secrets. See? More self-interest on my part."

He grinned and I smiled back. I *was* a sucker for confession, even one that was also a hustle.

"Now, Michael, I know very very little about the rest of your collection, though I'm intrigued by the possibilities. I suspect that the rest of your objects are much like this calligraphy. Displaying them would be perfect for my gallery. I hope you'll reconsider what would be an excellent financial arrangement as well—"

"I've never sold my objects. They're gifts."

"And you're cheapening your gifts and their revelations by giving them away. Now that was a very entertaining cab ride from the airport—the indifference of money, the poetry of insurance—but I have to disagree. People value what's *valuable*, what *costs*. Exchanging money for something creates an invisible bond, so if you want the treasures you bestow to *really* be treasures, I'm sorry to say that you'll need to make a bit of profit from them."

Preston tilted back his head and finished his drink. Then, with that familiar flick of his arm, he scattered the ice cubes onto the polished wood floor. They clattered and careened off the baseboard, splitting into jagged chips that skitted back toward us.

"An interesting pattern, don't you think? Maybe even worthy of one or two of the paintings on the wall. But the ice will melt, and then the puddles will evaporate. I can't sell this, it can't be owned. Besides the necessary pleasures, art *has* to give a sense of prestige and permanence, and this is felt most deeply when its purchase involves a sacrifice, a risk. It's my business to understand this."

"But you're contradicting yourself, Preston," I said, though with little sense of triumph. "You *gave* me a painting. A gift, remember? So where's my sacrifice?"

"Oh, what *does* a sacrifice constitute? When I decided to listen to you, I also decided to miss my plane and a very important meeting that cost me a great deal of time and effort to set up. And that has made the gift of this stone all the sweeter."

He kicked at one of the melting ice cubes and it spun away in swift pirouettes across the floor. "Look, Michael, I have another secret for you: I'm willing to gamble that your accepting my gift will be a first step toward your accepting my proposition. If you do, essentially you'll be releasing your precious objects for this one silk painting. Now *that's* a sacrifice worthy of the name, I'd say."

I turned back to the whirling brushstrokes of the painting that was now mine if I wanted it. I could simply roll it up, walk out the door, and add it to my collection. Or why not make a truly surprising sacrifice: first reject Preston's gift and *then* offer him my objects? Standing before the canvas, I was able to imagine that elusive, dancing figure as my own St. Vitus' Dance, suddenly arisen within to spin me away from every object I'd ever collected, to spin me away from the bric-a-brac of my life.

Extended Family

Up and down the block, one power mower after another roared a welcome to the beginning of spring, to the obligations of taming a lawn. Settled on my living room couch, I listened to the wavering intensity of each mower's back-and-forth growl. Before me on the coffee table sat Preston's catalog for his showing of my objects. I hadn't paged through it since the opening—an event so successful that almost nothing remained of my collection except a greatly enlarged bank account. But now those mowers outside sounded like an army of hungry creatures, and I found myself reaching for that glossy-paged, full-colored book, for what I already knew would be the last time, and I turned the pages to Preston's Introduction.

Virtually no object included in this catalog has any particular value in and of itself, yet each was once the center of a complex attachment, thereby accruing to itself a psychic patina, a glaze of significant drama that offers unique value for the collector.

There were pages and pages of this sort of prose, so I skipped ahead and stopped at the sight of an ordinary key chain. The color photo magnified the cheap plaster mold of a miniature bouquet and emphasized its one flaw: a dark orange petal, slightly chipped.

This object belonged to a woman who learned to drive a car so she could leave her husband, the text began, though this wasn't precisely true—at first she hadn't known what she'd end up doing. I could still see her surrounded by cartons of yard sale bargains in her front yard, watching me examine the key chain. Kate and I had just divorced, and that woman must have sensed my hidden rawness. Now remarried, she told a tale about an object she needed to let go. "But at one time," she'd said wistfully, "I thought if I lost this thing, I'd lose myself."

Her story, short enough and bluntly honest, often left me inventing my own details, beginning with the day she sat by the window of her apartment and listened to the steady whoosh of passing cars, an engine starting up on one of the side streets, the occasional car horn, or the squeal of tires. With eyes closed she imagined herself in a driver's seat, hurtling down avenues and weaving among reckless cabdrivers. But she never envisioned a destination in any of these private travels—the driving itself was the main pleasure.

When she decided to take lessons her husband mocked her: they lived in the city, he said, they'd never need a car, they couldn't afford one anyway. This time the familiarity of his arguments—yet another series of *nos*—made him strangely unfamiliar, and even as she nodded in habitual agreement she knew that she'd take the lessons anyway, behind his back.

Throughout those lessons she silently clung to words she shouldn't forget—ignition, clutch, accelerate—and each successful parallel parking, each left turn accomplished against traffic at an intersection must have become a secret declaration of her independence. She always drove with that key chain of small flowers hanging from the steering column, and as she followed the instructor's terse commands, those flowers gently swayed as if in the wind.

Though the woman never told me this, I'd always felt certain it must be true: when she came home from the Motor Vehicles Bureau after finally receiving her license, an odd emptiness blossomed inside her. With no car, what could this piece of paper offer her anyway? It was simply physical evidence supporting her husband's arguments, and all those lessons had been nothing more than a childish act of defiance. She hurled her key chain across the room, but when a piece snapped off, her anger broke too, transforming into regret. Picking up the key chain, the woman saw the chipped petal, the plaster interior revealed, and she tentatively scraped at it with a fingernail. A faint white cloud rose up. She sniffed the dusty dryness—the inside of this bouquet was as desiccated as her marriage. After scraping another wisp of plaster and watching it mingle with dust motes in the sunny air, she then—with surprisingly calm steps—approached the telephone. The receiver nestled against her chin, she flipped through the Yellow Pages for car rentals, already prepared to drive off into a new life.

The next object in the catalog was a car antenna with scratches down nearly the entire length of its silver surface to the jagged base. Preston had taken great pleasure in arranging the catalog's order of objects, making each one the segment of a larger story. "What we're offering is a Thousand and One Tchotchkes," he liked to joke.

The former owner of this antenna was a retired man who stood outside in rainstorms as often as possible, soaking one old business suit after another. He held this antenna high in the air, as if attuned to stations no one else could hear, always hoping that lightning might strike him.

Every thunderstorm his family searched for him, driving down side streets or along the edges of fields, and whenever they found him his two teenage grandsons had to chase him down. Despite the family's increasing precautions, he almost always managed to slip outside in any downpour, patiently waiting for his great moment. He was never struck, though once a tree only yards away was split into two giant slices by a sudden bolt. This near miss embittered him, and soon after he developed pneumonia and swiftly passed away.

There the catalog entry ended, though again there was more to this man's story than I'd revealed. After he died, his family found a newspaper clipping in his desk drawer, a daily science feature reporting that when lightning strikes a person, the victim's clothes are almost always torn off from the blast. Perhaps he hadn't sought only death but some sort of unmasking—the business suit he always wore in the rain exemplified a life of deals and payoffs that he wanted blasted away. But though he often stood only a moment away from a terrible flash, redemption proved elusive, as if his desire had created a magnetic field that repulsed its satisfaction.

A few glossy pages ahead was a dark green plastic figure that I'd found in a box brimming with old toy soldiers—a pioneer pointing his rifle at some unseen threat. His shoulders were hunched in concentration, the tail of his coonskin cap dangled down his back to a crossways slash that had nearly cut him in two, twisting him enough so that he couldn't balance on the flat, undamaged base. Another cut had nicked off a tip of his cap.

This plastic pioneer belonged to a young boy who owned many such soldiers: gladiators, Revolutionary War combatants, the Civil War's Blue and Gray, medieval knights, the doomed defenders of the Alamo. But this pioneer had been his particular favorite. So no one understood why the young man threw the figure into the front lawn one day and then, for the first time in his life without being cajoled, pulled the mower out of the garage and cut patient swaths through the grass.

But I suspected the reason. The wiry little man who'd sold me the figure was the father of that boy, now grown and living far from home. "He should have chopped up the rest of them," the fellow laughed. "He was nearly in high school, much too old to be playing with toys." As the man voiced his approval of the way school bullies had teased his boy out of a bad habit, I'd barely listened, wondering instead what liberating battles that son had fought with his soldiers, what inner violence he'd organized into play.

Finally, I lingered over the last photo: a silver serving plate, its surface embossed with flowery filigree much like an Oriental rug that Kate had drawn so long ago. That's why I'd stared at it so closely as it gleamed in the afternoon sun beside the yard sale cash box.

This serving plate once belonged to a sleepwalker, an elderly woman living with her son's family near the end of her life. Though once a devoted and accomplished cook, she was barely able to make a pot of tea. But at night, in a dream-like state, she set places for her family in the dining room. This silver plate was always in the middle of the table,

*always empty and yet, in her eyes, filled with never-to-be-forgotten del-
icacies she tried to serve to invisible guests until her son or daughter-
in-law led her back to her bedroom.*

As with all the other objects in this catalog, there was more to this
story than I'd admitted: one night, the family decided to attend one
of those midnight feasts. Three generations sat together, passing out
portions that weren't there from the serving plate, praising the grandmother's descriptions of what they ate. They all willingly entered her
dream, and she sat at the head of the table, transfixed with pleasure.

I closed the book and thought of some of the other people inside:
the woman who let her teakettle howl its shrill whistle whenever her
husband was late for work; the girl who filled the drawers of her toy
cash register with shredded photos of her prettier cousins; the man
who, continually afraid of losing his place, kept a bookmark in everything, even the television guide. They had once been my own extended
family, passing another sort of sustenance along a secret table.

I returned to Preston's Introduction, to the sentence he'd included despite my initial protests: *Those collectors who wish to purchase one of these objects should be aware of its potential as well as its
past. For who is to say that one of your own stories won't someday at-
tach itself to your new possession?*

My collection belonged to others now. Extended family or not, it
was finally time for me to let go of them and the remaining secrets of
their stories, just as I'd let go of my father, my brother, my sister. I
hadn't seen the Zombie Twins since my wedding day, couldn't bear
the thought of visiting them, and wherever Laurie might be, she no
longer sent postcards. As for Kate, Kate was only a husk in my heart.

I set aside the catalog and gazed outside: no mowers in sight, yet
still that restless keening continued. A jaunt through the peace of a
nearby park was what I needed. I passed through the foyer, pausing
at the hutch and what few objects I'd held back from Preston, and I
found my gaze lingering on that tape recorder with its fateful tape.
Shaking my head, I vowed to throw it out when I returned, along
with the rest. Then I picked up the afternoon newspaper from the
lawn and decided to bring it along, hoping it would distract me from
the urge to read the shadows of the surrounding trees at the park. I'd
simply settle on a bench, read about the dramas of others for a while,
and forget my own.

PART SIX

Pricey

Where is the voice that will speak to me now? I thought, straining to catch something of the disembodied conversations brimming about the diner. With my eyes still closed, all that interlocking speech became a single echoing voice, a voice that rushed along without a breath, reminding me of an auction caller's urgent tumbling sales-pitch and that caller was somehow speaking only to me but I couldn't quite catch the words, couldn't decipher what I should bid on.

Then I heard Sylvia swirling her spoon around the rim of a bowl, and I looked at her across the booth. Finishing off her rice pudding and enmeshed in her own thoughts, she hadn't noticed my brief retreat. But now, as she once again regarded me skeptically, I could see that I'd become just another unpredictable weather pattern. Perhaps this was true, since I found myself saying, even though I'd promised myself I'd never go to another one again, "When we're done here, how about coming with me to an auction?" If this woman was going to judge me, I thought, then there was far more of my life that she needed to see.

Sylvia contemplated the remains of her dessert. She gathered one last sweet spoonful of pudding, lifted it to her lips.

"You never know what you'll find at an auction—" I began.

"Sure, why not?" she said with a hint of wonder in her voice, as if that question was for her, not me.

At the cash register we picked up the local paper, and Sylvia searched through the classifieds for auction announcements. "Ah, here's one that's about to start. A farm estate sale. Sounds a tad dull."

"Not necessarily. Usually friends and neighbors show up with their eyes on something special. Where is the big show, anyway?"

"At something called The Auction Barn."

"Good—that's just a hop away," I said, marveling that I was actually about to reveal a secret pleasure that I'd never shown to Kate.

We took my car and headed north through long, sloping fields, quiet together until Sylvia, her dark hair swirling in the breeze from an open window, asked, "So, do you go to this sort of thing often?"

"Used to. And yard sales, too. But not these days. . . . I've tried to give it up, actually."

"Give it up? So this little adventure is a . . . relapse?"

I laughed. "Watch out, I might be contagious."

The parking lot was nearly full, and looming ahead of us was a huge building shaped like an airplane hangar. At the door we picked up bidding cards, and already we could hear the corrugated metal walls echoing with the caller's racing nasal chant: "Whatd'we have here—waterpump, FIVEdollarbillFIVEdollarbill. It'sBRASSit'sBRASS fivedollarbillgoingupgoingupgoinguptoSIX." He paused, then muttered into the microphone, "C'mon, ladies and gentlemen, we're *selling*, not renting."

At the sound of those cheerless words I said, "My God, the auctioneer's Jack Newly. I can't believe he's still at it."

"You know his name?" Sylvia whistled. "You really *have* spent some time at this."

We made our way among farmers wearing seed company caps, and weary-eyed, white-haired women; a wiry tough guy, biceps blossoming with tattoos beside a stony-faced girl, too young to be the mother of the baby in her arms; and cigarette and cigar smokers everywhere. This was a crowd of neighbors who knew the objects Jack called out, knew if any stories hid behind a pair of hammers, or a yellow hen tea cozy, a tire iron, a ceramic decanter in the shape of a tasseled Shriner's hat, a box of Christmas decorations, or whatever else was up for sale. If there *was* a story to be found, I wanted Sylvia to hear it too.

Jack kept rattling on at the back of a pickup truck that was parked about a third of the way down a tunnel of two long tables. "Whatarewelookingat, what'rewelookingat? TENdollarbill, TEN dollarbill. GoinguptoFIFTEEN—FIFTEEN. What'rewelookingat now, nowwhat'rewelookingat? Needalittlemorethere, morethere. TWENTYthat'sbetterTWENTYthat'sbetterthat'sbettermuch betterindeed. TWENTYFIVEthat'stheway, that'sjustthewaywe likeit, sowhatarewelookingatnow? If we had better light in here, it'd sell for *twice* that price."

Everyone about us affected boredom. Occasionally a numbered yellow card flipped up here and there. "If you show interest," I whispered to Sylvia, "the value of what you want goes up."

Sylvia laughed. "Giving yourself away is always pricey."

"Oh, there's always someone at an auction like this who can't keep a secret," I said. "If you examine something on one of the display tables long enough, you never know who'll end up telling you something about—"

"Wait a minute. You mean those knick-knacks of yours have—"

"Stories." There—I'd given myself away.

Sylvia spread her fingers through her hair and whistled a second time, just as Jack finished with a section of goods. He signaled to the driver and the truck inched along between the line of tables, the bidders following.

"C'mon," I said, and Sylvia and I walked ahead of the crowd and past the truck, to see what would be offered later. We passed an ancient food processor, a collection of car cables, two or three shovels, a sewing kit. I paused at a little plaster posse of eight identical John Wayne statues. Why so many? Then I noticed that one of the figures had been glued back together from four, maybe five pieces. I picked it up, examined the imperfectly painted-over cracks.

Across the table, a gaunt little man with a wispy flare of white hair took in my interest. I placed the broken John Wayne back down among his companions, picked up one more and waited. Careful, careful, I thought, a story might be on the way.

"You a fan of the Duke?" he asked.

I looked up at the old man's cautious smile that couldn't hide a hunger to speak. "Oh, just enough to maybe buy one," I said casually.

The man chuckled. "Not like old Tim. *He* had one for every room in the house."

"Every room?" I replied, my curiosity undisguised.

"I tell you, in his dreams he was John Wayne. Hey, you could probably buy the whole bunch for nothing. They're in good condition, except for that one—"

"I noticed," I said quietly. "Clumsy grandchild?"

"Nope. Tim himself. Threw it across the room, I've heard." He paused. "I don't mean to run the man down, you understand. Tim was the gentlest fellow you'd ever want to meet."

I regarded the broken figure on the table. "Well, I guess everybody's entitled to a lapse."

"That's the truth," the man sighed.

Now was not the time to say anything, not if I wanted that hidden story, and Sylvia seemed to understand this—she quietly moved a few steps away and examined an eggbeater, giving the two of us a little circle of privacy. I turned that statue over in my hand and waited for this man to restore the reputation of his neighbor.

"It's a sorry story, really," he finally said.

I met his eyes and nodded encouragement.

"You remember that Academy Awards when the Duke was dying of cancer?"

"Yeah," I said after a moment. "Barely looked like himself, if I remember—"

"Tim about cried at the sight. One of his daughters, the lippy one that went bad, saw him on the verge and said something sassy. He grabbed the nearest statue and threw it at her. Missed and hit the fireplace. At least, that's what his wife told mine."

The old man looked away, surprised, perhaps, that he'd spoken this much, and with an embarrassed nod to me he walked off.

Sylvia stepped back and whispered, "So you're going to bid for that broken one, aren't you?"

"Well, I'm not really collecting—"

"John Wayne. I know. You just want the statue as a souvenir of that story the old guy told you. An interesting hobby. How come?"

"Oh," I said cautiously, still not certain that Sylvia understood, "I used to think that objects like these, objects that came with stories, could be a kind of medicine."

"Horoscopes, medicinal knick-knacks—you keep getting more and more complicated."

"Well, thank you, I think." I looked over at the caller's pinched face, the semicircle of bidders around him, and I began to believe that my intuition to attend this auction might bear surprising fruit. "This is the first auction you've ever been to?"

"The very."

"So, bid for something," I said. "Anything at all. But bid to win."

Sylvia held up a green-tinted glass bottle and examined its dull sheen. "I haven't seen anything I like yet."

"Then let's keep looking."

We poked among the remaining offerings until Sylvia stopped at a cardboard box of toiletries and lifted out a cut-crystal atomizer. A long black tassel dangled from the pump, and she flicked at it with a finger. "My mother had something like this. I used to love watching her when she'd spray behind her ears. She'd get this goofy, happy look on her face, like she'd made it to heaven. . . ."

Sylvia pulled back her hair and pumped a little whisper of air from the atomizer, then paused. "What do you know," she said, shaking her head, amazed. "I just gave this thing a story, didn't I?"

"Not a bad one at all," I said, and looked down the length of table. "I'd guess we have a few minutes before Jack gets to this. Let's go see what he's up to."

Back at the pickup truck, Jack pointed to the shiny scoop of a metal scale. "HaveyouWEIGHEDyourbabytoday, weighedyourbaby weighedyourbabytoday? FIVEdollarfivedollar, fivedollarfivedollar, doIhearFIVEdollar? WAKE UP, people, you all weren't up *that* late last night."

A hand went up, then another, though the final bid closed at only nine dollars. Even at rest Jack's face tensed, eyebrows pressed close to his eyes. "*Every* hand should have been up in the air on that one."

Sylvia turned to me. "Is he joking?"

"Hear anyone laughing?"

"Nope. Mum's the word, apparently. So what's with him?"

"I've never quite figured out Jack. It might simply be a tactic to make people feel they're getting bargains, but I think his attitude actually tamps down the prices he's trying to raise."

Soon one of Jack's helpers was holding the atomizer up high.

"That'scutcrystalcutcrystalcutCRYSTAL, whatdoIhear? Bid'em atFOURbid'ematFOURbid'ematFOUR, FIVEoverthere, Iseeyou, FIVE."

Sylvia raised her card twice, warding off the interest of a stout woman in a flowery dress. When the bidding hit seven dollars the woman dropped out.

"OnlysevenonlysevenonlySEVEN?" Jack glanced over the crowd, then scowled at Sylvia as if he wanted her to bid against herself. "SOLD at seven dollars." He turned to the young woman recording the sales, his voice just audible as he said, "Mark that cheap."

One of the assistants brought the atomizer over, and Sylvia turned it and watched the crystal design catch the light.

"It's pretty," I said.

"Mmmm," she murmured flatly.

"Hey, how do you feel?"

"Well, to be honest, a little stained."

"You're right. Jack can take the pleasure out of an auction." When the John Waynes were offered, I picked them up as a single lot, for eight dollars and another of Jack's cracks. "Step right up folks, we're giving it all away here," he said, and I was glad he did, because I realized that Jack—poor, bitter Jack—had something of value to offer Sylvia.

"He goes after everyone, doesn't he?" Sylvia said.

"I think if Jack has an idea in his head about what something is worth, he gets annoyed if the bids don't match." Then, as casually as possible, I added, "Maybe he has this thing about . . . precise measurements."

"Precise measurements," Sylvia repeated. She watched Jack's gloomy face as he started the bidding on a tea cozy, and then she turned to me with a quizzical smile on her face that slowly widened. "So if this Jack fellow worried less about, say, the exact temperature or barometric pressure for tomorrow, then everyone would be having a much better time at the auction."

"Well, you're being a little too hard on old Jack. . . ."

"No, I think you're right. Jack needs to loosen up."

She picked out my sad little John Wayne statue in the box—his shoulder chipped and waist awkwardly glued in place—and sprayed air behind his ears with the atomizer. Then she pumped a ticklish breeze behind my ears too.

"Hmmm, nice," I murmured. "You know, I'm feeling lucky today. Let me in on another problem."

Sylvia stared off at the crowds milling about the tables, and when she turned her face back to me, I could see that odds had already been calculated, the same sort of terrible arithmetic I'd encountered when I first met Kate.

"Oh, I have a big problem. In this case, I *really* need to be saved," Sylvia said, her words strained and barely audible. She pulled at her turquoise ring, slid it down to the knuckle to show me what it hid: a much thinner, pale band of skin, certainly made by a wedding ring.

A False Road

As we drove from the auction those wooden John Waynes rattled in their box on the backseat, echoing the subtle struggles crossing Sylvia's face. She stared down at that turquoise ring and her hands clutching each other on her lap, and I kept trying to believe that this woman I'd pursued wasn't yet another of my mistakes.

"Yes, I *was* deceptive," Sylvia said, answering my unspoken accusation. "But I've been fooling myself too, trying to pretend I'm not married."

Pretending. "But you *are* married," I replied, my words clipped, harsh.

Sylvia grimaced, then rested a hand lightly on my arm. "Look, Michael, you just bid for that statue because you liked its story. Well, wouldn't you like to hear mine?"

Shamed, I nodded in agreement, then turned onto the entrance ramp for the highway. Easing into the swift passage of traffic, I waited for Sylvia's story.

We drove a few miles in silence before she finally began, with a weary shake of her head. "I've been floundering for months, for an escape. In all sorts of crazy ways. Last weekend I cranked up an old Stones song—'Gimme Shelter'?—and blasted it out the window. Y'know why? There's this moment when a backup singer takes up the melody and her voice just *breaks*, it actually seems to split in two, and I feel like something inside *me* is splitting too. So I played the damn song over and over, hoping somebody, *anybody* passing by would see me in the window and know right away that cracked voice was me."

I imagined Sylvia's sad face peering out through a screen window, the tight wire mesh like pixels on a television screen. Again my face was pressed close to her image during that weather broadcast, with little shocks of static electricity surging across my skin, and I almost forgot to turn off the highway for the exit back to the diner.

"Anyway," Sylvia said, "my little scheme never worked—not one taker."

She picked up the atomizer, idly fingered its tassel, and I thought she was about to lean over and once again lightly brush my face with air. But we merely passed a few more stands of trees, then the first strip mall, while she waited for me to speak.

"So, your husband, he . . ." I offered tentatively, afraid to hear the answer to this question I felt I had to ask.

"He works for a map company. He's off on a field survey now, checking the accuracy of a new map. His favorite part of the job, though, is working in the office, making trap streets."

"Trap streets?"

She nodded, her eyes keen with distaste. "Mapmaking is pretty competitive—what isn't, I suppose. Sometimes rival companies copy each other's maps but don't give credit, so they don't have to pay any royalties. That's why Richard adds a false road, maybe two, on each map."

"What's that?"

"A street that doesn't exist. If it appears on a pirated map, then there's clear proof of copyright infringement. That's the trap." Sylvia leaned back against the head rest and laughed a bitter laugh. "I'm married to a man who makes trap streets! And am I ever—"

"Wait a minute," I said, unhappy with the finality of *trap*, the constriction of its single syllable. "Didn't you call them something else, what was it . . . ?"

"False roads."

Yes, I thought with relief, as if I'd just discovered a hidden exit from my own troubles.

"Maybe that's a better description. You know, you took a wrong turn somewhere."

The diner was just ahead. I pulled into the nearly empty lot and parked besides Sylvia's car, too soon, too soon. With the engine idling, I turned to her and we exchanged wary glances. Sylvia closed her eyes for a brief moment, waiting, perhaps, for words she didn't want to hear me say. Then she opened the car door and a breeze gusted through her hair, unpredictable patterns of wind casting delicate strands across her features, turning her expectant face into a shifting map.

"*Wait*," I said, simply unwilling to imagine us driving away to separate destinations, and I brushed those weaving tendrils from her forehead, her cheeks, her eyes.

We straddled the wet spot on my bedsheets until Sylvia murmured, "I predict moisture levels, so why not lie on one?" She inched closer and pressed herself against me, whispering, "This time it's your turn to talk."

She clasped my hand, pulled at a finger until a knuckle popped, and I found myself confessing that secret knot I'd formed with my brother and sister in the face of our mother's performances. Sylvia tugged again, more urgently with each finger, setting free story after story: my mother's terrible, giddy escapade on the roof; her collapse among the clattering pins in the bowling alley; our reflection in her eyes as she lay on the lawn.

Sylvia listened in silence, her mouth a grim line, her eyes filled with a strange recognition. "Oh Michael, such a childhood!" she finally said. "If only I could give you mine. *My* parents played parts too, but I think you would have loved them. Every reaction had to be operatic. If Mom burnt the toast, it was a forest fire. For my dad, finding a lucky penny was like breaking into Fort Knox. I remember when I learned how to tie my shoes, they acted as if I was suddenly miraculously fluent in Sanskrit. But they *enjoyed* their acting, enjoyed it so much that I did too—each day was a kind of show." She paused. "I miss them."

"Sylvia? Do you mean—"

"A car crash. With a truck on some stupid icy road."

"I'm sorry, I—"

"Oh, it was a while ago, when I was away at college. It's taken me a long time to appreciate the irony of such a melodramatic exit, because sometimes . . . sometimes I wonder if it really *was* the icy road that caused the crash, or if they were in the middle of one of their B-movie scenes and . . . Anyway, I'll never know, will I?" She smiled a sad, brittle smile and sighed. "If only they'd been around on my awful wedding day, they would have gotten me away from Richard."

"Your wedding day?" I repeated, my voice the frailest echo of itself.

"Uh-huh. I should've gotten to this part sooner, but it's not something I like to talk about."

I couldn't reply, still shocked by her words.

"We'd just cut the cake," Sylvia finally began. "Richard's uncle was making a speech—a lot of bull about the age-old roles of husband and wife that I only half-listened to. But then he said, 'You're going to share a lifetime of meals, so when you feed your wife now you let her know who's boss.' Richard's family laughed, though *I* didn't see what was so funny. As for my groom, he kept flicking his fork back and forth a little nervously. What's going *on*, I thought, and then he speared a piece of cake for me.

"Well, when I opened my mouth he shoved that fork in so hard the tines scraped the roof of my mouth. I nearly gagged. But stupidly enough, all I could think was, Don't throw up, don't throw up the wedding cake, and somehow I managed to choke it down with the taste of my own blood. Then I managed to smile as if nothing had happened, and everyone applauded, and this man who'd just shown me he was the boss kissed me. I felt like I'd been raped in front of the entire wedding party."

I groaned at Sylvia's words, squeezed her hand as if to wring out her humiliation, but then I was far from her, standing on a dais with Kate, champagne glasses tinkling all about us. Kate flinched as I searched her eyes, and now I understood she must have felt violated by her own husband before all our guests. "My God," I heard my distant voice asking Sylvia, a voice racked with sadness, "what did you do?"

She let out a long, slow breath. "We danced. Richard threw my garter belt to the bachelors, I threw the bouquet to the girls. Then we left in the car for the hotel and I worked up enough shouting and crying to fog up the windows—a scene worthy of my histrionic parents, let me tell you—and Richard kept insisting he hadn't meant to hurt me, that he'd just slipped. I wanted to believe him. When we first met, he was trying to resist his family's tough guy ideal—they're such a cheerless, traditional bunch—and I guess, oh, I *know* I was attracted to his struggle. I missed my parents' melodramas."

Sylvia lay back on the sheets and stared up at the blank white ceiling. "By now Richard's perfected the art of bullying. He can make even an innocent phrase sound sinister. And when we're having an argument and really going at it, he makes this little gesture, this little offhand *flick*. Maybe it's unconscious, maybe it's not, I can't tell, but it reminds me of the way he shook that fork. Then I can't help myself, I just have to give in. And I hate myself for it. I want to leave him, but I'm afraid of what he'll do if I try."

I leaned over Sylvia. Her dark eyes were so filled with uncertainty that, although her strained face and marvelous hair were framed only by the white landscape of my bedsheets, once again I could see her on the TV screen, surrounded by flashing weather maps and longing for precise measurements, longing for *any* possible antidote to the terrors of ambiguity.

I reached out to stroke Sylvia's hair. But she held my hand and once again tugged at my fingers, and now I told her more stories: of my father's stony facade and the unexpected tenderness in his voice when he fired me; his battles with Laurie; my courtship of Kate. Then, unable to face Sylvia, I finally confessed my own terrible wedding day.

When I finished Sylvia lay quietly beside me, offering no comment, and I had to break the silence. "I *know* I should have protected her better, I know," I said, unable to face Sylvia, "but all I wanted was intimacy, really, that's all."

Her hand reached out again for mine, and she whispered, "That's what she should have given you, Michael. Right from the start." Then Sylvia touched her lips to mine, a delicate, healing kiss that we extended up and down our bodies until our skin fairly hummed above the moist sheets.

*   *   *

We met whenever we could in the next week, odd brief moments that wouldn't arouse suspicion now that Richard was back from his trip. And when we couldn't meet, Sylvia's weather reports served as a secret substitute: knowing I was home and watching her, she added a new feature offering a nightly tidbit of meteorology for her audience that was also a sexy little aside for me. With her face in giddy close-up she explained how water vapor in high-flying clouds can sometimes turn to ice and fall from its own weight, its chill melting into rain before hitting the ground; how air pressure is caused by the bouncing of uncountable molecules, creating "a microscopic tingling against our bodies"; how clouds warm up the night as they absorb and give off infrared energy, acting "a bit like an electric blanket."

I became an aficionado of innuendo, of Sylvia's growing confidence before the camera. And then one evening she stood with a sly smile before a new display of color graphics: a flutter of tiny wings in one corner of the screen rippling into a bank of cumulus clouds, which then swirled into a tornado that suddenly dissipated into clear skies and a goofy, grinning sun. With a flourish of her pointer, Sylvia announced, "Tonight I'm beginning a new feature for the weather report: Sylvia's Mea Culpa Corner."

The camera drew closer and Sylvia paused solemnly, taking us all in. "I'm sure you're more than aware that we had scattered showers throughout the region this morning, then two straight hours of rain in the afternoon with lots of lightning. Perhaps some of you remember that last night I predicted sunny weather. Was I wrong! I was wrong about the temperature too—off by eight degrees. And the rain completely blew my humidity count. So I'd like to apologize to anyone caught without an umbrella, to any family that had a picnic spoiled, to anyone whose morning paper got soaked on the porch, *even to anyone who kept the windows open thinking it wouldn't rain.* Mea, mea culpa! Unfortunately, there's really not much any meteorologist can do about it. Let me tell you about the Butterfly Effect. . . ."

While Sylvia began her description of chaos theory for the viewing audience, the curve of the globe behind her was covered with a black-and-white satellite picture of thick clouds spanning four state lines. She snapped her fingers and those weather patterns began gliding across the continental United States and Canada, then flipped back to the beginning and kept repeating at unlikely intervals as if affected by Sylvia's words. That same dizziness I'd felt when I'd first watched her forecast returned, not because of the computer graphics but because Sylvia had found her solution, asking forgiveness for mistakes large and small. I felt certain that at this very moment her viewers across our small city were gladly granting her absolution.

Her eyes peacefully radiant, Sylvia turned and waved her pointer at the clouds like a wand and the sky cleared, presaging sunny days from now on, rain arriving only at welcome intervals. "Even though I try to look authoritative in front of all these satellite weather films, I still goof up. So tomorrow, I'm going to tell you just how well tonight's prediction went." She paused, the camera moving in as she said, "On Friday, I'm going to give you my win-loss percentages for the week. I challenge my competition to do the same." Then Sylvia rattled off the numbers for the next day with a modest authority that somehow redeemed all the limitations of her predictive powers.

Sylvia's ratings rose high enough for her to be featured in the local paper and a radio call-in show, and then she quickly received invitations to give speeches at the Elks and Rotary Clubs, high school science classes and the Women's Business Council, the Masons and even the Mood Disorder Association. At the same time she began to suffer from a recurring dream, a dream she tried without success to laugh away when she told me: she stood beside Richard, sometimes on a windy boardwalk, or on a long line in an enormous bakery, once even in a nearly empty church, and he was caressing her shoulder gently, so gently, until his touch turned into a sharp ache like the stab of a fork.

This dream began to insinuate itself into Sylvia's weather report, and once again a hint of doubt colored her voice when she announced barometric pressures, her four-day forecast. One evening I watched her face grow increasingly strained while she predicted an ordinary, partly cloudy day, as if she couldn't bring herself to warn the audience of some terrible, approaching storm. "What's the matter?" I asked her image on the screen, and I paced before my television, anxious for the news to end so I could call her at the station.

When I finally reached for the phone it rang at the touch of my fingertips, and I lifted the receiver to Sylvia's breathless tumble of words. "Michael, that dream, I had that dream again last night, but this time it woke me up and my skin was tingling right at the spot where Richard touched me in the dream, like he really *had* been working at my shoulder while I was asleep. But he was just lying there in the dark, just sleeping, or maybe he was only pretending, because—"

"Wait, slow down. Do you mean—"

"I swear he really touched me, he must have, it felt so—"

"Was there any mark?" I asked, unable to hide a tremble in my voice.

"I, I didn't think to check. I just lay there, I was afraid to let him know I'd woken up, and then the tingling faded away. Maybe I'm making too much of nothing," she moaned. "But maybe, Michael, maybe that's what he wants me to think."

We both fell silent, reluctant to confront that possibility until I said, "Sylvia, if you think he could hurt you, you have to be very careful—"

"Michael," she cut in, "I'm sorry, but I just can't talk any more. I'm going to that new mall and Richard wants to come along. He's meeting me at the station and he'll be here any minute. I'll call you tomorrow, okay?"

"Okay," I replied to the dial tone buzz, and before replacing the receiver I decided to drive to the mall ahead of them. Whatever Richard was up to, the effect on Sylvia was clear: she'd become somehow less than herself, her spirit diminished. I simply had to see them together to judge, if I could, just what else he might be capable of doing.

I worried the gas pedal through the evening traffic and even sped past the occasional rumbling truck. In minutes I sat at a pizza concession at the corner of the mall's huge main thoroughfare, aptly dubbed The Sprawl. My back to the passing crowds, I stared at a wall mirror and hoped that Sylvia and Richard would pass by, so I could catch sight of them without their discovering my spying.

Nursing a diet Coke and slowly cooling calzone, I did my best to

take in the throngs of shoppers, but I might have missed Sylvia if I
hadn't heard a burst of her full-throated laughter. Yet it was tinged
with falsity, and her sleek image passed across the mirror too quickly
for me to get more than a glimpse of the short and wiry man beside
her. I eased from my booth and followed, unable to discover much of
anything about Richard by watching the back of his head, the sheen
of his dark hair.

Then the crowds thinned at a corner and I had to keep my distance as I watched Richard reach for Sylvia's hand again and again,
tugging her away from this storefront window or that, his movements taut with barely contained intensity. I drew closer when he
tried pulling Sylvia from a shoe store display and she broke from his
clasp. He yanked at her even harder, and then their angry faces were
inches from each other. I waited for Richard to make that flicking
gesture that so undid his wife, but too many people passed between
us—a clutch of hard-eyed teenage girls, a weary couple pushing at a
stroller, an array of boys with baseball caps on backward—and then,
moments later, Richard and Sylvia continued along too, the argument apparently having been decided in his favor.

They approached a video arcade. Just outside the entrance a
crowd circled a demonstration of a virtual reality game: six or seven
people stood in their own railed-in pods, harnessed to wired gloves, a
helmet with opaque goggles, a futuristic gun connected to various
tubes. I lingered behind a snack shop's canisters of caramel popcorn
while Sylvia and Richard watched those oddly bedecked warriors
squirm and twitch and aim their weapons at invisible targets. Then,
after a brief conference, Richard stood in line for the game, and
Sylvia walked off to a nearby fashion outlet well within her husband's range of vision. I watched him take in her slow, careful weaving among the racks of dresses and skirts.

Soon enough two teenage attendants fit Richard with the game's
unwieldy paraphernalia. Once those dark goggles were in place he
began twitching as he aimed the gun, and his compact body
hunched and dodged and sidestepped enemies only he could see. He
pointed here, he pointed there at only the air, clicking the trigger
again and again, and as Sylvia returned with a shopping bag in tow
he swiveled and aimed that space-age gun directly at her. Though it
was only for a brief moment, and though I was sure he couldn't pos-

sibly see her, Sylvia dropped her bag and stood transfixed, in the line of fire and unable to run. Her face distorted with a terror that I instantly understood and felt run through me: Richard was somehow stalking her in that strange virtual world.

The following morning I parked five doors down the street from Sylvia's home, a small colonial bounded by neat evergreen shrubs, its bright blue shingles gleaming and strangely heightened in the early summer sun. I'd seen enough last night to convince me that Richard had something terrible coiled inside him, and I unwrapped a sticky bran muffin and settled back in the front seat, prepared to track my lover's husband. Inside my shirt pocket nestled the hollow, quiet presence of a gift shop trinket I'd bought at the mall for this occasion: a scallop shell, both sides glued together and painted a glossy black. It had no story, but somehow I knew I had to give this to Richard, imagining that when he held it this shell would reflect back a dark, distorted version of his face.

The front door opened and Richard sauntered down the brick steps in his slippers for the newspaper. Idly slapping the morning edition against his hips, he then turned back to the house. What was their breakfast like inside, I wondered—did they sit across the kitchen table from each other, steam rising from their coffee cups, with Sylvia still cowed by the memory of the sweep of his aim last night, and did Richard take in her quiet, wary face as if he still had her in his sights?

Before long the garage door opened and Richard backed a blue sports car down the driveway and pulled away from the curb. I waited until he nearly turned the corner before following and kept a car or two behind, just as I'd seen in countless TV dramas, yet each time I pressed the accelerator or flipped a turn signal, I felt that if I wasn't traveling on my own false road, then I was far off any map I'd ever imagined for myself.

I'd assumed Richard was heading for work, but he skirted downtown and instead drove along a road lined with strip malls and fast food franchises. After much start-and-stop traffic he pulled into the parking lot of the very mall he and Sylvia had visited the night before, and I knew he'd returned for another try at that virtual reality game.

I cruised slowly, one lane away, until he finally parked his car. My engine idling, I watched him make his way to the mall entrance, and when the glass doors closed I continued down the lane, still not sure how to approach him, or if I should even try. As I neared Richard's parked car, saw the rear lights and trunk framed by my windshield, I imagined I faced my own video screen, not merely following him but actually chasing him, about to smash into his car as he tried to escape. Suddenly my foot pressed on the gas pedal, and with a terrible there's-no-turning-back twist of my arms I turned the wheel sharply to the left and my car tore into his, my bumper shattering the brake lights.

Red plastic shards spun wildly into the air. My hands shook so much they thrummed against the steering wheel as I remembered in quick succession Mother slamming the broken glass into a cantaloupe, Laurie flinging the inkwell at a mirror. Was *this* the secret place where I'd been heading? Somehow I managed to put the car in reverse, and in the rearview mirror I saw a white-haired woman, her hand waving like a flag in distress. She'd seen everything, witnessed the violence I'd discovered within me. With a sleepwalker's muted energy, I waved back, pointed to a nearby parking space and eased in.

Stepping from the car, I turned to the woman approaching me and exclaimed, "Can't understand it! The engine just revved up and took off—it's never, *never* done that before." And this lie slipped from me so suddenly that I surely did appear shaken, for the woman nodded, seemingly convinced.

Emboldened, I continued, "I feel so bad about this," and then stopped: I couldn't possibly let anyone else know what I'd just done. Quickly I added, "But I've got to, got to . . . rush home. So I'll just leave my name and address here on the dashboard. Could I borrow a piece of paper, a pen?"

Still silent, she nodded again, this time with less enthusiasm, as if she already suspected that I was about to write down anything that came into my head. Yet she drew what I needed from her purse.

"Thanks," I said, affecting gratitude, and I leaned against the hood of Richard's trunk, wishing this woman who hovered too close to me would finally say something. Distracted, I scribbled away with nervous energy and then stared in horror at the notepad: out of habit I'd written "Michael Kirby," and the beginnings of my real address.

But then, with an eerie calmness, I thought, Why not use this to my advantage?

"Here," I said, turning to my skeptical witness, "why don't you make sure all this is correct?"

"I'd be glad to," she replied, her voice surprisingly firm. She compared my note and driver's license carefully for any subtle discrepancy. Her small, delicate hands softly worked at the paper, and then I knew she wanted to believe me.

"I'd appreciate it," I said, adding a worried twinge in my voice, "if you'd leave your name and address too. You never know, this person might try to claim more damages than we got here."

Her last suspicions withered away with these words. She took back her pen and through the invisible armor of my successfully feigned innocence I watched the pale lips of her pinched mouth, the slight flare of nostrils as she worked out a spidery handwriting. Yet she also seemed utterly far away—I imagined that if I reached out to touch her, my arm would have to stretch for miles. Was this oddly intimate distance what my mother and Laurie had grown addicted to?

The woman's small script filled up the bottom of the page so slowly that I was afraid Richard might return before she finished. My eyes were on the mall entrance when she finally handed me the note paper. "If more people were like you," she said sadly, "the newspaper would be such a bore to read."

I'd actually disappointed her! Without waiting for a reply, she turned and walked off to the mall, and I crumpled the incriminating list and stuffed it into my pocket.

Then I examined Richard's damaged car with my practiced eye: this minor accident wouldn't top the usual deductible. He'd have to pay for all the repair work, a small enough price for the fear he'd instilled in Sylvia. I jangled the keys in my pocket and considered making a long jagged scar down the length of his car, a little road he wouldn't find on any map.

A strange tickling at the back of my neck made me glance up at Richard returning from his little game, a few cars away and his eyes already on me. I wanted to kick at the red plastic pieces on the ground, anything—why had I lingered here? Now it was too late to slip away. If only I could become someone else, and then that eerie sense of intimate isolation took hold again. With secret deliberation I shook my head in disbelief at the shattered rear light, and as Richard drew near I asked, "Excuse me, are you the owner of this car?"

Scowling at the damage, Richard muttered, "What next what next what *next?*" He kicked at the broken pieces and I cringed inside at this echo of my own impulse.

"Well, I saw the whole thing," I offered, trying to calm him. "By the way, my name's Tommy Gibbons."

Richard's hand reached out and slipped through the air like a blade, and I pulled back, then recovered. The faintest twitch of amusement crossed his lips, and I felt Sylvia's dread run through me. It was gone at once, and we shook hands.

"I got a pretty good look at the car that backed into you," I announced with a hint of a drawl. Surprised at this folksy touch to my voice, I kept talking, afraid to lose it. "A little red Chevy compact. I got some of the license plate, but not all of it, I'm sorry to tell you. G 56, and then after that maybe an 11, or a 17."

"Thank you," Richard replied curtly, "thanks for all your trouble, really."

"Or it could have been a 77," I continued, warming to my character's single-mindedness. "Or a 71, now that I think on it. I'll guess the police know to figure out the combinations."

"That's okay, I'm sure my insurance will take care of this," he mumbled with a dismissive glance. He took his keys out, ready to leave.

I wasn't going to let him do that, not yet. "You're right," I said, stalling, "small bad luck is no bad luck at all."

Richard tried to slip past me to the car door, but I ignored his impatience. "That reminds me of my . . . my Uncle Henry. He knew all about bad luck."

Richard sighed—he was going to have to hear this odd bird out. "How so?"

"All because of . . . a little shell a man gave him."

"A shell," Richard repeated coolly, though his eyes revealed a brief flash of curiosity. He was suggestible, after all, I realized—hadn't he followed his uncle's cruel advice on his wedding day?

"That's right," I said, stalling, for I really had no story to offer. Yet as I clutched that shell in my pocket, the smooth ridges seemed to speak to me. "It was a little shell, painted shiny black and glued together like something inside shouldn't get out. He won it in a poker game, from an old man who had nothing left to gamble with. Oh, my Uncle Henry used to bet on just about anything, and after he won this shell, the old man let him in on a secret. The shell wasn't ordinary, it could keep him from misfortune or rain it down on him, depending. The depending was this: if something went wrong in his life, Uncle Henry should accept it or it'd just get worse. Only if he learned to accept the trouble would his life ever get straight again."

Richard nodded again and again, urging me to the end of my peculiar story, but there was little hesitation in my voice—ideas were leaping over each other like a game of interior hopscotch. "Well, my uncle threw that thing away his first chance, in the town dump on the way home. But that night he burned his finger lighting a cigarette, and even though all he did was put on a band-aid, the next day another cigarette started a fire on the arm of his easy chair. Of course he had to put that out. Then he remembered the shell, and he ran back to the trash heap and got himself a nasty cut on the hand before he finally found it. But he'd learned his lesson—he just let that cut fester and swell and stink until it finally healed up on its own."

"This is all very interesting," Richard broke in, "but you'll have to excuse me. Thanks again for your help." Sliding past me, he opened the car door and settled behind the wheel.

Determined to appear as hopelessly ineffectual as possible, I pointed to the dashboard and said, "Say, maybe that fellow hit you harder than I thought! What's that flashing light mean?"

"It means I haven't been given the opportunity to *connect my seat belt.*" He slapped at the steering wheel with an exasperated grunt and I flicked my shell onto the backseat. It bounced lightly against a briefcase, the dull *ping* masked by the ignition turning over.

He drove off, down a false road I'd just given him—perhaps he'd find it longer than any street he'd ever made up, with misfortunes looming everywhere. Then I returned to my own car and rode away, still unsettled by the frightening ease with which I'd disguised myself, and I kept glancing in the rearview mirror, as if I were being followed by my own inventions.

* * *

Sylvia sat beside me in a corner coffee shop, shaking her head at the scare Richard had given her outside the video arcade. "I thought, This is it, I'm finished," she whispered, with a cautious glance at the nearby tables. Murmuring reassurance, I held her hand that groped for mine and said nothing of my spying, or the easy violence I'd discovered within me. How could I? Sylvia might find me as suspect as this husband she feared so much. So with the same ease with which I'd slipped into someone else's voice at the mall parking lot, I assumed the gestures and inflections of another me, finally saying, "Can't you just leave him?"

The door to the coffee shop jangled open and Sylvia lifted her head sharply, but only two young women in identical black dresses had made their entrance. She turned back to me, her lips tight and drained of color. "Oh Michael, I'm closer, much closer, but I can't do it yet. It's going to be so ugly."

I only nodded, offering whatever patient words she wanted to hear, but Sylvia interrupted. "I should have told you this first: last night I had that dream again. Richard and I were at the movies this time, watching some awful action picture. His hand was stroking my shoulder, and the more people on the screen that screamed and died, the more my shoulder hurt, it hurt until I felt like screaming—and I woke up. It was so dark, and my shoulder throbbed, almost in time to Richard's breathing, until I couldn't stand it any more, I got out of bed and checked in the bathroom mirror. I had to twist a little, and the pain had faded, but right where I still felt tender, I'm sure there was this faint pink line, like the imprint of a fingernail."

My face so stiffened with shock that Sylvia hesitated, undone herself by what she'd said. "But maybe it was a, a rash, you know? It could've been . . ."

She hedged and reconsidered for the rest of our brief rendezvous, and though I said nothing to contradict her, I was convinced—by now I knew how possible it was for anyone to be overtaken by a fierce and frightening urge.

"I've got to go," Sylvia finally said, rising, crumpling her paper coffee cup, "the bus'll be here in a minute."

"Bus?"

"Richard's borrowing my car while his is in the shop." She tossed the cup in a wastebasket. "Somebody backed into him, or something."

So her husband had heard no warning in that story about the black shell. I nodded casually, disguising my alarm, and kissed her good-bye.

That night I parked near Sylvia's house, prepared to wait out the night, as if my presence might somehow prevent trouble. But before an hour passed, Richard tramped down the brick steps and drove off in Sylvia's red compact. Was she all right? I thought, ready to leave my car, but when I caught a glimpse of her slim figure passing by the living room window I sped after Richard, now nearly two blocks away.

I expected to be led back to the mall, but after a few miles he cruised down the center of our small city's modest downtown, slowly exploring block after block for a parking space. Since Richard knew what I looked like I kept as far back as I dared, and when he managed to find a space on a dark side street I quickly drove past, my face averted.

I circled the block, returning to Main Street just in time to see him open the door to Tammy's Tavern and vanish inside. I smiled. If he'd taken to haunting a bar, maybe he wasn't so sure he could manage whatever trouble came his way. I could even imagine he'd found the shell and kept it hidden in a drawer, a secret waiting to reveal itself.

Again and again I rode around the block, waiting for Richard to settle into his first drink, and each slow circuit echoed that distant carousel ride with Kate when I'd discovered just how relentlessly I'd been pursuing her. One last time I turned down the side street where Richard had parked and I idled a few yards away from the red compact. I hated the thought of ramming into Sylvia's car, an act as cruel as anything Richard had inflicted on her, but how else could I fulfill the prophecy of the mysterious shell and show her husband just what kind of trouble could be had when you ignored the warning signs? If anything, it was *better* that I hit her car, so Richard would feel singled out by fate even more.

Twisting my front wheels carefully and using all my experience as an insurance agent, I gauged exactly how I might do the most damage. The driver's side door should collapse, and the window glass shatter into sharp rain. The side mirror should easily shear off from the impact, and already I could feel its untethering. Was this an-other secret poetry of my profession, a familiarity with wreckage and ruin so intimate that it reflected my own?

I scanned the rearview mirrors for any passersby. With only the empty street as my audience, I gunned the engine and tore into the little import. It groaned and crumpled and I urged against the seat belt that held me in place. I sat there a moment, utterly calm, even satisfied—Good, let that bastard consider what could have hap-pened to him if he'd been in the car. The ease of this appalling thought so shocked me that I almost forgot to escape. But I man-aged to back up and speed away, and my car's mangled hood helped frame every quiet residential street I passed through, as I searched for the safest, most deserted route home.

For most of the night the memory of that battered car haunted me: I'd disfigured my love for Sylvia while trying to release her from her husband. I turned from one end of my bed to the other, searching for sleep but unsettled by the fear that Richard might not take this lat-est warning. If not, what was I prepared to do next? I pressed my hands against my closed eyes, afraid to imagine any further escala-tion, yet still it faced me: Richard's car forced off the road and up-ended in a ditch, its dark wheels slowly spinning, spinning like a drive around the block, like a carousel, spinning until elusive sleep slowly offered me an escape.

It was no escape at all. I dreamt I was one of those John Wayne statues, somehow life-size and trailing a couple across a parking lot, a man and woman who could have been Sylvia and Richard. I hur-ried to catch them, but my glued pieces came undone—first an arm, a shoulder, then the bottom of my legs lopped off, and I di-vided at the waist and tumbled to the ground. I tried to reach out and repair myself, but my body was wooden and my unblinking eyes could only stare at a long row of tires and the painted lines of park-ing lanes.

I rose to the alarm's grating buzz and faced the familiar walls of my bedroom. I didn't dare rise, frightened by what I'd done last night and what I still might do, and I knew this crazy knight-to-the-rescue spiral had to stop. I reached for the phone and dialed Sylvia's number, prepared to confess everything.

She lifted the receiver in the middle of the first ring, as if she'd been waiting for my call.

"Sylvia, I have to tell you—"

"Michael? You wouldn't believe—it's . . . so strange, I mean—"

"What?" I rasped out at the wonder in her voice. "Tell me, please—"

"Well, I . . . I don't know how to describe—"

"Is it Richard?"

"Uh-huh." She paused. "He came home last night with a tow truck. My car was *so* messed up, and his *breath*. He swore he hadn't been driving and drinking, though—he told another story about some hit-and-run with the parked car. But he was real . . . subdued about it. And this is the really weird part—this morning, after he called a car rental he rang up the repair shop and told them to stop work on *his* car—"

"*Stop* work?" I repeated, not sure if I'd merely heard what I wanted to hear.

"Yeah, can you believe it? He told them to quit working on his brake light. But he didn't stop there, then he told me not to bother fixing *my* car and I said, What do you mean, how am I going to get around, I have to—anyway, he got *furious*. He screamed and screamed at me that the car was totaled, we'd just have to live with it, and then he flicked his hand and I swear he was going to . . . but he just *stopped*. All the fight left him. He looked . . . terrified, I mean—scared of himself. I swear he was."

Suddenly weightless at Sylvia's words, I clutched the receiver, its dangling cord my only tether to the world. Somehow all my foolish risks had succeeded, *succeeded*, and now, before I could reconsider, I took one more: "Sylvia, if Richard's scared of himself, then now's the time to ask for a divorce."

"Oh Michael—"

"No, listen to me, you have to do this quickly. If he's uncovered something inside himself that's so terrifying, then don't wait for anything else to happen, take advantage of the moment. Ask and he'll let you go, I'm sure of it. I have this . . . intuition."

"This doesn't have anything to do with the horoscope, does it?" Sylvia replied and I knew she was nearly ready, if only I'd keep at her. "Look," I said, continuing my performance, "tell him somewhere . . . public, like a restaurant, where he can't give you any trouble."

Sylvia said nothing; she wanted to hear more.

"I can wait nearby if you need help, I'll sit a few tables away. Just don't tell Richard anything about me—it'll complicate everything. You want this simple."

"Simple," she finally replied. "Short. And sweet."

"Then call him up," I said, now pacing along the edge of my bed and barely able to contain my excitement. "Call him now and invite him out for dinner tonight."

I set my glass down again and again, leaving a spiral of moist rings on the bar counter, and slowly worked my way through this ale that grew more sour with each sip. The morning's exhilaration now long lost, I stared in the mirror at the reflection of the restaurant's front door, directly behind me, and waited for Sylvia and Richard to arrive.

They were late. Perhaps Sylvia had decided against such a difficult meeting with her husband, perhaps she'd even resigned herself to living with the ambiguity of Richard's intentions, however fraught with danger those might be. I took another sip of my bitter drink and considered once again the bleak possibilities even if she *were* able to leave him. How could I tell her what I'd done—for all Sylvia's fear of her husband, he'd never accomplished the sort of violence I'd proved myself capable of. Yet if I didn't confess, I'd have to remain a stranger to Sylvia, my secret transforming all our intimacies into a sham.

I heard the door behind me open and I glanced up at the mirror again, but only an elderly couple made their way to the hostess' table. I turned back to my own reflection, at those calculating eyes in my haggard face, and there was the family resemblance to Mother and Laurie, clearer than ever. Play acting had brought me to this unhappy point, and now I understood their great loneliness, the isolation created by the stories they'd woven around themselves.

Again the door opened and now Sylvia and Richard walked in. *She came, she came*, I thought, elated that at least I might do Sylvia some good. With a nervous sweep of her eyes she quickly located me at the bar, and I stared down at my drink, afraid Richard might follow her gaze. When I looked up again I easily found their reflection in the mirror: an ordinary young couple sitting together at a table near the window, though their faces were both terribly strained. Richard kept working away at something buried in his jacket pocket, and I knew he was turning that little black shell over and over in his hand. His own face ashen, he was far along on that false road I'd given him. I had to look away, thinking of all the other objects I'd given to people or had Preston sell at his gallery. Why had I been so certain they'd be a comfort? Some of them might have proved to be delayed explosions, their shards slowly ripping through the lives of their new owners.

As we'd planned, Sylvia sat facing me, and I took in through the mirror the features I was afraid I'd soon have to give up: those large dark eyes, that sheer drop of cheekbones. The tense lines of her distant mouth moved silently, her voice lost among the nearby conversations and the sound of food served and enjoyed, and Richard nodded, following whatever it was she said. Then her face slowly broke through the mask of her fear, and I knew she was speaking the words that were about to change her life, and Richard's, and mine.

A Matched Set

Without our usual breezy jostling and teasing, Sylvia and I prepared dinner together in silence, just as we'd done the night before and the night before that. Now she stirred a cream sauce for the chicken breasts with tight turns of her wrist and stared down at the tiny white whirlpool she'd created. I imagined her brooding over Richard's sad decline, and I chopped away at a thick, sweet onion as if I could somehow rearrange the pieces of his story. But I knew the details far too well to accomplish that. Immediately after agreeing to the divorce, he'd insisted on giving Sylvia his own car, and he had hers towed off to a junkyard—a mystery to Sylvia, though I knew he was trying to reverse the influence of that scallop shell and win her back. At first he took the bus to work, then he walked to work, and when it was clear that Sylvia wouldn't return, he walked but didn't always make it to work, sometimes wandering aimlessly along the city streets. Eventually he quit his job at the map company, and when the divorce was finalized he split the sale of the house and left town.

I reached for a tomato, slit it in half, and thought of that postcard Richard had sent Sylvia weeks later: an oversized slice of cake, layered with dark gummy icing; on the other side a faraway postmark but no return address, and one little word—*sorry*—repeated as many times as his cramped handwriting could possibly squeeze into such a small space. "Too late," Sylvia had murmured, crying as she read it, "too late," and then I'd held her in my heavy arms, wanting to repeat that same simple word myself, for the secret that I still kept from her.

"Michael?"

I turned to see Sylvia with her hand hovering above the wok cover. "Taa daa!" she sang out, lifting it off the counter with a flourish, and there was the Felix the Cat night-light that I'd kept hidden on a corner of a closet shelf.

"I'm sorry to be so dramatic," she said, "but when I found this thing I was sure it had a story. You're collecting again, aren't you?" Sylvia held the night-light in her hand, now adding wearily, "Well, I like the stories too, so why keep them from me? Please, Michael, don't turn me into Kate."

So this was the reason for her recent long silences: my own false face, which had grown as smooth as these objects that I was indeed now secretly collecting. There were others she hadn't yet discovered—a set of Swiss Alps coasters, a hand-painted doorknob, and a Davy Crockett toothbrush—but none of them had stories. They were merely things I'd picked up, small, empty stages for a play acting I tried so hard to contain. Whenever I was alone I whispered to their quiet surfaces, confessing the gift of a black shell and my dangerous stalking of Richard. At the end of each telling I imagined confessing to Sylvia as well; sometimes she forgave me.

"I don't know what you mean," was all I could offer.

"Then let me ask you this," she said, her mouth grim, eyes uncertain. "It's been months since my papers were signed—when are you going to pop the question? What's the trouble?"

"I don't know," I said, miserable as I reached for another tomato.

"Why not? It wasn't that long ago you said it was what you always wanted."

I only nodded, concentrating on cutting through the soft red pulp, sliding the knife down until a sharp ache stopped me. I huffed out a shock of breath and reached for a paper towel.

Sylvia grabbed my finger, examined the neat flap of skin and welling blood. "Oh no, you need some first aid *here*, kiddo." Pulling up her T-shirt, she held my hand to her belly and smeared my blood against her warm skin. "You want to be chased? Is that it? *I'll* chase you." Sylvia led my finger under her pants and the elastic band of her panties until it fit snugly inside her. The cut tingled with pain and I tried to move away, but she pressed against me. "Hmm, keep it there, love," she whispered hoarsely.

I slipped my finger partways out and then in, again and again, my palm pressing against the thick coils of her hair. Perhaps I *could* be healed by our desire. My other hand groped for hers, held it, squeezed it, just as I'd squeezed the tiny hand of that doll's arm I'd given away so long ago. But our hands were warm and alive—so much better able to see us through the world together. It is possible, it *is*, I thought, and though our mouths sucked at each other I managed to say, "Marry me?"

"Marry you?" She laughed with delight. "Honey, I've had a minister on hold for a long time now." She unbuttoned my shirt, her fingers lightly stroking my chest. "He's a member of some Protestant denomination you've never heard of. Now I want you to lie down, Michael, because I know you won't believe this. In his spare time he's an auctioneer."

We drove through long stretches of a gently sloping country landscape, the rise and fall lulling my fears and letting me hope that with a single ceremony my deforming secret might fade to a faint white scar. We finally arrived at the outskirts of a small town and stopped before an ordinary, one-story, whitewashed building. Besides the sign, NEW LIFE CHAPEL, only a cross on the lawn and a tiny stained-glass window on the front door lent the place the look of a church.

The door ajar, we knocked once, twice, then entered. With a single portrait of Jesus on the wall, a cross here and there, a small electric organ in the corner and folding chairs lined up into makeshift pews, the very self-denial of this interior promised a wedding as simple as our first ones had been ornate.

"Hello?" Sylvia called out over the echo of our footsteps in the room.

A side door opened and a beefy man peered out of a dimly lit room, his eyes blinking. "Mr. Kirby, Miss Mathews?" he asked, his voice oddly suspicious.

"Yes, that's us," Sylvia replied.

"I'm Reverend Coslow," he said, beaming now as he stepped out to greet us, and at once I remembered his beatific grin and the lilt of his chant at a charity auction I'd once attended.

I shook his thick hand. "I saw you work an auction a year or so ago. You had great style—"

"Yes, your fiancée explained to me how you first met at an auction."

I turned to Sylvia with a questioning look, and her replying smile disguised any hint of this little lie she'd told. It was, after all, true enough.

"Actually," the minister continued, "I'm happy to be able to bring together my worldly and my godly . . ." His voice trailed off when a broad young woman now stepped from that same side room. As she approached I saw she was older than I'd thought—her crown of dyed black hair only accentuated those dull eyes, that hardened face.

"This is Mrs. Renée Thomas. Our organist," Reverend Coslow announced, looking away. "She'll be your witness. After the ceremony she'll give you some good conjugal advice—included in the wedding fee, of course—because she's our marriage counselor too. I don't know what we'd do without her."

Renée smiled as modestly as she could under the minister's praise, but when he turned to us and explained the details of the paperwork, I caught her secret glance at him, a mixture of suppressed longing and resentment that she swiftly extinguished, her mouth clenched against words she couldn't say.

We quickly paid the fee. Then Renée sat at the organ and poked out suitably solemn music while Sylvia and I walked down the aisle together, dressed so casually we might have been merely rehearsing the roles of husband and wife. We'd just arrived at the altar when the minister leaned into the microphone: "Whatdowehavehere, dearlybeloved, whatdowehavehere? ABRIDEabride, amostbeautiful beautifulbrideandaGROOM, agroomheretoo, notabadgroom, betterthanmostbetterthanmost, betterthanmostI'veseen, anexcellent groom."

I gaped at Sylvia's radiant, grinning face and, grinning now myself at this surprise she'd planned: here was a ceremony that just might erase the memories of those disastrous weddings we'd each endured. But the music had stopped with an electronic squeal, and I glanced over at Renée—her fingers worked the cross at her neck and her wide glistening eyes seemed to say *He's gone too far*. The minister, however, was already off again: "Asyoucansee, asyoucansee, asyoucansee, theymakeanexcellentCOUPLE, anexcellentanexcellentcouple, atruly atrulystunningpair, andtheyare HERE, theyareheretheyareherehere here, dearlybeloved, theyareheretotakepart, totakeparttogether, to takeparttogetherintheHOLYriteoftheHOLYriteoftheHOLYriteof matrimonymatrimonyMATRIMONY, theHOLYriteofmatrimony."

Renée hacked out a mild coughing fit, but this protest wasn't enough to stop the proceedings—in rapid tones, Reverend Coslow announced that Sylvia and I, both previously married, were used goods, bidding for each other. "ButintheEYESoftheLordtheLordthe HOLY LORD OUR FATHER, youareNEW, mychildren, youare newtoeachotherandnewtotheworld. AnyoneELSEwantstomakea bidmakeabidabidaBID, forthisbrideorthisgroom, brideorgroom, afineafinematchedset, averyfinematchedset, makeitnowmakeitnow makeit*now* . . . orforeverholdyourpeace."

In the silence I imagined those empty rows behind us filled with our particular ghosts: Sylvia's parents and mine, Laurie, Dan, Kate and Richard, and all the other characters of our lives. How would *they* calculate our worth? And would Richard, finally recognizing me, rise from his chair and raise his voice in protest?

Sensing I'd drifted off, Sylvia nudged me with her shoulder when the minister continued. "NowwehaveaRING, aringaring, awedding band, agoldGOLDfourteencaratGOLDweddingband, agoldwedding band. HasaninterestingSTORY, asignificantSTORY, thebridewantsto tellyouitsstory."

Sylvia held out the thick gold band and spoke quietly, even shyly. "Michael, this ring belonged to my father, and its story goes back to the summer when I was nine. My parents were having one of their angry melodramas on the porch—they both could get buggy from the heat—and in one of Dad's usual B-movie gestures he pulled the ring off and threw it at Mom.

"It flew right past her and into the empty lot next door, and we all ran down the steps after it, Mom already crying and Dad apologizing like mad. That lot seemed huge to me in those days, an entire country of grass and dirt and weeds, and we looked and looked until it was nearly dark. At least Dad and I did—Mom was inside, crying in the bedroom as loud as she could to inspire us.

"Somehow I thought that my parents wouldn't be married any more without that ring, and I told myself I'd *starve* before giving up. It got so dark that Dad decided to get flashlights, and when he turned on the porch light on his way inside, I saw a glint of something a few feet ahead of me.

"It was the ring, halfway down the dried stem of a stalky weed— God knows what the odds were for it to land like that—and it looked like a demon had stuck it on his finger, trying to steal my parents' marriage. I pulled at the weed and grabbed the ring, but I didn't say anything right away. Instead, I thought how powerful I was. I held my family's happiness in my hand. All alone in that huge lot, I'd defeated the demon."

Slipping the ring on my finger, Sylvia added, "But who's alone now?"

I stared down at the ring and wished I deserved the story held within its smooth circle, wished I had the courage to tell Sylvia why I didn't deserve it. Instead, I took out a simple gold band I'd chosen for her and said lamely, "No story yet, love." Sylvia nodded, her disappointment showing through the tiniest flinch, and I hurried to add, "We'll make our own, okay?"

In a moment the ring fit her finger and we said our *I do's* to the minister's rapid-fire vows. Then he paused to say, "I now pronounce you husband and wife." Behind us Renée punched out a march on the organ and we kissed, long and sweet, as the minister called out, "Soldsoldsoldtoeachother, soldtoeachother in the EYES of the LORD, soldforakissakissakiss, onekiss, SOLDforakiss."

The organ sputtered to a stop, but we held our embrace—all alone in that quiet, with no past or future to pry us apart, until the minister finally said, "Congratulations." Then, with a glance at Renée, he added, "This certainly has been a one-of-a-kind service, never to be repeated, but I'm glad I could help you."

He motioned us in the direction of the side office. We followed, signing the necessary documents, and when Renée entered the room

Reverend Coslow said, "I'll leave you now in our counselor's able care."

As he walked off, Sylvia whispered to me, "Aw, can't we skip this?"

"Shh, how can it hurt?" I returned. "If he can break the rules for us, we can follow his."

Waiting patiently behind a desk, Renée held a printed list in her hands, and we sat down, preparing ourselves for a well-meaning lecture. Barely nodding, she began reading in an odd, affectless voice. " 'Number One. Now you are one person, not two, and your time is each other's.'

" 'Number Two. Always tell the truth as gently as you can, and always accept with grace the truth you're told.'

" 'Number Three. Having children is a blessing, and keep your heart open for each new arrival.'

" 'Number Four. *Never* go to sleep angry.' "

"*I'll* say," Sylvia murmured, and she leaned in and nuzzled my neck.

Renée frowned and put down her list. "Excuse me, ma'am. I'm not finished."

"Sorry," Sylvia replied, straightening up.

She regarded us with a mixture of envy and distaste. "I know you're happy and want to go off. Well, you should be happy. Lots of folks never marry the one they'd like, or they marry the one they shouldn't. You both know that. Honey, you got your man, but the hard part's not over, it's just the beginning. I've seen many a happy couple pass through here, and I've given them all advice. I wish most of them listened better. There's hardly a soul in this town who doesn't wish for a better marriage."

She paused and closed her eyes for a moment, and I knew that thin line of her mouth wasn't caused by us. "I was very interested in that story you told your new husband. There's stories I might tell you both."

"Please, tell us one," Sylvia said, sweetly trying to placate this unhappy woman.

A hint of pleasure forced itself to Renée's lips. "All right. I will. Instead of reading this tiresome list." She swept it away with such coiled energy it flew from the desk and twisted to the floor.

"A boy and a girl here, they worked at the luncheonette in town—

he tended the grill, she waited tables. After hours they got to talking about the highs and lows of the day and they just fell in love. They were nice kids, but they weren't ready for what makes living together so hard sometimes."

In a clear, steady voice, Renée seemed to talk past the open door behind us, where I suspected Reverend Coslow lingered by the altar. "They argued over nothing, the little types of arguments that quick get bigger, and soon enough they closed their hearts to each other without even knowing what they were doing. I've seen it happen so often. One night they were cooking and it wasn't enough to disagree, snip snip snip, they had to get mean. He hollered something terrible to her, she ran to another room and he followed."

Renée paused, now staring straight at us, her smile turning nasty. "They screamed for a while longer and forgot about that frying pan on the stove. When they remembered, the fire was already spreading."

"Michael, let's get out of here," Sylvia murmured, standing. "We don't have to listen to this."

Renée wouldn't let us get away so easily. "Ever try to put out a grease fire?" she asked, her voice rising sharply as Sylvia tugged me from my chair. "Well, they got burned so badly nobody around here can bear to look. Though we try to do our best by them!"

We were out the door by then, hurrying down those aisles of chairs still filled with all our invisible guests watching as Renée followed and shouted out, "Their lack of faith in themselves was the kindling! And their anger at each other was their own hellfire!"

We tore down the steps outside and across a few feet of parking lot gravel to our car. Grappling in my pocket for the keys, I looked back to see when Renée would be upon us, but she'd stopped at the top step, fairly spitting out, "And *that's* one of *my* stories!"

Reverend Coslow appeared in the screen door behind her, his round pale face nearly collapsing when Renée shook her fists at the sky and howled, "May the good Lord take pity on us all! May the good Lord take pity on us all!"

Ecstatic Wings

Sylvia and I lie together, and even in sleep she needs to touch me—a leg lined along with mine, an arm around my chest, her chin nuzzled against my neck. Is she afraid that I'll slip away from her on our first night of marriage, that I've already begun the first secret steps of escape and in the morning she'll awake to find her hand grasping at the empty half of our bed? I shift my body into her sleeping embrace, let my fingers stroke her hair in reassurance. I can only imagine how much worry Sylvia has kept from me these past few months, and my tender gesture can't sweep away what I've kept from her.

She shifts again, her instep brushing against my toes, and when I hear her faint sigh I echo it, hoping she somehow hears me, even if it's not enough to drown out those terrible words that still ring inside me—"*Their lack of faith in themselves was the kindling! And their anger . . .*"

Outside, the relentless chorus of cicadas rises, like the first cracklings of a grease fire, and now I think of my false face above Sylvia's as we made love tonight—how is my face any different from the scarred mask that sorry husband will have to endure for the rest of his life? I can too easily imagine what he confronts in the mirror each day—two holes for a nose, his mouth a lipless slit, his eyes worlds away, surrounded by the stiff cruel sheen of reconstructed skin.

The cicadas continue their furious music, eerily synchronized surges that seem to grow ever louder and I simply can't stay here, I ease away from Sylvia and pad from the room as silently as I can. In the hall I head for the stairway, then walk carefully down the dark to the living room. With the faint moonlight contained by the curtains, I have to ease around the edges of the furniture, my hand reaching tentatively before me, and as I take one step, then another, I suddenly imagine Richard trudging through the darkness of a tunnel with two—no, three men. A work crew, perhaps.

Surprised by the thought as I think it, I sit down in the nearest chair, unwilling and yet unable to prevent myself from imagining Richard's new life in a distant city. He spends much of his time underground now, I think, traveling miles of passageways as he maps the repairs and renovations that work crews make for an intricate new subway system, checking that the electric cables, phone lines and emergency sprinkler systems are accurately marked. There are no trap streets possible here, no false roads.

So there he is, wearing a hard hat with its own search light, turning a dark corner with a crew he's followed before—they're hard workers and give him tips on what to look for, though he hasn't yet been included in their easy joking.

They stop before a phone box that's gone out, they form a small cluster, their tools out and loosening screws. "Shit!" someone cries out, and the others stop and gather around.

The crew foreman, Pete, laughs and says, "Aah Joey, it's only a little nick. What're you whining about?"

Joey's the youngest of the bunch . . . and the most impressionable. This could be the moment, Richard thinks, stepping back. He'll slip the little black shell into Joey's open tool chest now, and on the way back to the station platform tell the kid a story about the dangers and promise of a simple, blackened scallop shell. Then I can quit this job in the morning and move away, Richard tells himself, thrilled at the possibility that he might finally be released from the grip of this damned thing.

The men are busy, they've forgotten him for the moment, and

Richard lifts the shell from his shirt pocket. But he hears the passing rumble of a subway on a distant line and remembers wandering through town in those days before the divorce, so distracted by remorse he was nearly hit by a bus one morning. It passed by inches from his face with a roar and rush of air, and he'd fallen to his knees, shaking his head as if to clear it, understanding that he had to move away, had to let go of the hope that Sylvia might ever return to him.

"I can't pass this on," Richard whispers to himself, easing the shell back in his pocket. Yet now he *has* to rid himself of this shell, before he's tempted again.

He returns to the men, checks his charts with what they've done. When they finish up he makes a few corrections in pen, satisfied. Then they return through those dark passageways together, but after a few minutes Richard lingers behind, he bends down beside one of the tracks and takes out the scallop shell. It's as dark as the tunnel they've been traveling through. He places it on the cold track, where the wheel of a subway car will eventually crush it to powder. A dark mist will settle over the gravel bed and then the chain will be broken. No one else will ever have to be haunted by this awful thing's story.

With this thought, the shell—so tiny on the long, long track— loses its power, becomes just a silly knick-knack. Did it ever have any power? Richard wonders. Maybe it was just my . . . excuse to escape from the kind of person I was turning into. Richard shakes his head, amazed.

One of the crew turns around, the beam of light on his helmet arcing back and forth until Richard is caught in its glare, crouched beside the track. "Hey, Richie, what're you doing, taking a piss?" Joey calls out. "Watch out for the third rail!"

It's an old joke they've all heard before, but this is the first time, Richard realizes, that he's ever been included. Then Pete feigns annoyance and offers the usual response, "Hey, what're you warning him for? I thought you liked barbecue."

The men laugh easily, in almost ritual fashion, and they continue on, but slower now, so Richard can catch up. *This* is the moment he's been hoping for. These men like him. They know he does good work and doesn't mind the odd hours or getting dirty. He's a regular guy, someone they wouldn't mind introducing to their friends, or a lonely cousin, maybe even a sister—

A dog barks in the distance and I'm surprised to find myself sitting in the dark of my own living room. I laugh quietly. My sister would be proud of me, now that I've imagined Richard offstage. It's just the sort of scene she might have created. The dog's yelps die away down the block and I still sit here, somehow lighter, feeling as released as Richard from that shell. Why *couldn't* this story be true, or true enough?

Yes, I think, this is the sort of imagining that gave Laurie so much pleasure: rewriting the script, changing the possibilities for the people in her life. For all her troubles and anger, wouldn't she too, at least sometimes, try to bestow upon them a story more bearable to follow?

I want to think this of my sister, and I want to imagine her, imagine where she might be at this moment. She's lying in bed, I think. But she's awake, too. She's listening to something . . . someone. It's her latest man leaving her apartment—yet another lover disappointed in ways she knows he can't articulate. She stretches lazily on the twisted sheets, savoring how she'd changed the tone of her voice, the pattern of her gestures and facial expressions slightly every few minutes, so that this man—an ambitious member of the chorus who liked the idea of sleeping with one of the leads—felt so unsettled by her subtle shifting that even when he came inside her he suspected that she somehow eluded his grasp.

And of course she has, because now he's gone. She knows that he won't flirt with her again backstage tomorrow, at least not in a way that signals real desire, and this is the way she likes it—all intimacies brief and on her own terms. She doesn't have enough room inside her for a lover's slowly escalating demands, for someone else's need for an audience.

But there will be other nights, when a woman leaves her, that Laurie lies in bed and regrets the quiet exit, wishes she hadn't so artfully feinted and parried. If only she'd taken a chance with this lover and stripped off her entire cast until she was down to a one-woman performance. This sleepy regret transforms into a dream that Laurie's had many times before. She's herself, an adult, yet holding hands with Mother on the roof of our old house. She looks down and the backyard is no backyard at all but the floor of a stage, all scuff marks and taped stage directions, and now the roof where she and

Mother perch, precariously balanced, is the ledge of the theater's balcony. The audience below stares up at them expectantly and Laurie can't remember her lines or even her part—she's dizzy, unsure of her footing. This is always the moment when she wakes, and she can't help but feel lost those first few moments in the dark before she finally finds herself, alone in bed.

But this is too sad, not at all what I want for Laurie. Perhaps all her bizarre play acting had only been a show for my benefit: the Uncontrollable Sister dancing at the edge of the cliff. Even if she danced with well-practiced steps, she couldn't possibly maintain such a balance day in, day out, so why not imagine my sister in repose? She's at home with her feet up on the coffee table, a bowl of chips nestled in the crook of her arm, and she's absolutely herself, Laurie to the core. She picks up a book of short stories, a nice fat anthology, and dips in, lets herself become who she reads. And when she's done there's always something serviceable on the tube. She clicks on the remote control and lets herself wander about the set of a soap or sitcom, among the other characters. She has this little vice, equivalent to a nicotine fit, that keeps her company whenever she needs it.

This is better, I think, closer to the peace that Laurie needs, and I can try again another time, can't I? Because I'm eager to take on someone else, and an image comes to me of Father and Dan, crouching silently before a few sickly shrubs that need quick tending. They don't need to speak, they know so much about the nursery: if they were trees their branches would have long ago entangled, each dependent on the other for sharing shade and light. They're the Zombie Twins.

But this is Laurie's name for them, and how did she ever know what went on when they were alone? She was only imagining, as I am now, watching Father and Dan stand in the doorway, returning home after a hard day of pulling weeds and stacking sod, planning the orders for next season and forcing out smiles at short-tempered customers. The key's in the lock, and they enter.

They slap together their usual workmanlike dinner, and Father watches his son carefully. After an especially trying day, Dan sometimes slams a cabinet door shut, or grasps a steaming cup of coffee too roughly and splashes his drink on the tablecloth. Once, without any warning, Dan smashed his fist through a wall and Father had to drive him to the emergency room, calming him while they waited for the nurse to finally take down their names.

So when Dan curses at his steak knife when it doesn't slip smoothly through a thick lamb chop, Father waits until after dinner before saying offhandedly, "It's a nice night for a walk."

Without another word, they leave the house and its shining porch light and set off on a long walk through one neighborhood after another, commenting on a patchy lawn or an unruly hedge along the way. Then they stop: a home with three days' worth of newspapers sprawled across the front stoop looks promising, though down the block is the shell of a house that's under construction, its wiring and plumbing unprotected for the night.

Dan chooses the half-built house and, filled with nostalgia for his old days of wreaking havoc on our block, he slips along the side of the construction site. Father lingers behind and leans against a streetlamp, his son's lookout.

I'm stunned as I imagine this, but I'm convinced that it could be true, that Father needs Dan so much he's willing to take part in such escapades. He has, after all, worked his way down to one lone family member, and perhaps this is all the intimacy he can manage. As he glances up and down the block, does Father admit to himself that he condones his son's spurts of rage because, except for toppling one frail triangle of bowling pins after another, he'd never, never given himself permission to do this on his own?

Dan eventually returns, grinning and empty-handed, though he's become a collector all the same—a collector of all the little vandalisms that Father helps him with. As they walk back home, Dan tells Father a story about a man who wanders in a dark, unfinished home, searching for something that might easily snap off, or loosen with enough tugging. He's become a storyteller too, and understanding that Father doesn't want to hear what really happened, Dan embellishes these forays into spy missions and narrow escapes.

And if you were sitting on a porch one of these nights, you might hear the full, appreciative laughter of an older man. When he'd finally come into view you'd see him walking side by side with a younger man clearly his son—the same short curly hair, the barrel chests—and you'd have to smile to yourself at this brief glimpse of a happy family.

I hear a car pass by outside—someone as restless as I am perhaps, a man returning from a long trip, so anxious to arrive home that he's driven through the night rather than stop at a motel. Now just a few blocks from his driveway, he's no longer tired. I wish him well as his car's engine fades in the distance, and I close my eyes and prepare to face the hardest ones of all for me to imagine: Kate, and my mother.

I begin with Kate, elusive Kate, and remember how, in our last days, she couldn't stop washing: taking two, even three showers a day, scrubbing her hands more times than I could count, rubbing lotion into her face and spraying herself with perfume again and again. My poor, hunted wife must have been trying to lose her scent, to give me the slip in a cloud of artificial smells.

I imagine her now lying in a tub, hair tucked up at the back of her head like a pillow, the steaming water up to her collarbone. Her body shimmers under the water, it barely seems to belong to her, especially when she shakes her shoulders and sets off riplets and waves. She's floating above herself, listening to the subtle sounds of the house around her: the distant chug of the dishwasher in the kitchen; a soft sweep of the wind outside and a branch scraping gently at a screen window; the footsteps of someone walking down the hall outside the bathroom—who? A man, I think, a new husband who gratefully accepts her quiet ways and seeks the same harbor she does. He doesn't enter the study while she's drawing, and she knows he won't check on her in the bath as she's happily hovering above her new life.

Then she opens the drain and listens to the suck of escaping water, she stands and feels the soapy droplets on her skin already evaporating and tickling, and she giggles giddily. Her husband's footsteps stop briefly, then continue—he's heard her laughter, she knows, and her happiness is enough for him, he doesn't need to know its source to be pleased himself.

She looks in the misted mirror and doesn't rub her hand over the steam; instead, she watches as she gently, slowly reappears to herself, a familiar face that not long ago had seemed frighteningly unfamiliar and lined with a premonition that something terrible was about to happen. She'd been right, she'd been wrong, for now she regards her divorce almost fondly, as a stepping-stone to this present contentment.

Kate breathes in the humid air. There's just a faint film hugging one corner of the mirror, and she turns a shoulder, a hip, modeling what she can see of her naked body. She's safe, her face settled into a calm I've never seen, and even though I feel on the verge of discovering one of Kate's secrets, I open my eyes and let her go, freeing her from any further, unwanted probing.

I blink, my eyes now so accustomed to the dark that the furniture in the living room has taken on dim outlines, familiar patient shapes that wait as my mother waits for me to imagine her. She must be amused by the daunting task I face.

She's dead, of course, yet I'm certain that she's ideally suited to the afterlife: every character she's ever assumed—however briefly—is mirrored within her transparent shape, a protean pulse shifting into whatever she wishes, braiding an infinity of improvisations that all began with a bit of a story over breakfast so long ago, a little butterfly wing of trouble, a dangerous flutter that couldn't stop once it started.

Who can ever say *why* such a small flutter set off such a storm? But she needs no family now, for we're all within her, Dan and Laurie, Father, myself: fellow cast members and eternal audience. From time to time she tries on our intimate strangeness, seeking out the origin of every expression she can remember from our faces, even becoming all of us at once, for she is a virtuoso, she is version after version of all she's left behind, and she settles into our sadness and fear of her and then goes further, finding in us that time of contentment before she split into pieces.

The complex tussle of voices within my mother has become both a single voice and a marvelous harmony that echoes throughout the afterlife, a startling music in that unimaginable other world where we'll someday join her, twisting ourselves into competing possibilities of who we were and are and might be. But such a future is so far off. Until then, I can always imagine another ending if I need to, something happy, or bittersweet, or whatever I wish.

For the moment I'll keep these acrobatics at bay. I need to return to Sylvia and I climb the stairs to the bedroom. Though I want to wake her and tell her all these stories, I let my wife sleep and lay my head beside her on the pillow. Sylvia stirs and I shift under the covers, attuned to the subtle movements of her sleep, and this gentle brushing of limbs is a slow dance I hope we'll always continue—why couldn't we be two ecstatic wings, stirring our own sweet turbulence, creating new stories together?

Then, suddenly, it's morning, the early light strangely soothing. I turn to see that Sylvia's awake too, her dark hair tangled about her forehead as she takes in my still sleepy face. Before I can speak she closes her eyes, a faint, mysterious twist to her lips. I imagine that bits of dream still drift within her reach, that she manages to recall a scene of us jogging, matching each other's stride as a storm she hadn't predicted approaches. She can still feel the dread rising inside her as the downpour washes over us, lightning and echoing thunder on all sides. It passes as quickly as it came. Yet the puddles—and our wavery reflections within—still seem to grow, and as we run we splash them into even smaller puddles. No matter how they divide, each tiny pool contains both of us shimmering together, our swift alternating steps locked in rhythm as we hurry home.

"Listen," I whisper in Sylvia's ear, because it's time for me to tell her my first, my most difficult story. She opens her eyes and sees mine filled with words she's long waited for, words she can't predict. She shivers, whether in fear or relief I'm not yet sure, but when her hand searches under the blanket for mine, I know she's ready to hear what I'm about to say.

ABOUT THE AUTHOR

PHILIP GRAHAM is the author of the story collection *The Art of the Knock* and a memoir, *Parallel Worlds: An Anthropologist and a Writer Encounter Africa*, coauthored with his wife Alma Gottlieb. He has received a National Endowment for the Arts Fellowship, the William Peden Prize in Fiction, and the Victor Turner Prize. His stories have appeared in *The New Yorker*, *The Washington Post Magazine*, *North American Review*, and *Missouri Review* among others, and are frequently reprinted, most recently in *The Norton Book of Ghost Stories*. His second story collection, *Interior Design*, is forthcoming from Scribner. Graham teaches creative writing at the University of Illinois at Urbana-Champaign and lives in Urbana with his family.